THE PRISON TANGRAM

OTHER BOOKS BY CLAIRE HUOT

China's New Cultural Scene (Duke University Press, USA, 2000)
La Petite révolution culturelle (Arles, France, 1994)

THE PRISON TANGRAM

A MYSTERY NOVEL

BY CLAIRE HUOT

THE MERCURY PRESS

Copyright © 2007 by Claire Huot

ALL RIGHTS RESERVED. No part of this book may be reproduced by any means without the prior written permission of the publisher, with the exception of brief passages in reviews. Any request for photocopying or other reprographic copying of any part of this book must be directed in writing to the Canadian Reprography Collective.

The publisher gratefully acknowledges the financial assistance of the Canada Council for the Arts, the Ontario Arts Council, and the Ontario Book Publishing Tax Credit Program. The publisher further acknowledges the financial support of the Government of Canada through the Department of Canadian Heritage's Book Publishing Industry Development Program (BPIDP) for our publishing activities.

The author wishes to thank the Canada Council for the Arts for its support in the writing of this novel.

Editor: Beverley Daurio
Cover design: Gordon Robertson
Composition and page design: Beverley Daurio

Printed and bound in Canada
Printed on acid-free paper

1 2 3 4 5   11 10 09 08 07

Library and Archives Canada Cataloguing in Publication

Huot, Marie Claire
The prison tangram / Claire Huot.
ISBN 978-1-55128-131-5
I. Title.
PS8615.U69P75 2007   C813'.6   C2007-904903-6

The Mercury Press
Box 672, Station P, Toronto, Ontario Canada M5S 2Y4
www.themercurypress.ca

感谢翼波：我的超级编辑兼本之本。

PROLOGUE

I chose that particular bar because the terrace seemed to be suspended over the lake. I'd been walking Otis all evening and even the dog needed to take a break. I'd forgotten how noisy Saturday nights could be in Burlington once the bikers came. Thankfully, the music seemed less loud on that terrace. I took a table right above the water's edge.

Water was one of the things I'd missed most about Burlington: the way the town sloped down to the shore of big Lake Champlain to the west, while the Winooski River snaked through the rolling hills of the north end.

A waitress brought a pail of water for Otis and two pink drinks for me. "Two for one, tonight, sweetie." She bent to pet the dog, who immediately started in on the water. "That's three for you, I guess."

I sat there looking at the moon, and listening to the tables filling up around me. I turned to have a look: WWW was an all women's bar. Which was fine. I wasn't looking to meet guys. I'd left my boyfriend back in Beijing. To his mother's great satisfaction; she'd never liked her son getting mixed up with a white foreigner. And yet, thanks to email, Huiru and I were still hanging on.

The girls in the bar all seemed to know one another; they moved from table to table, clinking glasses and exchanging wisecracks. Otis settled in for a snooze and I went back to staring at the moon.

"Grad student?"

"Anthropologist."

"Archaeologist."

"Right, looking for Mr. Bones."

The dog's ears pricked up at that last word; he came awake and lifted a paw onto my leg. I knew the routine: I opened a Ziploc of dried liver treats, offered him a piece and patted his head.

Howls of "Woof! Woof!" pealed around the terrace.

I dug a cigarette out of my bag.

"Look! She's got two doggies."

They were referring to my shaggy handbag. I loved that bag, the thick woolly shag, the way it swung when I walked. Before I'd taken over responsibility for Otis, that bag had kept me company on many solitary walks. I didn't have a friend in this town; I'd been away too long. Really, I felt no different here than I had in Beijing. I was used to being an outsider. Always a little out of place.

I lit my cigarette and sipped my pink drink, a daiquiri I think. I guess cocktails was another gap in my education. My fellow cadets at the academy had taken to calling me moon-girl, meaning that's where I'd come from.

I picked up my courage and turned to the woman sitting closest to me. She was all decked out in black, including her lipstick and nail polish. "Cop," I said.

She gave me a quizzical cock of the head.

"I'm a cop," I told her. "Not an archaeologist."

She shook her head and pointed a long black fingernail. "You're a writer. Like me. I'm Petunia, pen name Bethune."

"Hi, Petunia," I smiled, and added for no reason I can explain, "I'm Lily-of-the-Valley."

"Come and sit with us, Lily. You too, pooch," said Petunia, her long black hair brushing my cheek as she twisted my chair toward the already crowded table.

I looked at the beaming faces, wondering for a moment whether they'd all taken Xtasy. Hothouse flowers, all long hair, arms gesturing, touching each other, blowing kisses at me.

"What are you guys drinking?" I asked to break the ice, though it was obvious they were also into pink drinks.

"Bazooka Bombs!" someone blurted, and they all laughed.

So I sat tucked in next to Petunia. Beside her were a couple wearing matching his and hers fifties bowling gear; across the table, Anita, a black woman with a gigantic Afro, tiny granny glasses and a pink leatherette mini-skirt had started talking with great animation to a couple at another table. "Are you saying there's no such thing as unbranded space?" Anita asked. "What about my own body?"

The couple — whom I instantly nicknamed Metallica, because of the chain-link tattoos circling their upper arms — conceded, in stereo, that okay, one's own body was still unmarked territory, but every other space had been conquered. "Even in prisons, everything, even their bleach's got a brand," the elder Metallica said.

The younger Metallica chimed in, "Yeah, the no-choice brand."

I've always thought of myself as someone who spurns brand names, but there I was wearing my Swatch with its Edgar Allan Poe face, and with a purebred Lab lying at my Adidas-clad feet.

Petunia grabbed my wrist in a black claw, "You're not really a cop, are you?"

"Oh give her a break," Anita said. "She's not going to bust you for under-age drinking."

Petunia's grip tightened on my arm. "A cop could get me into Montrose."

Anita scoffed, "Here we go again. Petunia's always on the prowl for sensational stories. You gals remember her big push on homeless women? Last year was the year of the bag lady."

Petunia removed her paw from my arm, and cast a murderous glare at Anita. I figured they were ex-lovers. "You were supposed to talk to Clo's mother," she said. "Clo was going to get me in there."

"Who's Clo?" someone asked.

"Isn't she Nicole's girl? The one who's a student?"

"Right." Anita replied. "That's the one."

"She volunteers at Montrose," Petunia said. "And Anita knows her mother. But will she set up a meet? No, that would make my job too easy."

"Maybe Anita's the jealous kind," the younger Metallica suggested, which set off another round of raucous laughter. Only Petunia was not amused.

"Why don't you get arrested?" Anita suggested. "That's one way you could get into that prison."

"Montrose is not a prison. Or so they claim." Petunia put on an official tone: "Montrose is an experiment in reform."

"You just watch," the elder Metallica said, "they'll shut down that experiment pretty soon. Nobody in this town likes it, anyway: it's too expensive keeping all those ladies happy and well-fed. Once the politicians get hold of the story…"

Anita nodded. "You publish a piece about it, you'll just make it worse."

I could contribute nothing to this conversation. I'd heard of the Montrose Detention Center for Women; I knew the experiment in campus-style living was only in its second year of existence. And that was all I knew.

"Well, someone's got to get in there," Petunia said. "That's our sisters they're experimenting on." She looked at me slyly. "You're not really a cop, are you?"

Someone broke the spell: "All right, grrrls. Let's have a toast to all of our sisters."

"To the girls inside! To the panthers and Amazons!"

Echoes of "Grrls!", "Amazons," "Chicks!" rippled out across the lake.

By the time I left the women's bar, I felt more like a zombie than an Amazon. Petunia had slipped her card into my shaggy bag. Under her email address imbedded in the image of a petunia, she'd written: "Cuff me anytime, Officer Lily."

Of course, my name wasn't Lily. And, that evening, I was barely a police officer yet. But a brand new blue uniform was hanging stiffly in my closet.

PART I
PAVILION BY THE WATER

"I'm assigning you to Sanitary Collection," Warden Segal told May Ho and waited for a reaction from her newly arrived convict.

Ho, wearing jeans, a man's Vichy shirt and a corduroy jean jacket, sat expressionless behind heavy black-framed glasses, on the pink brocade settee across from the warden's desk.

Warden Segal was a petite woman, dressed in a shapely pink jersey two-piece. Squinting slightly as she tried to peer into the eyes behind the inmate's glasses, Warden Segal continued: "Facilitator Walker will take you through the routine tomorrow morning. Work starts at 8 o'clock sharp."

May Ho nodded respectfully. She felt a little out of place in the dainty sun-washed office. And in the whole detention centre, for that matter. As though they had tossed her into a community college where everything was bright and colourful, and everyone, nice and cheerful, instead of the prison where she belonged. There were no bars in sight, and women seemed to be wandering around freely in the yard without chaperones. While the warden riffled a bound manuscript on her desk, May glanced out the large bay window into the yard. Shrubs of holly created a prickly fence around a quadrangle dotted with green plastic benches. In the centre stood a single young scraggly maple.

"Everything I've told you can be found in our manual." Warden Segal dropped the wire-bound manuscript in May's lap.

May adjusted her glasses in an unconscious gesture and sat up to peruse the *Manual for New Arrivals*. She leafed quickly to the index, letting her eyes fall on random entries — Bleach, Counts, Personal Effects, Visits. The manual had some eighty pages.

Warden Segal checked her Longines watch, and stood to survey the courtyard: "Here's Elizabeth Rich. On time. As we expect everyone to be." The warden and the new inmate watched a blond woman cross the yard and knock on the door to the left of the bay window.

Introductions were made at the door. "Elizabeth will be your buddy," Segal told May. "Of course, if you have questions, you can always come to me." They were dismissed with a flick of the warden's manicured fingers.

Following Elizabeth Rich's long blond ponytail out into the yard, May thought: dog owner. A pretty face, finely etched features, bit pudgier than the warden. A little dumb? In her early thirties. Her clothes matched the ponytail: faded jeans, running shoes and a powder blue sweatshirt over a white turtleneck. Big box stuff.

In the courtyard, the blond ponytail swung around and Rich extended a soft hand. "You can call me Liz."

Those few steps had given Liz time to conceal her surprise. May Ho was not what she'd expected when the warden told her she was going to be a Chinese woman's buddy. May was tall, and she looked straight at you. Liz took in the strange haircut, layered, uneven, short, short bangs, black-rimmed glasses. Where the hell did she come from with that funky professor look?

"May Ho. May as in 'maybe baby'; Ho as in... Santa Claus."

Liz nodded, smiled, and led the way.

The moment they walked into the cafeteria, the smell of sour armpits told May lunch was puréed tomatoes and onions. She got into line, behind the ponytail. A thick silence surrounded them. May wiped her glasses with her shirt-tail and waited her turn. She could have guessed without looking that the smallish cafeteria was painted Anita Bryant orange. Out of the corner of her eye, she surveyed the hall. There weren't as many women as she'd expected. Maybe fifty. Not the endless rows you saw in prison movies. The women were mostly young, many in their twenties. Several were checking her out.

Two looked eerily like twins: not only were they wearing identical outfits — black bomber jackets and black jeans — but they also had the same bleached hair. Both were staring at her, puckering. Amerindians, maybe. May concentrated on her tray, watching as the inmate on duty piled it high with the *menu du jour*; she rejected the rice pudding, and wisely reached for black tea instead of coffee. At Liz' silent invitation, May followed her to a plastic blue picnic table that could seat up to six. So far they were alone. Liz almost trailed her ponytail in her spaghetti sauce as she slid in and along the bench.

Liz decided May must be in her forties. She'd spotted a streak of gray on May's head when she bent to sit under the neon lights. Well, she'd have plenty of time to dye her hair in here. Liz stole quick glances at her new buddy. A hard jaw line and tiny wrinkles around the eyes confirmed May was older than Liz. Who the hell over 40 would have a punkette hairdo? A weirdo. Liz ploughed into her spaghetti with her blunt three-pronged fork. Soon she stopped. May was twisting the odd noodle with her soft spoon.

"Is it always like this?" May asked without looking up.

"You mean quiet."

May nodded.

"Whenever we get a newbie. Sizing you up."

May did not reply immediately. In her mind she was recalling scenes from *Papillon*, or the more recent *Shawshank Redemption*, wild fights erupting suddenly in chow halls. Her brain camera-panned to a scene from *Family Game*, the Japanese comedy by Yoshimitsu Morita, in which a family is lined up on one side of a table, silent but for the noisy slurping of noodle soup, as though the director had put mikes right up against the actors' throats. She smiled and turned her attention back to Liz: "So, buddy, where do you live?"

Liz pushed back a strand of hair: "We're both in B, short for Begonia. I'm right below you in Block 3, Room 1. B3-1. Bingo."

"You in garbage duty, too?" May asked without the slightest curiosity.

"Geez, no. I'm in laundry."

As they exchanged these civilities, a buzz had been building around them. Now May distinctly heard the words "Korean," "Viet," "Jap" being tossed back and forth at different tables. The red table was the rowdiest. She spotted the bleached twins. Finally she heard the inevitable "stinkin' Chink." She pulled a cigarette and lighter from her shirt pocket, stood up, froze a moment to give them all a good look, and exited from the Montrose Penitentiary cafeteria, unlit cigarette in the corner of her mouth.

✪

May stretched out on her monk's cot in Montrose's B3-7, her new home for the next four years, minimum, and closed her eyes. The sound of a loud television rose from the foyer. A commercial for improved business management set to a Nina Simone tune. At least there were no phone calls here. Someone growled in the foyer: "Eileen, get your ass over here." May heard the echo of another harsh voice in her head. "May, it's your mother. Have you forgotten me?" The memory sent a shiver down her spine. Her mother's feeble voice on the answering machine: "Hello, is that you, May? May? Where are you?" Sometimes there had been five or six messages a day. Occasionally May had tried to forestall the dreaded calls by phoning first. But not every day was Mother's Day. You had to feel pretty good to call your mother, and you had to have something to talk about. Nothing about politics, religion, her lover, her work — those subjects only led to raw disagreement. Which left what? Strictly over-the-counter topics: girlfriends, her health, house cleaning, family stuff. I went to a movie (no specifics required); Joe and I went out to eat. No, he doesn't have a girlfriend yet. And how's your health, don't clean too much, did you go to the bridge club this week? How's Sam?

Play it again, Sam. May was amused at the association. Bogie's gangster voice interpreting her big brother Sam! Ludicrous. But, then, they were both short and suave. Bogart's foolish magnanimity. Poor, dumb Ingrid. Why was passionate love always so lofty on the silver screen when it was so twisted and ugly in reality?

"Eileen, what the fuck? Get down here: *The Sopranos* is starting."

"Shut the fuck up, bitch. I ain't comin' down."

May stared up at the ceiling — white, unblemished, but for the smoke detector — and the walls — more bare white. She pulled her cigarette pack and lighter from her shirt pocket and moved toward the window where she'd set her miniature silver ashtray. No bars. But a security system in the insect screen. A glass of wine would be nice. She let herself be guided by *The Sopranos*' opening theme and projected herself on the highway, crossing the bridge, past the electric pylons and oil refineries, speeding until she turned into a gentrified neighbourhood and stopped at 20 High Grove Crescent. A quick caress and a few pebbles for Mimi. A change of clothes and a glass of wine. Lee would be arriving any minute now. They'd drink and kiss until the bottle was empty. Mimi would try to get between them. May would feed her a treat and drag him to bed. Pull his clothes off.

"It's your favourite part, Eileen: he's with the shrink. Come on!"

"Leave me alone, for Chrissake: I fuckin' mean it."

May retrieved her earplugs from her polka-dot toiletry bag on the shelf. She lay on the bed, opened her shirt and pulled her nipples; her pants now half down, she rubbed her clitoris roughly until she produced a weak orgasm.

※

May came down to Begonia's foyer at 0800 sharp to meet Facilitator Janet Walker.

Walker's round face framed in straight bangs belied a no-nonsense manner. "As you were told by the warden, you've been assigned to Sanitary Collection You start at the Eagle."

May made a funny face.

"The Eagle building. Didn't Elizabeth Rich show you?"

May gave her a non-committal shrug.

"That's our services building, where the laundry, the food and other supplies are kept. And the clinic. It's on the other side of the courtyard. Let's go." Facilitator Walker pivoted soundlessly on her flat shoes, and May followed the flaired skirt and occasional glimpse of cellulite down the half-moon path that linked the residences A-B-C-D to E for Eagle.

Facilitator Walker pointed to a gray plastic cart on wheels in the corner of the laundry room. "Mornings, you collect the residents' individual refuse and put the bags in this container."

May spotted Liz, but the latter, almost buried under mounds of linen, didn't acknowledge her.

"Each resident is required to put her garbage bag outside of her room, to the right of her door by 0730."

May noted Facilitator Walker's use of the terms "resident" and "room."

"Every resident is provided with Kitchen Catchers, like these." Facilitator Walker pulled from the right pocket of her skirt what for a split second looked like a rabbit but turned out to be a transparent bag. "You must notify us if you find other types of garbage bags. On no account should you touch any other type of bag."

The transparent bag, May realized, meant no intimacy, not even in one's garbage. Part of the punishment.

"The three residences we just went by each have four blocks, and there are twelve rooms per block: in theory you have 144 bags to pick up. After your tour of each residence, you will come back here to the Eagle to empty your cart in the dumpster."

In theory? May was amused to find theory even in here. What, she wondered, did a theoretical garbage bag smell like? How many bags were there in actual practice? Certainly, there was now one more in Begonia: hers. And there was nothing theoretical about it, her period having started overnight. She followed Facilitator Walker outside into a circular parking lot where she was shown the dumpster. A single van with the red lettering HANNAFORD BROS. CO. was parked in the lot. Food. Not drugs.

"Oh yes," Facilitator Walker plunged a hand into her skirt's left pocket. "These are your gloves. Do not lose them. They are to be returned after work, at the Eagle. After lunch, you will move on to the cafeteria and the washrooms where the girls working there will help you put their large garbage bags onto your cart."

So they were all "girls" here. May felt like she was back in the convent.

"And, one last thing, Miss Ho: do not think that, because you're a college graduate, you'll get extra privileges in here. You're already privileged to be in Montrose and not at the Singer Center, believe me." Facilitator Walker pivoted one last time on her silent soles and vanished.

May preferred her "collection" job to working in the kitchen or laundry. Theoretically, she thought, she was a dog rummaging around for choice scraps. The interest lay in the different shapes identically sized plastic bags could take. Some would be bursting at the seams with candy boxes, cigarette packs, hand lotion bottles and depilatory-wax containers; others would be so light as to hold only a few Kleenexes smeared with snot and mascara and cheap lipstick. Probably it would all be predictable. What was a person allowed to consume in here, anyway? Canteen treats, Mini Oreo, Chips Ahoy! Ritz Bits, Cheese Nips; a lot of hair care products, nail buffers, ridge fillers and roll-on deodorants. All alcohol-free, of course. After all, what do women do? Eat, smoke, make up and over, menstruate — the puffy bags gave away who had the curse — and not much else.

A for Acorn was the staff housing, and off-limits. So May's alphabet began with B. Begonia, her building. She started on the first floor and, well, it turned out the little transparent Kitchen Catchers weren't exactly to the right of each door. Beside some doors there were none — no occupants, maybe — others had two, three. At the end of Block 1, she picked up an innocent looking package that was almost impossible to lift. It turned out to contain a free-flying weight from the gym. Still, May figured she was doing okay, no punctured glove yet, no dirty tricks. She became careful as she encountered more obstacles. In a bag on the second floor, a handful of blades which had been removed from the plastic razors. The idea of alerting Facilitator Walker never crossed her mind, even when at last, on the second floor of Block 2, she came up against the most predictable prank: shit. Not only inside the bags, but outside too. Shades of September initiation rites in her undergraduate days. She picked up the foul brown bags, put them in her container and, before heading to the Eagle building, let her soiled gloved hand trail along the wall of the entire block. It wasn't her block. Tough shit, ladies.

✡

Liz was feeling sorry for herself. She sat on the side of her bunk in B3-1, kicked off her running shoes and dangled her white-stockinged feet, legs apart, head falling forward. Another fucking laundry day. First towels, all rosewood pink. Then sheets, all singles, off-white. Scrubbing menstrual stains. How could people be such porkers? The weird texture of the suicide-proof sheets. No wringing. And a hundred head-fucking dryers spinning. Not different from way back when. She'd never had enough quarters for the laundromat. Washing baby diapers, baby sheets, and keeping an eye on Bing. Washing her own bloody sheets and clothes at home, her body a fountain of liquids. Liz got up to look at herself in the long mirror she'd hung by her door. Awful pale today. She half turned. And getting a little plump, too. She combed her hair and pulled it back into a ponytail, tying it with a flowery band. Put on a happy face.

By the time Liz got to the cafeteria, May was already seated at a yellow table, next to a skinny girl with gray-streaked hair and glasses. Her tray filled, Liz made her way over. "Hey, Laura, what's up?" She didn't expect an answer from the bespectacled mousy girl, but she always greeted her all the same. She turned to May: "You still here? I thought you'd be fed up and gone home by now."

"I thought I'd finish reading the manual first. Impressive set of rules."

"You ask any of the ladies around here, they'll tell you: this place is pretty cool. You know fuck all about P4W. Ask Eileen or Chris or even fat Gloria: they were in Singer first… Come to think of it, take my word for it." Liz whispered in May's ear: "Those gals over at the red table, Eileen and Chris, they don't just bark."

May stole a look in Eileen and Chris' direction. The two bleached heads were sitting face to face, hunched over their plates and scarfing down their food with spoons. They were wearing their black bomber jackets. May turned back to Liz and smiled, nodding at her buddy's hands: "Seems to me you could be in trouble with those nails."

Mousy Laura chipped in: "'Page 37, section 5.6: Nails must not exceed three millimetres.'"

Liz speared a few peas with her fork. "Laura, count your peas." She pierced more peas but they were so overcooked and the fork tines so dull, she only managed to create mush. "Ah, love that canned feeling. From the Valley of the Jolly, ho, ho, ho, Green Giant. number two peas. Shit, I must've eaten a goddam sixteen-wheeler of number two peas in my life."

She gazed down at the plate, until her eyes glazed over for an instant, then shifted her mood: "Chicken à la king, peas and mashed potatoes. Now that's grand wedding fare. You married, May? Kids?"

"Was. Nope."

"You, married? I can't fuckin' picture you in front of the altar. Okay, what'd you serve up at the banquet?"

"Joe had my red shoe."

"What?" Liz stopped making canals in her mashed potatoes and brandished her fork as a question mark. Laura, meanwhile, had turned her peas into abacus beads and was busy making arcane calculations from the shifting configurations.

"Joe, my groom, got smashed," May said. "We're standing on a table by then. He gets down, takes off my red high heel, fills it up…"

"Sure, sure, Joe fills it up with champagne, drinks it down, and bingo! He tumbles down, taking you with him, your white dress stuck in the chandelier, and so on. I saw that movie."

"I figured it was something in the shoe, put him over the edge."

"So what was the meal like?"

"Can't remember. Lots of ginger and saffron. And booze. Mostly booze."

"And what happened to Joe?"

"He became a drunk."

Side by side in silence, they ate their brown chicken, yellow clotted mashed potatoes and assorted peas, number ones, twos, threes… while Laura arranged her peas into clusters of two, then three, then back to two.

May was the first to rise, unlit cigarette in her mouth.

Liz followed. She was tired, PMSed. Felt like wet garbage. She'd always thought she would end up getting married. Wanted the house, husband, the whole deal. Never happened. Now she was feeling even sorrier for herself. May was wrong to shrug it off. Marriage, and a splashy wedding, too — red shoes, ginger and saffron, for chrissake. Did they do it at the Sheraton? Shit, you can put an alcoholic on the wagon.

☼

May figured the Montrose's inner yard would look okay over the summertime. Right now, the dried up February brown clashed with the pink of the directional signs. From left to right, May ran through the corny alphabet. The name she found most amusing was Ivy Institute: the library and classrooms. Somebody had high hopes. An untagged maple tree stood, leafless, in the centre of the yard. May sat on the green plastic bench facing the cafeteria, her back turned to Warden Segal's office in, what was it again… the Hollyhock. She lit a cigarette and tried to locate the bird sounding a two-note tune. Not in the tree, it would have been a breeze to spot; nor on any of the signposts. A bird in hiding, then. Those two-notes were getting to her. Plus her ass was cold. As she extinguished her cigarette, she spotted Liz moving between the cafeteria and the library in a slow stagger, hands to her stomach, hips forward, gaze turned inward. May lit a second cigarette and called out: "Hey, Liz, you okay?"

Liz stumbled towards her, steam pouring out of her mouth and clouding her features.

"Looks like you're cold."

Liz was again wearing that ponytail and those jeans and pastel sweatshirt under her open blue down jacket. She didn't speak, just stood there rubbing her belly.

"What the hell you doing? Exorcising your demons?" May offered her cigarette pack.

"Don't smoke. Never did, never will. Don't like the stuff. You smoke a lot?"

"As much as I can." May paused a moment, as though her answer was as surprising to her as it appeared to be to Liz. "I feel alive when I smoke. It's like I'm taking it all in, good and bad." She nodded her head. "Smoking is this girl's best friend. They can take away coffee, wine and all the wham whams, but I won't go without my fags."

"Shit honey, that's pathetic." Liz resumed massaging her belly with her two hands moving clockwise in small gyrating motions.

"Breathing is something you can do anywhere. But breathe in more than just air you're getting extra. It's life, scorching your throat, burning the inside of your nostrils."

"Enough already. May, you ought to take up qigong!"

"Chee-what?" May laughed at Liz' pronunciation. "What the hell you know about qigong?"

"That's what I was just doing: qigong!"

"Wonderful, now the inmates are doing qigong." May slurred the word with a sneer. "Well go rub yourself over there, why don't you. Lot of good it's doing you. You look green, I mean canned-pea green. Is that the qigong look?" May took a long last drag and dropped the cigarette under her heel. "Have you ever noticed that qigong practitioners all have pot bellies?"

"Well, I don't." Liz pushed back her ponytail and resumed her belly massage.

"How long have you been into this bullshit?" May lit yet another cigarette; they were the cheap ones provided by the facility: tubes you filled yourself with generic, dry tobacco. That bird was still tut-tutting, and still invisible. May eyed Liz' belly. "So Ms. Hong Kong, when did you pick up the Chinese exercises?"

"Oh, that was Jane Spitzer. Long time ago. She was staying at my place for a while, after the bastards threw her out of her apartment. I swear that girl was 48 or 49 and drop-dead gorgeous. And giving off all this energy. I never seen anyone looked like that. It was qigong did it. She never missed a day. Jane taught me. And she gave me her book. I have it with me, if you want to take a look."

"No thanks. Opium will give you a peachy complexion, too. Could be your gorgeous lady was an opium flower? Or maybe a crazy Falungonger."

"You're full of shit, May. Come on, get off your ass and walk a bit." Liz grabbed May's arm and forced her up.

"Only if you stop gyrating." They started down the path toward their unit, Begonia residence, but veered off and headed toward the letter F, as it was chow time.

A group of women was barring the entrance to the cafeteria.

"So Ee-lee-za-bett, looks like you found yourself a pet!" It was one of the two black bomber jacket girls.

Liz forced her way through. "Fuck off, Chris."

"But ooh, what an ugly one," Eileen, the other black-bomber-jacket girl, added.

"Look at those glasses."

"And those slits for eyes." Chris grabbed May's glasses and threw them to Eileen, who swirled them dangerously, as though she was going to smash them on the door.

May lunged in vain to get them back. Several other women emerged from the cafeteria and joined in, passing the glasses from one to the other. Finally, Chris put them on and said: "Wow, no wonder those Chinks squint. I can't see a fuckin' thing."

May was bombarded by questions and light shoving from all sides. Without her glasses, it was hard to tell who was asking what.

"So, Yellow Slit, when'd you land?"

"What you in for, Chink, killed kitchen cat?"

"Hell, Judge, she was hungry."

"Whatever it is, must be pretty serious — she's in the Bygone B, right?"

"Wanna be my pink pen pal, hey? How about it?" Someone started feeling her up from behind. It was Eileen. She unhooked May's bra and grabbed her breasts.

But Chris punched Eileen in the belly. "What the fuck, Eileen?"

Eileen let go.

A large dark-haired woman wearing a wide smile, oily pancake make-up and a generous royal blue pantsuit approached the door and interrupted the gang meeting. "Hey girls. Give Miss Ho her glasses back. Right now. Now!"

"Ooh, Gloooria! Yes, Your Majesty, whatever you say, Your Majesty."

Gloria swung her wide hips, bumping away the women barring the door, and proceeded in dignified manner to the chow line. Eileen dropped May's glasses on the ground, crunched them under the heel of her running shoe, and handed them to Chris, who returned them to May: "There you go, Ho. Ho-Ho!"

◘

A sweet pungent smell flooded Liz' room. Her single bed was littered with two dictionaries, ragged exercise books, brushes, and old newspapers. Liz was sitting at the built-in desk, which was also covered with newspaper. Between the bed and the desk, on the gray industrial rug, a brush was soaking in a cup of blackish water beside an ink bottle. Liz was drawing on grid paper with another brush, which she regularly dipped in a saucer of black ink. Her eyes stayed riveted for a few seconds on the top right corner of the book to her right, then moved to the page in front of her. Again and again, she repeated the same motions.

She was learning the Chinese character *ni*, meaning "you." The order of the strokes was crucial. First, one left-falling stroke, from top-right to bottom-left. Then, one vertical stroke from top to bottom. Another stroke from right to left downwards. One...? Shit. Liz flipped back to the table of contents. Okay. One horizontal hook stroke; first, from left to right, then lift brush to make the hook. One vertical stroke with an end hook, down from top to bottom, lift brush to make the hook. Then the two dots: from right to bottom-left, and lastly from left to bottom-right.

Is that it? Liz looked at the model, then at her own version.

Okay, let's do it again. She threw the used newspaper in the wastepaper basket to her left and stretched to grab more of the sheets of paper on the bed. Better this time, this *ni*. Now, how do I write me, myself and I?

She got up and eyed her work critically. Looked more like a kid's writing, bending this way and that. Unsteady. The *Practical Chinese Reader* said they should be "units of energy, each with its centre of gravity." Instead, she'd produced mouse droppings. Nausea swelled in her belly. Blocks. Bing's bright plastic blocks, red and blue, green and yellow. The way he tossed them all over the living room. Angry, so often angry. She had to stay in control, breathe in, calm down, hands to the navel. A little of this every day. And a little of that. Every day. There were 214 radicals and 858 phonetics, which combined to make thousands of characters. A lifetime. Liz stowed her writing implements on the windowsill and her books on the shelf on top of the desk. She reached for the photo album, but stayed her hand in mid-motion. Not tonight, or sleep would be peopled with them. The sweet pungent odour lingered.

In the cell above, May was lying on her bed, having just finished reading Montrose's *Manual for New Arrivals*. Good thing she wasn't farsighted; she could still read without her glasses. She pulled out her earplugs, and was immediately assailed by the canned laughter of a television coupled with the loud reactions of the viewers downstairs. She checked back to the "Schedule of Daily Activities." To her relief, there would be a head count in exactly twenty minutes. At least they'd be back in their cells soon. Her ashtray, filled with butts, had spilled over the bedcover, which looked less like a quilt now than a sleeping bag after a rainy camping day. Her funny hair looked even scragglier, bits spiking straight up here and there. She went to the window. A night bird somewhere. But without glasses, there was no hope. What was it like to be a bat? Sleeping upside down, prowling at night. Qualities unknown to humans. Joe probably knew, instinctively, as usual. Lee would have been clueless. Never up to much of anything at night, except nocturnal fears. A wet puppy afraid of storms. Though not when he was horny, more like a bear rushing at her, all senses open, though the arms didn't stay open for long. So much sex and yet so much longing, never enough. Never touched her enough. Big, useless arms. She'd turn him into a shaggy sofa, sink into him forever, drive her elbows in, drown in the plush. Boys. And where did it get her? Nailed him, screwed him and killed him. May sprawled on her stomach across her cot. The nylon quilt smelled of Sebreeze and nicotine. She checked again the number of books allowed in the "List of Permitted Personal Effects": ten, not including schoolbooks.

A hoarse voice rose from below: "You fuckin' bitch! Can't you see it ain't over! You bitch, turn it back on, you gotta see the outtakes, for shit's sake. I'm gonna…" May screwed her earplugs back in and returned to her thoughts. Which of her ethology books would she ask to have brought in? She got up again, opened her window wide to let in as much air as the thick screen would allow. Smoking did have that drawback. Yellow air, yellow teeth. She emptied the mini-ashtray and sat on her bunk bed, flipping through the "Permitted Hobbies" and waited for count.

✿

"HA-HA-HAPPY BIRTH-DAY TO YOU…" At lunchtime on an otherwise ordinary prison Monday, Liz walked into the cafeteria and straight into a loud chorus. Chris, her bomber jacket tied around her waist, was standing on a table, using her fork and knife to conduct the inmates in an impromptu celebration of Eileen's happy 24th. Chris bent over Eileen, serpent tongue probing, and was rewarded with a French kiss. For a delicious moment, the two bleached heads became one The birthday girl pulled up her bubblegum pink T-shirt over her tits, offering them to the serpent tongue. Oohs and aaahs all around, clapping, fists banging on tables. Liz ignored the celebration and made her way to a yellow table, where Laura Elmsley was sitting alone, cutting away Chiclets-sized morsels of the daily mystery meat.

Laura stopped slicing long enough to reposition her glasses and identify the person in front of her: "Hey Zil, what's up, Zil?"

"Zil?" said May, coming up from behind and setting her tray down beside Liz'. 'That's cute. How's tricks, Zil?"

"And who are you?" Laura asked May.

"It's May, for chrissake, Laura," Liz said. "You've already met her."

"Didn't recognize her. No glasses." Laura repositioned her own specs again to prove her point.

"That's right, I'm spec-less May, now. Anyway, the less I see around here the more I like it."

Again Laura secured her own eyewear, as though May might try to steal it.

Liz, with her 20-20 vision, ignored them both, brandishing instead a cold-cut slice. "Donkey dick," she declared, loud enough to turn heads. "The guys in the men's pen call this mystery meat 'donkey dick.'"

"Dicky dung," echoed Laura, resuming her slicing.

"Hey, Lizzie, why don't you come over here and suck my dick?" yelled Chris, who had seated herself with an arm draped over Eileen's shoulder and two fingers pinching the birthday girl's left nipple through the bubblegum T-shirt, which read "BIG FAT MAMA."

Even squinting, May could barely read the T-shirt. Incongruous declaration, she thought, on this thin, rather frail girl. May turned back to her plate. "Boys and their dicks," she sighed. "Doesn't make this baloney taste any better. What is it? Spam?"

"Fuck me, May, now that you mention it..."

"Fuck who? Hey, Lizzie? Fuck who?!!" shouted Chris.

May and Liz lowered their voices and hunched closer together.

"I'd go for sukiyaki, right now," said May, pushing her plate aside.

"Make that two. And a jug of sake."

"Right, sake. And sushi, sashimi, a bowl of clear miso soup with wakame seaweed."

"I used to make miso soup with doufu almost every day. Very healthy, no fat."

"And I'll have green-tea ice cream for dessert, please," added May to the invisible waiter.

"Sure, this is on me. With my alimony, I'm rolling in doufu."

Laura, left out of the banter, put in a belated word: "I don't think it's wa-me-ka, I mean wakame. It's wa-sa-bi, I mean, wa-bi-sa. Am I right or am I right?"

For one giggling moment, they were teenaged girls. Then Liz got serious, dropped her fork and leaned closer to May's ear.

"You wanna know what I'm doing while I'm in here?"

May eyed her warily. "No, I don't think I do."

"You can't guess." As May didn't look like she'd be drawn into guessing, Liz continued. "Well, I ain't tatting lace doilies for my love chest."

Suddenly, May decided to play. "All right, so you're learning to make noodles by hand."

Liz concentrated her attention, for a moment, at scraping a minute spot of something off the table. "You can't guess." Liz lowered her eyes and aimed a shy smile at the table.

"Learning the bible by heart? Both testaments. Backwards."

"Backwards? The bible is written from right to left, from back to front, from.... Not back," recited Laura.

Liz gave her the finger. "Laura, eat this right to left."

Laura set to work slicing her Chiclets once more, into halves.

"All right, May, can't guess?"

"You're studying something. That's it, isn't it? Something useless."

"Maybe. But it keeps me going." Suddenly Liz raised her head and confronted May defiantly. "Don't laugh: I'm learning Chinese. Just started learning how to write."

"What the... what for?" May shook her head slowly. "Talk about hard time. Well, you're in it for life. Your life, not mine."

"Okay, okay. Never mind. Fuck you anyways." Liz had turned deadly serious. Her ponytail hung along her nape down her back. "I want to learn a method. I mean I want to learn something methodically. Step by step. One, two, three. For once. I mean, shit. I've got all the time I need, don't I?"

"I can't argue with that. Time is the one thing you've got, Zil. But why Chinese?"

"Why not." Liz hesitated, "Well, it makes sense, you know; I mean, in a fucked-up sort of way. Like you draw the character for woman next to the one for child and you get 'good.' There's a natural order..."

May laughed. "Very natural! A female with a baby — and it's a male baby, by the way — means good. Who do you think thought that up, Liz? And how about women who don't have babies? I guess they're not 'good'?"

"I just like the order..."

"You're going to need glasses, Liz. Zil, glasses you will soon need. I'm telling you. You're going to end up with a pot belly and two-inch thick specs."

"So what, I don't care... You're joking, right? Anyway, when I need them, I'll wear them. What's the matter with you — too vain?"

May pulled out her broken glasses, laid them on the table. They both fell silent, sipping their Lipton tea while Laura, opposite, juggled a red Jell-O cube on her knife.

"Christ, May, I'm just trying to find something to get my mind off my dog dirt of a life. By the time I get out of here, well, if I'm ever outta here, I won't… I mean, well, I won't be fertile any more. But I want to be ready. I want to have peace of mind. Chinese will do that for me."

"Bullshit. You just don't know, Liz. You don't know what you're getting into. You think Chinese is some kind of magical mystery tour… Nirvana-on-earth. All human language is the same, more or less. Just like humans. Disappointing."

Liz straightened and her jaw tightened. "You've got a bug up your ass against Chinese. Some sort of prejudice, for who knows what fucked-up reason."

"It takes a white girl to love all things Chinese."

"Get off my back." Liz stood abruptly, crashing her tray and Laura's. General applause throughout the cafeteria.

"Hey, sweet Lizzie, come over and push Big Mama!" yelled Chris, or was it Eileen? Liz raised a finger in their direction and marched out of the hall, ponytail spinning. May remained motionless for a moment, then turned her attention to rolling a cigarette, fiddled with it, put it in her shirt pocket. She waited for the birthday girl and gang to go before leaving.

○

The showers at Montrose were particularly busy on Wednesdays. Maybe because Wednesday was shrink day and the inmates felt a need for purging, some before their interview, some after. Although an effort had generally been made to render the pen convivial, the showers were a far cry from private. They were communal, without curtains, probably to discourage shower-mates. But then again, so many nooks and crannies elsewhere offered potential lovers' nests: so why the taboo in the bathroom? Perhaps it was simply that the contractors had changed in mid-course, and the money for the construction of the new women's detention centre had run out? Whatever the reason, the showers were basic no-nonsense, to say the least. Of the twelve, four produced no more than a trickle, and four would scorch you. The women gathered around the remaining few. Some clever ones, like Liz, and now May whom she'd let in on the secret, came during meal times.

May was massaging her thighs with tight fuzzy purple gloves in clockwise circular motions. She glanced up from her labors to look at Liz, white-haired with conditioner.

"Well, Miss Rice Queen, how is lesson number two coming? Which radical are we doing today?"

"Eat shit and die."

"Okay, I was a little rude. You were right. I'm totally subjective, I'm biased, I'm misanthropic, I'm…" May stopped her massage to beat a mea culpa into her chest.

Liz turned away.

"Oh! Look at that, she's got a tat!" May's fist stopped beating and floated an instant between them. She stepped closer and stared at Liz' left shoulder. Liz didn't move away, but rolled her back slightly to enhance the view. The tattoo was a greenish-black lizard, without eyes.

"So you're into body art, uh? Any piercings? Seriously, Liz, this thing looks beautiful on you, perfectly targeted."

"Bullshit. I mean it wasn't… Christ, think what I'll look like when I'm an old fuckin' granny? Fuckin' cheap is what."

May laughed. "What's the likelihood you or I will ever be grannies, so I wouldn't worry about that. But why a lizard?"

"It's a cha-me-le-on." Liz recited in the tone of someone who has explained this many times before. "All possibilities, always changing. Small and unobtrusive." She darted her right hand over her shoulder, rapidly concealing and revealing the lizard, in a playful show. "Now you see it, now you don't."

May laid both gloved hands on the lizard. She scratched a little. "It's really permanent."

Liz put her left hand on May's. "Yeah, yeah, the REAL thing," she shouted into May's ear.

May moved both hands around Liz' shoulders and kissed the spot where the reptile's eyes would be. She hugged Liz under the shower. Her nose filled up with the smell of apricots and almonds. Again she kissed the eyeless lizard.

"Liz, tell me, Zil, why no eyes?"

"To make you talk, stupid."

May slid her tongue into Liz' ear. Liz pulled away.

"Turn around. Let me look at you."

"No." Liz shied away, rinsed her long hair once more, wrapped her hair in one towel, turban-style, and swiftly dried herself with another. In a minute, she'd put her sweatshirt and jeans back on. She hurried out with her bra and panties in her hands.

◘

Facilitator Walker was doing the day's second count in the Begonia residence. The "residents" were assembled in the foyer, in the prescribed fashion: the first-floor inmates with their backs two feet from the wall according to their block and room numbers, and the second-floor inmates facing them from across the room with their backs two feet from the windows. The five daily counts were the only moments in the day when they were reminded they were prisoners, not college girls. Liz grinned at May who was last to get into position, opposite her. As Janet Walker, stern-faced, standing in the middle of the room, counted: "Bee One Dash One, Bee One Dash Two," she was answered by the corresponding inmate, who spoke out her name, Danielle Badger, Sue Mann, Bridget Fox, and so on, while another facilitator — today it was Monica Haynes — checked off the occupancy list. During the count, other facilitators, two per block, conducted cursory inspections of each cell, the doors of which had been left open by the inmates. Count took no more than 5 minutes, unless something went wrong.

At 11:22, as the inmates dispersed, Facilitator Irene Hill arrived in the foyer, in her thick woollen sweater, pushing the mail cart. "May Ho: you've got mail! Hey… Ho!" May turned back down the staircase toward Hill, who was waving a letter in her direction. "There you go, your first letter. Some girls sure are lucky."

May tucked the letter in her shirt pocket without opening it. She headed for the stairs but was stopped by a firm hand. It was Gloria, smiling: "Miss Ho, you know you're eligible for visits after a week. A girl's got to know her rights."

May didn't reply. Instead of racing back to her cell, she went outside and lit a cigarette before looking at the dollar-store envelope. Just one glance at the handwriting told her who the sender was. Ant tracks in black ink: "J.T., Weeds Ln., Enosburg Falls, VT 05450." The unpleasant feeling only got worse when she noticed her own new address, "Montrose Detention Center For Women, Rivers Bend Line, Williston, VT 05495." The letter had been opened.

Back in her cell, she finally and reluctantly tore open the envelope. The top of the sheet had been stamped in large red letters: "A P P R O V E D."

The letter was dated February 22 — it certainly hadn't taken long to get here. But then Joe didn't live far. The salutation simply stated "May." Not even a "Dear." *I am rushing to write to you because I want to come to see you <u>as soon as possible</u>.* Rushing like the Falls. Joe, as neat as ever, was still writing ruler-perfect lines. Not the slightest ethylic tremor. *Last Wednesday morning, as I was crumpling newspaper for the stove, my eye caught something in the Classified Ads: "Auction at 20 High Grove Crescent, Burlington." An auction at our old place? I know you get funny ideas at times, but an <u>auction</u>?! There had to be a mistake. I smoothed out the paper to read about it.* He would smooth it down with an iron, if he could. *The auction is taking place this coming Saturday, February 26.* May dropped the letter, went to the electronic mosquito screen and lit a cigarette. 20 High Grove, that damned townhouse. Well, 20 High Grove had been heaven, for a while. What was there to auction off? Stacks upon stacks of books. No furniture to speak of. The kitchen things, Mimi's litter box? A good bed, though, and a decent work station. She retrieved the letter and carried it over to the window.

I picked up the phone and called our neighbour, Carole. She hung up on me. I'm sure I had the right number: you know I always remember phone numbers. Yes, Joe was irritating that way. *I called back and said: "I know this is 862-3888 and you are Carole. I'm Joe, May's husband." She cried and then told me to get off the line, never to phone back. So I hitchhiked down to Burlington and by the end of the day, I had the full picture.* May didn't want to imagine how he'd gotten "the full picture." *What a mess. Why didn't you tell me? My dreams are filled with flashes of you and him. And Mimi pops up, too. Let me come to see you. We'll talk. Please.* His letter ended with an elegant, albeit evasive, *As always.*

Carole. . May had forgotten about her. So she was back in 24 High Grove. Neighbourless, not even Mimi to feed. Of course the whole disastrous string of events was all Mimi's doing. Mimi had made it happen by falling in love with their neighbour. That cat had broken Joe's heart. And then Carole's. Did Carole miss Lee as badly as May did? Not possible. Not that gut feeling. It was all over. Even Mimi was dead. May had seen it coming; for weeks she'd carried the cat from her desk to the litter to bed. Arthritis in the animal's bones, infection in her mouth. Straying over to the neighbours' mirror townhouse had turned out to be her last adventure. They had better sofas, a nicotine-free environment, and plenty of yogurt and other feline treats to offer. May missed her, more than Lee, maybe. She got her purse mirror and eyeliner from the polka-dot bag. She drew her fishtail eyes, dabbed her neck with Roger Gallet eau de cologne and lay face-up on the cot. Missing Lee's smell. On his nape, on his gloves. Never could get enough of him. Still sitting on the edge of her bed, May opened her legs, reached under her panties to rub her clitoris till it ached. A tingling all through her sex and inner thighs. May looked up at the unblemished ceiling, then at Joe's letter, on the bedspread. Joe wanted to visit. Yes or no? Yes and no. Yes. May reached for the *Manual for New Arrivals* and detached an "Application for Visits." Relation to detainee? X.

✡

Visiting days, Liz got a little edgy. Even newbie May had a visitor. Joe might be a drunk, and her ex at that, but he still came to see her. As for Liz' family. The usual story. Mutual repudiation. Even K hadn't contacted her, never got back to her after her phone message. But did Liz really want to see him? Sorry creature, that K was. White man, pink dick, brown suit. She was glad he hadn't tried to come around. She'd say no, if he asked. Definitely no. Liz looked at herself in the mirror and repeated: "NO WAY JO-SE!" She picked up her writing implements from the windowsill and brought down her Chinese exercise book from the top shelf. Okay, Elizabeth, get to work. She picked up the brush and began by rehearsing in the air. A cross between a cheerleader and a music conductor. On today's menu: the word *hao*, "good."

Hao: six strokes, 3 on the left for "woman," 3 on the right for "child." Even immersed in her Chinese practice, she couldn't get away from motherhood. Got it. So that's "good." She wished May hadn't been so negative. Sure, just because a woman never had a baby, didn't mean she wasn't a woman. But could such a woman understand mothers? Weren't women with children more whole? Was Dr. Leo a mother? Liz bet the prison shrink had two beautiful children, a boy and a girl, three years apart. The boy went to private school, the little girl was still at home with a nanny. They lived in a colonial mansion in Shelburne. Dr. Leo's husband, a big-shot corporate lawyer, would drive them all to their lakeside cottage on weekends. While she mused, Liz continued her writing. She repeated the same strokes over and over, her hand gradually overcoming her mind, the gesture overriding her thoughts. She became a perfect scribe, unthinking, at least until the day's last count.

◘

May was drying herself when Liz arrived with her shower caddy. May nodded at her and started putting her own toiletries — soap, brush, massage gloves — back in her polka dot bag. She watched Liz undress swiftly and hop under the shower. May hesitated, dropped her bag and towel on the floor and got under the same nozzle as Liz.

"I thought you'd washed already?" Liz smiled broadly.

"Not behind the ears." May put her tongue on Liz' lizard and her hands on her breasts. She pinched Liz' nipples softly and gently bit her neck. Soon, she'd wrapped her legs around Liz' body. Liz acted as though nothing was happening, and started to lather the shampoo on her head. May's right knee slipped between Liz' legs, pushed upward and pressed firmly on Liz' pubis. Liz stopped washing her hair and stood there, eyes closed, shampoo trickling down her face. She crossed her arms, but her legs were relaxing. May felt Liz' juices flowing and soon she heard her moan. She kissed Liz on the nape again and moved away.

"See you later, salamander." May quickly toweled off again, dressed and exited the communal shower.

Today, for the first time, I doubted my little red book. Not Mao's little volume of quotations; I mean the miniature bilingual edition of ancient Chinese proverbs. At the crack of dawn, still in my fireman red PJs, I starting flipping the pages of the tiny tome. Once I'd formulated a question about my first police assignment, I stopped flipping and jabbed a finger on the page at random. I landed on "Advantage: a pavilion by the water: you have the best view to see the moon." This answer to my question made no sense. It was as though the book of proverbs was referring back to last night's hanging out at the WWW bar with the grrrls. But the proverb book was never wrong.

It was Liu Qi, a schoolmate at Beijing's Number 3 middle school, who'd taught me this peculiar form of bibliomancy. You were supposed to formulate a question, then think of a page and line number at random. The proverb thus located provided the answer to your question. Over the years, I'd made so much use of the proverb book I found myself remembering specific page and line numbers and cheating, so that I had to switch to just poking my finger into the book. And poke I did, especially in times of crisis: after my foster parents died in a plane crash en route to Hainan province, leaving me entirely without family. And then again when I learned that they had left me a good sum of money. And more recently when I had to decide whether or not to go into the police academy. I'd been hesitating between literary critic and crime solver, because on my first try the book had fallen open to "Read between the lines," whereas on the second try it had suggested I "Follow spider webs and horse tracks." But, in the end, I couldn't imagine Rey a.k.a. Lily-of-the-valley, signing my autograph on a book tour à la Petunia a.k.a. Bethune.

At the police academy, the first lesson was patience: how often we'd been reminded that rookies invariably spent their first months behind a desk. So, now, I consulted the book a second time in search of a clearer explanation. The second proverb promised imminent radical transformation: "You cast off your bones and emerge a new person."

Bones? I checked on Otis through the sliding patio door. He defecated, moved over to chomp on a clump of grass, sprayed a nearby shrub, and confirmed his mark with a long appreciative sniff.

Otis is a handsome Lab. Well, handsome as far as I can tell, my knowledge of canines being limited to a brief introductory police course in sniffer dogs. Otis came with the condo, which belonged to dotcomer Max Foe, a childhood sweetheart of mine, from the days before I moved to Beijing. I'd been very lucky to bump into him again so many years later, just before my graduation from the academy. Turned out it was a good deal for both of us: he was relieved to find a dogsitter, and I didn't need to go apartment hunting. I'd never had an apartment to myself and it was a privilege to stay, if only until Max returned, in his renovated turn-of-the century townhouse in the heart of downtown Burlington. I could never afford anything like this on a third-grade cop's salary.

Otis? He must have disappeared behind the dogwood shrub. A bee was hitting, one by one, the pistils in a cluster of narcissus.

It felt strange being back in Burlington after so many years. On the one hand, there were bad memories here, my mother's death, not to mention all the debris of childhood one prefers not to revisit. But, at the same time, I felt an attraction to the area. It was no great metropolis like New York or Beijing, but it had a lot to offer. First and foremost, the range of geography concentrated in such a small area: in Greater Burlington, you can still go from urban to suburban, from small town to rural, all within twenty minutes of driving. There are flat lands and hills, cliffs and bluffs overlooking the lake, and the Winooski River turns and bends into rapids, falls, and bogs. And then there's the way Vermont has clung to the northern edge of the US, almost Canadian in its weather and its politics, yet drenched in US history. Unlike China, and most of the world for that matter, Burlington, I figured, was one place you could still be a cop in the service of the state without being an enemy of the people.

I'll also admit I was getting more and more nervous that Sunday morning, as Monday approached. I abandoned my proverbs and went to the closet to check on my brand new uniform, as though it might disappear on me the day before my first day on the job. It was still there, complete with high-polish kickass shoes and cap. I slipped the jacket off its hanger and put it on. It looked good, though a bit kinky over my red PJs. Quickly I dropped my pants and donned the entire uniform. I imagined tomorrow's first encounter with the chief and my peers at the police station. I walked into the living room, sat down and practised pinching the pants so as not to crease them. There I was, the perfect blue figure of the law on a red sofa, immaculately neat, except for a strand of hair that had broken free of my three-bobby-pinned chignon. Okay, so maybe I looked more like a mischievous kid in her daddy's police outfit. I liked the look but...

Even with the most conventional clothing, I've always enjoyed making my own little fashion statement: my straight hair, which I like to pull together with a barrette in the shape and colours of an HB pencil, is never entirely tame; my nails, which I often paint blue — though I'd refrained on that Sunday — are always slightly too short; my shoes, mostly high-heeled and red, rarely match my absolutely minuscule or oversized handbags. I like to mix but not match Chinese things with Western accessories, men's with women's clothing and, of course, retro with new.

But my admittedly offbeat clothes were not what drew so much attention in Beijing. To fellow Westerners, I suppose I was a five-foot-five, 110-pound brunette with grayish-green eyes. But there were few Westerners in Beijing back then. For most of the seven years I lived there, Chinese who met me referred to me as the big, yellow-haired girl with blue eyes. Somehow the Chinese described all shades of hair or eyes that weren't jet black as respectively blond and blue. In the countryside I had sometimes been asked what sex I was. Maybe my lack of make-up, my short nails and the absence of a hip swing in my walk somehow turned me into a long-haired boy with breasts. Or else the rare Westerners in China all looked strangely sexless and alike. Occasionally I took satisfaction in the look of surprise I'd get from a Chinese person who heard my fluent Mandarin before turning around to see me. I had assumed all that would change when I returned to the West, but it seemed I'd picked up something in China that now made me look as odd to people here as I'd been to the Chinese over there.

Otis threw his 80 pounds at the sliding door at the same instant as the phone rang. I sprang up, glancing at the dog, then the phone, and then my watch. Caught *in flagrante*: for a brief moment, I had the idea that I ought to take my police uniform off before answering the phone. My Swatch's hands pointed through Edgar Allan Poe's jaw and skull: 0700 hours. On Sunday morning? I took off my cap, tucked it behind my back, and turned myself into the house servant. "Max Foe's residence, may I help you?"

"Officer Pirelli?" It was Captain Carter's firm but gentle voice. "I need you to get down to Montrose, ASAP." As the Chief spoke, I had to struggle to control my excitement and keep track of his words. "Officer Pirelli," Captain Carter repeated, as though he wanted to be sure I was still on the other end of the line, "there's been some trouble at the women's detention centre. It's Easter Sunday, I don't have any manpower… I mean personnel." He cleared his throat. "You go down to Montrose Pen… Montrose Detention Center… see what the fuss is about, and file a report. As simple as that. Got it?"

"Yes, sir, file a report."

"Just a FOOS, Officer Pirelli, that's all. You're the first officer on the scene, you file a report. And get your ass out of there."

"Yes, sir, file a FOOS and get my ass out of there."

There was a pause while I wondered whether I should hang up or wait for him to sign off. Then he cleared his throat again. "Officer Pirelli?"

"Sir?"

"You do know where the Montrose Detention Centre is, right?"

"Yes, sir."

"All right then."

The line went dead.

Fluttering about like a schoolgirl, I forced Otis back inside the loft-like living room a little roughly. I treated him with the remains of my breakfast, one steamed white bun and half a boiled egg, and sat down again on the red couch with my cold espresso, and the Security System reference card. But it was too late to figure out how to bypass open sensors so that Otis could go in and out of the fenced yard. Tough luck, dog.

I dropped the alarm system manual on the kitchen counter and plunked my coffee cup back on top of it. I looked straight into the oval mirror by the front door, readjusted my cap, tucked in the wild strands, walked past the alarm system without pausing, and closed my eyes to recite my mantra: *Nan-mo-a-mi-tuo-fo*.

The library at Montrose Pen was located on the third floor of the Ivy Institute, the building with a mind to shape minds. On the second floor were the core programs: living skills, cognitive skills, substance abuse intervention, sex-offender treatment, family violence. On the first floor, the vocational and basic education programs: highschool education, literacy, home economics, carpentry and the recently added computer skills. Cool Clo was the nickname by which both staff and inmates called the graduate-student volunteer who supervised the compulsory "free" reading periods in the library. Cool Clo wore a T-shirt and Gap stretch jeans, and her hair in multiple braids. She was a semiotics student in the comparative literature department at the University of Vermont. Her job was to walk through the library sections, making sure everyone was keeping busy.

The computer stations were the hot spots of the library. The eight computers were always occupied. Surfing was what inmates did on the computers, and though porn and hate websites, as well as the sending or receiving of emails, were disabled, there were still sites tailored for the female inmate, sites like "In(ti)mate Valet" and "Love behind Bars," which promised anything from intimate apparel to a husband, all on the buy-now-pay-later plan. Although a sign limited use to 15 minutes, few inmates got a turn on the machines. Cool Clo didn't check time.

Most of the others could be found in the periodicals section, browsing through old magazines. Who knew? In less than five years, those outmoded elephant pants and rounded shoes might swing back into fashion. The most dog-eared sections of the magazines were the questionnaires on your sex drive, sex appeal, social skills, and ideal partner. They had been filled in by numerous residents. If all those answers had been collected and fed into a profile program, the machine would have overloaded. Grrrls.

Gloria Fletchard was among those who were content in the periodicals corner. She could be found ensconced in the two-seater, which her royal-blue suit pretty well filled up. Next to her, in the little remaining space, she piled up issues of a zine in which no one else had expressed the slightest interest: the high-brow *Gourmet*. The Ivy Institute had an enormous collection, decades' worth, of the magazine, donated by a rich patron who, some people said had given up eating to join an ashram in southern California. Others claimed the donor had rebelled against the magazine's editorial bias against *nouvelle cuisine*. This didn't bother plus-sized Gloria, who pored over hundreds of recipes, although she would never actually make or taste the dishes. She was not allowed in the kitchen at Montrose. For Gloria, reading was eating, and everyone was the better for it, because Gloria was serving a life sentence for the murder of both her parents, her husband, three children and an aunt. She had accomplished this pruning of the family tree with an elaborate 10-course meal.

Chris and Eileen were also frequent users of the periodical section. Though they wouldn't admit it, they were computer illiterate and never seemed to get their asses to class. They preferred movie star-gazing and any mags catering to curiosity about the lives of the famous. Eileen usually came up with the best finds, mainly because she was a slightly better reader than Chris.

"Can you believe this?" she told Chris, "Liz Taylor didn't know how to make a fuckin' bed before she got to the Betty Ford!"

Cool Clo approached to listen in. Clo's girlfriend was writing her dissertation in Comp Lit on the discourse of celeb-reality shows.

"Don't wet your pants, honey," Chris said. "Nick Nolte just figured out he's colour blind: at Silver Hill, he had to choose his own socks in the morning and he kept puttin' on a red with a green!"

Eileen flipped a page. "Guess what Anna Nicole used to feed her French poodle: Prozac 'cause he's depressed."

Chris didn't like to be undone. "Who the fuck cares about fat tubs like Anna Nicole and Liz Taylor? Maybe, our own fat Gloria? How many hubbies did you turn into stew, Gloooo-reee-ah?" Gloria ignored her. "Hey," Chris shouted, "what's on today's menu? Fat fart soup à la arsenic?"

Eileen chimed in: "Pocket pizzas stuffed with Paul's pepperoni."

Gloria caught hold of Cool Clo's sleeve: "Please, Miss Clo, some folks here are disturbin' the peace." Then she stuck her nose back into a Shandong lacquered duck recipe, part of the special issue on Chinese regional cuisine in the 1984 fall edition of *Gourmet*.

The decibel level was rising, but Cool Clo just nodded sympathetically to Gloria. A little noise was acceptable, so long as they were talking, not using their fists.

"Hey, lookee, lookee, she's planning Liz rolls and pineapple chick balls for Yellow Slit," Chris announced. "Right, Liz?"

May moved deeper into the stacks. Earplugs blocked out noise but, somehow, the racial stuff always seemed to get through. Liz, on the other hand, hadn't heard the mention of her name. She was one of a group of inmates sitting at the long table in front of the windows facing the inner courtyard. She brought her own books to the library: her *Practical Chinese Reader* and character exercise manual, and her bilingual dictionary. Today, she was practising the characters *ma* for "mother" and its homophone, the particle signalling an interrogation, or so she told Cool Clo, who was genuinely impressed. Laura sat next to Liz. She was diligently copying words from the *Webster's College Dictionary* into columns and rows, formatting them exactly like in the book. Today she was at page 124, "bed jacket" topped the first column; the second column contained an illustration of various cuts of beef. Cool Clo wondered whether Laura would copy this too. Other women at the long table were writing letters home or their own diaries. Clo caught sight of many false starts. Even the initial salutation of a letter written from the inside required meditation. Clo found much inspiration during her twice-weekly surveillance periods at the Montrose library.

Cool Clo drifted through the few aisles of bookshelves in the library. May was holding volume 23, "Li- Mu" of the 1973 edition of the *Encyclopaedia Britannica*. As Clo passed, May took the large tome over to the long table.

Liz looked up and to her left, past Laura, and spotted the volume. What was May looking for in there? Mother? Mummy? Murder?! Jesus. What was May in here for, anyway? Would she tell? In any case, such things had a way of leaking out sooner than later. Liz thought she must tell May her own story before it was too late, before someone else — mousy Laura, maybe — tattled. But when? How? Of course, there was no way to explain. Liz broke off her Chinese lesson to write May a confession:

> *Ni hao, May!*
> *Sitting here wondering what you're searching for in that fat book: new info on mothers or monsters? I guess it's about time I told you why I'm here, don't say you don't care or you know already: you don't, I know you don't. If you knew, you wouldn't be talking to me any more. I can't say it to you, so I'm just writing this letter. May, I killed my boy, Bing. That's his name. It wasn't an accident, I killed him on purpose. He was a monster. Seven is awful young, I know. But seven's the age of reason, he knew what he was doing. Now you can stop speaking to me, sit someplace else in the caf.*
> *Liz, the not-yet Chinese whiz*

Why try to make it funny? Nothing funny about it. If you want to write it down, then just do it. Tell it like it is. *Mother Kills Own Son on Hallowe'en*. Not funny — scary.

> *May,*
> *Check under "I" for infanticide. That's me. I killed my son, his name was Bing, he was seven. He killed my newborn baby, Ann.*
> *Liz, the monstrous mother*

Drop that last line. And the smart-alec reference to the dico. No use even trying to be cool about it. Don't even think for a moment she won't be turned off.

Cut some more. Cut. *May, I killed my son in cold blood*. No, cut the act. *May, I killed my own son. Liz*

At 16:45, facilitators Haynes and Walker, with Cool Clo's assistance, conducted the head count in the library. The women at the long table by the window were the last to leave. Liz was putting her papers in order, throwing some out, sticking others inside her dictionary. May watched her absentmindedly. Liz felt herself blushing, as though May could read what she'd written.

"Read this." Liz plucked one version of her letter out of her dictionary without choosing, and thrust it in May's face. Then she strode quickly away, back to her cell.

May couldn't figure out why the sleeping pill wasn't working. Something was disturbing her more than usual. Couldn't be Liz' letter. At first she had thought it might be a love letter. Or a poorly phrased "Women Unite" pamphlet. Instead, a vulgar confession. It wasn't called infanticide when the kid was seven. Murder. Liz, a murderess. May had assumed she was in for petty theft. Acupuncture couldn't buy you a whole lot of groceries. Infanticide, matricide. It had long been May's opinion that all mothers should be separated from their kids before they got a chance to do away with them, even if it was only by grinding them down.

In spite of herself May found herself flashing back to a cold room, she and Joe lying on separate cots, with electric wires attached to their lower bellies. They were in the basement of an acupuncturist's home. Dr. Perlman lived next to the pink brick synagogue on Archibald. He had opened the door, his ringlets tucked behind his ears and his prayer shawl sticking out below his jacket. Entering the house was enough of a shock: the strong smell of boiling chicken and the dozen children, three in diapers, others ranging from kindergarten age to pre-teens, the eldest holding a newborn, sneaking glimpses as she and Joe crossed the ground floor, past the kitchen, on the way to the clinic downstairs. Dr. Perlman certainly didn't require his own services, or perhaps he'd been overindulging in his fertility enhancement techniques. But electro-acupuncture, which the good doctor called beebuzzing because of the high noise it produced, hadn't saved May's marriage. She and Joe had gone back to lie there for a good five sessions, cold jelly spread over their vibrating bellies. Even then, she knew a baby couldn't save them. Dr. Perlman began every session with the stipulation: "You must be relaxed and put your faith in God." After a week off for Hanukkah without the cold and noisy treatment, Joe and May had decided to let God do his work without Dr. Perlman's help. God, in his merciful wisdom, had chosen not to transform them into parents.

May tossed and turned. She heard her mother's voice drenched in self-pity: "May? I'm lonely. I don't know why, but I'm so lonely." What could she say? Tough, get a pet? Get a life? Your own life. What did her mother hope to accomplish with her emotional blackmail? To force May to take her in? Or simply to rob her daughter of the freedom she'd never had? "January is so long... I just don't know what to do with myself." May stretched her imagination to come up with things an 83-year-old might do: go for a walk, Mom, go down and see if Mrs. S wants to play cards. Take a day at a time, Mom, look, the sun's shining. Have you heard from big brother Sam?

Of course she had, twice a week, without fail. Why not go visit your nice son? Her mother only sighed. May's suggestions never worked. It was dead of winter, an old lady couldn't walk on those slippery sidewalks. Her majiang pals were dead, or blind, or gaga. And Sam was too far away. Slowly the sentimental blackmail began to eat away at May's brain, though both right and left hemispheres were already filled with grief.

By the time spring break came along, Lee wouldn't see her any more. Mimi was dead, and the big bear too. The thing with Lee had been a roller coaster nightmare. Now he was back on the needle. More than she had with any man before, she missed Lee. No more petting, no more kisses. Still, May couldn't figure out what got into her to take her mother to Mexico. It took some convincing. And who could blame the old lady? Sure, she wanted the sun, the heat and company, anybody's company. But to be alone in a foreign land with her strange, unpredictable daughter… All through the month of January, she kept phoning, asking if May hadn't changed her mind about going after all, asking about that Riu Hotel, was it clean, free of roaches? Threatening to cancel her ticket every second day. Clearly Mrs. Ho didn't have much trust in that wild daughter of hers. Now, if Sam had offered to take her somewhere. She'd have gone anywhere with Sam. Sam, so nice, so considerate. Well, he could afford to be. He was a long way away. Such a good son, writing weekly, phoning twice weekly. Always willing to swap small talk. Whereas May… With May, it was all teeth and nails, and you never knew where you might end up.

Perhaps her mother was worried that May would abandon her under a parasol with no one to talk to. An old woman, unaccustomed to travelling, stranded in a foreign land, albeit a seaside resort, but the strange money, strange language. As soon as they arrived at their five-star hotel on the Mayan Riviera, May regretted it. They both did. Mexico, paradise on earth. Mother and daughter in a single hotel room for one long week. Scorching hot weather Couples, all heterosexuals, on the beach, by the pool, everywhere. With the exception of May and her mom: aged mother and middleaged daughter. May couldn't bear to watch the couples mock-burying each other in warm sand, smooching in the turquoise water. Drove her nuts. "Disgusting," her mother said, though she constantly made remarks about how "nice" the young women with two-pieces and matching shirts looked. And how ridiculous May looked in her bikini: "You're not going out with that, are you? May, do you realize how old you are?! No wonder you can't keep a husband." By the third day, Mrs. Ho retreated to their room, complaining of the heat. Wouldn't even get on the tour bus to visit the Mayan ruins.

The ride took all morning, freezing inside the air-conditioned bus. They arrived at noon. Too hot to visit, really. Anyway, they only had one hour. May, determined, scrambled to the top of the pyramid. The sun was at its zenith and, for a moment, she felt on top of the world. Must have been a touch of heat stroke. But she did feel something in the air around the Mayan pyramids, in the noon silence. A predatory bird floating off to the west. A place to bring the old to die. Good thing her mother hadn't come along. Too steep, too hot. And coming down! May had to zigzag left and right to negotiate the sharp drop.

It was past midnight and sleep would not come. She was only issued one sleeping pill a night. And no glass of wine. May got up, smoked a cigarette, half of it by the screened window, the other half pacing between the window and the door. She lay down in bed again and tried to put her body to sleep by making each part of herself numb, from the feet up. When she got to her belly, where her hands were resting as though she were in a coffin, the game stopped working. May was too wide awake and her mother wouldn't get out of her head.

Three o'clock: a white sun flooded half the hotel room. May finished her mom's beauty treatment and moved her from her chair in the shade, laying her in the sunlight on the bed with her freshly done red nails crisscrossed on her stomach — at least she'd be properly manicured for viewing. She wasn't heavy, frail bones and loose wrinkled flesh, sagging even more now. May put away the Kleenexes, and the tweezers she'd used to pluck the few facial white hairs, as well as the Christian Dior lava-red nail polish. She poured herself a glass of rosé wine, lit a cigarette, then dialed 0. "*Reception? Mama muerte, si muerte.*" She couldn't remember the Spanish word for "quickly." Instead she said "*Speedo, por favor.*"

The consulate put them on a military airplane home. Why the urgency to transport the dead? A perfunctory coroner's examination had taken place. "Heart failure. Yes, an 83-year-old woman with high-blood pressure, the plane trip, the heat, the strange food, *la turista.*" "Very hot this week, Senorita," Dr. Saura declared, and then, as if to confirm his diagnosis, wiped his thick neck and brow with an immaculate cotton handkerchief. As she listened and nodded, May couldn't stop thinking she'd used the word "Speedo" on the phone to the receptionist. In retrospect, she felt foolish. What did it matter: her mother was dead. Had the receptionist found it funny, in spite of the situation? Probably laughed out loud as soon as she'd hung up. Did they have Speedo bathing suits in Mexico? Of course they did. Later, she phoned big brother Sam to break the news. To her surprise, he cried over the phone. Which made her feel worse. Heartless. Poor Sam, Ma's golden boy. And now he wanted to visit May in Montrose. How strange that what stuck most in her mind was her stupid use of the word Speedo.

¤

"Out! Now. Step out of your room, right now, Gloria Fletchard. Don't take anything, leave everything behind." Monica Haynes' high-pitched command rang through the block.

"Excuse me, ma'am, but I need a hygienic pad right now. I've got the feminine... you know what."

A cry went out from somewhere on the block: "Oh, shit, get your life preservers, Big Mama's got the curse."

"I've got some paprika here: you wanna stop it."

"Stand against the wall. Now! To the left of your room. Like the others," Haynes' partner, Janet Walker, added in a lower, harsher tone.

Haynes and Walker, standing one next to the other, both dressed in brown, offered a striking contrast; Haynes was all height, whereas Walker's dimension was horizontal. Gloria, on the other hand, radiant in her tangerine outfit, occupied all three dimensions.

The facilitators were doing another random search on the second floor of Begonia's Block 2. As ordered by the warden, who decided such searches on a monthly basis. The residents were, from left to right: Hillary Cox, prostitution and drugs; Gloria Fletchard, murder, murder, murder; Eileen Shaw, burglary, assault, forgery, drugs; Chris Morrison, ditto; Pat Machin, armed robbery; Shelley Barry, more prostitution, more drugs. With bee-like intensity the two guards buzzed the rooms, searching in what the warden called "improbable" locations, all of which were well-known to the inmates. Nevertheless, the searches provided an effective deterrent. Tall and skinny Haynes did the first three rooms, B-2:7-8-9 while short, plump Walker did 10-11-12. The inmates were surprisingly quiet during the rummaging.

Suddenly Haynes called Walker: "Better get Paul over here."

Walker squeezed her walkie-talkie to contact the guard. Paul was quickly on the scene, examining their find: white granules that looked to him much like Drano. "All right, let the others back into their rooms, and you can go," he told the facilitators. "I'll take over." He turned his attention to Gloria.

"They're too small to be pills." Paul said.

Gloria was trying to conceal her feminine hygienic pad in her chubby hand. "I guess you've never heard of homeopathy. It's for my thyroid. They go under the tongue." In spite of her thick make-up, Gloria's face was flushed and glowing, perhaps in the reflection of her orange jumpsuit.

"How did you get them? I oversee everything that comes in to Montrose. Never saw these." Paul put one tiny granule up to the light and then to his nose. No smell.

"Nurse White, she got them for me. On request. Check it out. 'Purple Shutter Herbs,' the place is called. On Main Street. Listen, I've got to go to the ladies' room. Urgently." Sweat was rapidly turning Gloria's pancake make-up into orange mud.

Paul took a step toward Gloria and laid a single finger on her double chin. "Listen, Fletchard, and learn. Nothing comes in here except through me. Understand? Never mind the nurse. From now on, you want homo pills or anything else, you ask me. Okay?" He smiled briefly, pocketed the Ziploc sandwich bag and stepped out the door.

✵

By the day's last count Liz was wiped out. Another laundry duty day. And Thursday was macaroni and tomato sauce. When it wasn't menstrual blood, it was tomato stains. Red on white. She was getting fat. May had said so. Liz checked herself out in the mirror, inspected her exquisite tattoo, mentally comparing it to Chris' crude homemade jobs. The tat queen had been thrown in the dissociation cell. Something about a haemorrhage, according to Laura. Or did she mean rage. With Laura, language was always slippery. Eileen, a more direct if not reliable source, said Chris had cut herself up pretty bad. Slashed her arms and burned them with cigs and then swung her seared flesh into a facilitator's face. Which facilitator? But Eileen was always inventing the weirdest things about everyone. What she said about May. Liz got into bed and lay very still, a mummy wrapped in her suicide-proof sheet, looking at the ceiling where rays from the fanlight were creating a sash bar effect. Why did they have to leave the corridor light on? Liz had never been in the dissociation cells. Were there lights in there? Maybe they were always on? More likely it was totally dark. Which was why some Singer girls called it The Box.

Liz closed her eyes and that semi-circular shape turned into a light at the end of a tunnel. Soon, Batman emerged, his midnight-blue cape spread wide, the oval yellow insignia flashing. And it was Hallowe'en again. Liz turned over on her stomach. Her lower back was throbbing. But not as bad as it had been that Hallowe'en. She must have twisted something during her labour. Her back had been bad ever since. The slightest wrong movement and it jammed again. Bing and Batman. He'd wanted a pumpkin, but that was asking too much. Hadn't she made his Batman suit? Even though she could hardly sit down, her ass was so bruised and scarred. And her breasts overflowing, no more Kleenexes in the trailer. She sewed the night-blue cape, found him last year's black mask and sewed on bat ears, concocted a yellow and black bat decal to glue on his gray-black PJs. And a yellow Batman belt. She'd even glued some fins onto his winter gloves to create the hybrid animal look. Pretty good, she'd thought. He seemed pleased, though Bing was never too pleased. Like his fuckin' father. Couldn't even smile for the picture. Between the baby and Batman, Liz had lain her bruised body on the bunk. She couldn't satisfy him. Of course, he wanted to go trick-or-treating. But she couldn't. She just couldn't.

Could you break a seven-year-old boy's heart? The neighbours were no help. The Fosters were drinking and fighting again. The Priestleys, sweet but too old to go door to door. In the end, she'd phoned the least likely candidate: K. She got his answering machine: "You have reached eight-sssix-fffour—fffcrty-ssseven-eightteen." Even his recorded message was dripping with that fastidious tone. She'd been a fool to think he'd take Bing on the trick-or-treat ride, that he'd play Robin to Bing's Batman. And Bing had overheard her pleading. "I can't take him, could you help me out this once." A seven-year-old might be just a kid, but a kid can read the signs. He knows when he's become a burden. How had she misread him? Spinning the wheels of his Batmobile on the mini kitchen counter, over and over. Wouldn't stop. Totally ignored her. And the baby. No questions, never said a word about her. He'd barely said a word at all during that entire week. Liz had tried to feed him, as usual, but there wasn't much to offer. Just peanut butter, bread at first, then Melba toast and Kraft dinners. And milk, well the first few days. How was she supposed to manage? Go out and leave little Ann alone with him? Send him to the store some ten minutes away, with a highway to cross? Still, he asked no questions, didn't speak. She didn't say much either. He watched TV: cartoons, soaps, cop shows, talk shows. Liz dozed off, even while the infant was breast-feeding. He never looked at his mother and her baby. After he opened the bathroom door and saw her splayed out on the floor, with a head coming out between her legs, he'd simply disappeared. Liz had called out to him for help; he wouldn't come. Her own face in the mirror: blood, sweat, panic. Who would cut the umbilical cord? Not exactly the birds and the bees for second-graders. The aluminium door banging shut, as he ran out. Probably better that way. With the tiny bundle in her arms, Liz had gone to fetch a clean knife. The knives were all dull. In the end, she used the scissors, the same scissors with which she'd cut the Batman suit.

That trailer was so small, and yet she had not been able to keep track of everything. Late in the afternoon of Hallowe'en, K. had still not returned her call. Liz had gone to the toilet. She was still bleeding heavily. Her body was a fountain of milk, blood, and now diarrhoea. When she came out, Ann's head was under the cushion Liz used for breast-feeding. Bing sitting very still in his Batman suit next to the lifeless infant, staring at the floor. Liz saw red.

She turned over again, on her back, fixed her gaze on the fan shape on the ceiling.

The entire time she'd worked in vain to revive the baby, Bing hadn't moved. She had pressed him down with one hand like a rag doll. Unswerving, her professional acupuncture hand had targeted his CV14 right in the centre of his Batman decal. She had held her middle finger pressed hard under his sternum. He hadn't suffered.

She was crying now, silently. To soothe herself, she extended her left hand to her sex, but immediately sat up, on the edge of her bunk bed. Her mind was totally out of order. She was twelve again, feeling guilty because she played with herself. You're so ugly, Betty. Fat. And covered in pimples. Betty went to the washroom to pick up her mother's handheld mirror. On one side, it was plain Betty; on the other, it was huge Betty with blackheads and pimples, ten times bigger. Ugh. But Betty couldn't help looking at herself on the magnifying side. The nose was amplified; you could see every little hair on your face, every ugly bump and pit. Betty took the mirror to her room and closed the door, twice, it only clicked the second time. She didn't turn on the square ceiling light, and made sure to close the milky curtains. The sun's rays spread across the floor, and over the pink bedspread. She sat on the edge of the bed, holding the mirror like a sceptre. Betty the Queen of England, Queen of Sheba, Queen of Wonderland. The Queen looked at her face, her neck, unbuttoned her white blouse and looked at her chest: two pink bumps. She buttoned her blouse, unzipped her pants and pulled them down a little. Her favourite paisley corduroys. The Queen got braver, pulled down her pink cotton undies. She couldn't see a thing, so she pulled them down to the floor, but without taking them off. In case. Now she picked up the mirror again and tilted it so that she could see inside. She spread her legs and, holding the mirror with her right hand, opened the flesh with the fingers of her left hand. There was a bulge with a slit almost in the middle, the left side was thicker than the right. Her fingers pried their way in a little and a bright button popped up. And when the middle finger touched there, it hurt a little. Her fingers moved in deeper and the two folds opened up gradually; there was always more and more red flesh. It felt good. Someone was at the door. She froze.

"Betty?" The door opened so fast, she had no time to pull her pants back up. She threw her head down between her legs. "Betty? What the hell?" He came in he hadn't knocked, he'd opened the door and walked right into her room. He was going to beat her, he was angry, he was going to call Mom, he was going to run out and tell everyone. Instead, he sat at the edge of the bed. Right beside her. At first, she couldn't move and, once she could, she tried to pull up her pants but he stopped her. He put his foot down on her paisley pants and forced them with a kick to come off. She could smell his sweat, his neck was right by her nose.

"Betty." But Betty was frozen. He put an arm on her back, his mouth on her nape. She was feeling silly, and looking at her feet. A ray of sun was right on her panty. "Please, don't... please." She was so polite. He drove his fingers inside, hard. In and out, in and out. He was breathing loudly when he knelt down, on the cold hard floor, lifted her legs with both hands, and opened them up. It was all so quick, she wasn't sure what he'd done. She thought he stuck his tongue inside her, he licked where she shat, too. Then he was gone She was wet. She smelled of tobacco, sweat and sour armpits.

She hurried to bring the mirror back to the washroom before her mom came home. Because her mom would kill her.

¤

On Sunday mornings, Montrose inmates tended to stay in their cells. There were no activities worth getting up for, if you discounted the religious ceremony, and few were interested in Irene Hill's smorgasbord of group confessions and good intentions. You stayed in bed, or you plucked your eyebrows and shaved your legs, varnished your nails, dyed your hair. May was alone in the central courtyard with the scraggly maple tree. It wasn't showing any signs of life. The two-noter bird was on the job, but she was used to it by now. She sat on a bench onto which the sun's rays were beating a steady rhythm. Eyes closed, she sat lizard-like, enjoying the early spring warmth and her second cigarette. Liz appeared, massaging her belly, her ponytail swinging to and fro. She stopped in front of May and stood with her fleshy arms slightly raised above her head.

"You communing with Li Hongzhi?" May asked. "Ask him what the weather's going to be like this afternoon."

Liz was baffled. "Who's Li Hongzhi?"

"You know the Brooklyn guy who makes his disciples stand like you're doing in front of Chinese consulates all over the world. Leader of the Falungong, who else?"

Liz didn't bite. She lowered her arms and sat down next to May, fanned her cigarette smoke away with broad exaggerated motions, then delicately brushed a caterpillar of ash from May's thigh. "I ain't no specialist, but I think those sticks of yours are pretty dry, Ma'am." Liz blew more ashes away from May's clothes and started massaging her own hands, finger by finger, pressing here and there. Then her ears. "You should at least do your ears. Let me." Liz got up and went behind May to massage her ears.

"That's okay, Liz, no thanks."

"But it'll make you feel so good, come on."

May let her do it, but then on the fourth rotation, she took Liz' hands in her own, kissed the palms and brought them down to her breasts. Liz slowly removed her hands, and sat back on the bench, next to May.

"Not much to do here on the weekends." Liz played with her ponytail, crossing her legs, then swinging them over the other way and re-crossing them over and over again.

"Got the blues, honey? Let me be your rocking chair. Let's have a little fun." May tried to pull Liz on top of her.

Liz moved away, though not off the bench. She sighed once, long and hard. "Don't you get the blues on Sundays?"

May shrugged; she'd never thought of Sunday as particularly different from any other day.

"Well, I always do. Even when I was a kid, I dreaded Sundays. Doing family stuff, like car rides, going to see some aunt or cousin, stuffed into those Sunday clothes you especially don't like. My brother Dan used to get car sick. I had to sit in the back with him and the stink of puke."

"Ah, poor little thing, you. What a miserable life." May tried to get closer to Liz' body. She put her hand between Liz' legs and gently eased Liz' head onto her shoulder. "I'll bet they always made you eat the maple-nut ice-cream 'stead of the strawberry you wanted. Come on, talk to me, honey. I'll be your red stressless couch. Let my shirt-tail be your crying tissue." May slipped into a German accent: "Alzo, Meez Reech, you have zee nauseah of Sunday, ya? You pleaz to tell Herr Doktor everyzing, Frau Reech."

"How about a drink, Doctor."

"Ah zo Alcoholicalitosis, of course. Your papa was ze drunk. Am I not correct, Frau Reech?"

"How do you know that?"

May lowered Liz' head onto her lap. "Ya, it eez. Herr Doktor knows everyzing. Vee must to exorcize your childhood, Frau Reech. Let us pretend I am being your papa, yes?" May gently opened the zipper on Liz' jeans, moved her hand inside.

Liz didn't budge. "My dad's a funny guy. Or so they say. They say I'm funny like him."

May moved her hand in Liz' pants.

"Make me laugh, May," Liz whispered, and almost immediately she moaned.

May continued talking, as though nothing was happening. "Unt your mama, Frau Reech? She vas so much a mean beetch, ya?" She rubbed her whole palm over Liz' sex.

Liz stiffened and moved as though on a rocking chair. Once the pleasure had subsided, she reached up to redo her ponytail, which had slid below her nape. She said: "You've got a thing against mothers, May. I'm a mother."

"Sure, you can be my mama, ya."

Liz, suddenly impatient, sat upright.

"What's on your mind, Liz?" May grabbed Liz' two hands and tried to get eye contact.

"Grow up, May. You just don't get it, do you. My babies are both dead. Died the same day."

May played with Liz' blond ponytail, letting the sun shine through and turn the hair colour to Venetian red. She had a momentary vision of Liz, naked, bending over the bathtub, each hand pushing an infant under the water. "You have a boyfriend, Liz?"

Liz shook her head in the negative.

"See, we're not so different. I don't have a boyfriend, either."

"I hear you killed him," Liz blurted.

May was silent.

Liz was embarrassed. She added: "Eileen told me," as though this confession could make up for her bluntness.

May hesitated as though she were about to reply something nasty but changed her mind. "I don't care who knows it."

The two sat silently for a moment.

Finally Liz said, "A drink would be nice, right about now."

"A Tequila Sunrise."

"A Margarita!"

"Make that two!"

Liz cupped her hands around May's ear: "Gloria used to make booze. She may be still brewing something in her room. Wanna ask her?"

"Are we that hard up? Fermented oranges?"

"It's not as bad as you think. The Singer girls did it almost every weekend. Ever wonder why it's especially rowdy on football nights? Well, it's not just the blood on the field and the punched-up boys with their tight little asses that get them excited. Fuck, how I hate football. All my life, I've had to listen to it. My dad and my brother Dan, and then Rick and then Phil, right up to Don. Slapping each other on the back, slapping high-fives and fists, guzzling beer, and the announcer screaming his head off. TOUCHDOWN!" Liz fell silent. She hadn't shaken off her Sunday blues after all.

"I never listened to football. And my brother certainly didn't either." May laughed quietly at the thought of Sam watching a football game, drinking beer and eating pocket pizza.

"He must be gay."

"Bingo, give the girl a kewpie doll. Sure Sam's gay. Not your brother, I gather."

"Ooooh no! Tell me about your brother, May."

"Why? You want to talk about brothers, you talk about yours. Or would you prefer to talk about homosexuality?"

Liz did not reply.

"Oh all right, my big brother Sam is a very sweet guy, a loving son, considerate to others, and very cultured in so many ways. He does everything well. He's a traditional herbal pharmacologist."

"Really?! Where, in Burlington?"

"In New York. He's coming this Thursday if you want to see him. Check out his stationery." May raised one buttock to retrieve the letter from her jeans' back pocket. The fine ricepaper was decorated with a delicate red line-drawing at the top. Unfortunately, the "A P P R O V E D " stamp ruined the elegant balance. The black ink handwriting was refined, slightly idiosyncratic and neatly centred.

"He's left-handed, isn't he?"

"My, aren't we fine-tuned today. Actually, Sam is five-foot-two and weighs 95 pounds, he has buck teeth, he's cross-eyed and wears thick eyeglasses. And his nails! He has long, pointed nails, longer than yours…" May got up, squeezed her eyes almost shut, put her teeth forward and extended her fingers as if they were nails towards Liz. Her version of Fu Manchu.

"Hmm. My brother Dan's average height, but he's a good 200 pounds overweight; he's pimply, pussy, flabby and smelly." Liz stood and walked around, stretching her pants a good foot away from her waist, and adjusting an imaginary cap. 'Always wears a baseball cap. Plus he blows his nose like this." Liz blocked one nostril and blew snot into the wind.

"Hey, hey. What's this: charades?" Chris and Eileen suddenly appeared behind Liz.

Liz spun around: "I was imitating you, bitch."

"Is that so?" Eileen and Chris plunked down on the bench, squeezing May between them.

"OK, Liz, share the wealth."

"Leave her alone," Liz warned.

"Your dope, asshole. You can keep your Yellow Slit. Get your shit, we want some too."

Chris grabbed Liz and dragged her down onto the bench.

"Fuck off." Liz yanked free.

"Listen fuck-face, get your powder out, now." Chris twisted Liz' ponytail.

"I don't have any." Liz replied. She looked at May.

"All right, so maybe Yellow Slit's got some 'O'? Isn't that what you Chinks smoke? Share the wealth, Chop Suey."

"I thought they put you in segregation?" May was trying to keep cool.

"Eh, nobody keeps Chris for long in diss. She finds a way." Eileen said proudly.

"OK, fuckhead, Queen Liz, fuck off. Go to church. Go wash out your panties." Chris pulled Liz off the bench by the ponytail and kicked her in the ass. "Not you, Chink Dyke." Chris and Eileen clamped May down on the bench. Liz moved a few steps away, hesitating. "Get lost, bitch," Chris warned.

Liz stood for a moment, but there was no appeal or even a shared look from May. Liz turned and marched off.

"OK, Yellow Slit. What you got? Where's your stash?"

"In my slit, you moron." May stared at both women, one after the other.

For a moment Chris and Eileen were taken aback. Then they went for her, first emptying her shirt pocket to produce tobacco, rolling papers, lighter, then ripping open her undershirt. Nothing. Chris pinched May's tits hard. "Pull her pants down," she told Eileen. May struggled to get free, but the two women were too strong. They didn't get her pants off, but their hands rammed all her cavities. "Ain't nothin' there." Chris finally concluded. "Dyke's all bones. And dog piss. She ain't got nothin'. We're outta here."

They moved to go, Chris turning to say, "Go douche with Pepsi. Beats Coke. It's the real thing."

PART II
FROG IN A WELL

I was on the sidewalk outside Max Foe's condo before I remembered I had no car. Naturally there were no cabs on Easter Sunday. I started running toward Police Headquarters. By the time I got to the garage I was sweating profusely into my brand new blue uniform. The attendant was a civilian, and he was clearly amused by my breathless, rumpled plea, but he could see the uniform was authentic. He dug up a report form from the drawer, and let me sign for a large heap of a Ford. I was too embarrassed to ask him for directions to Montrose, but I should have, because I had no idea how to get there.

Lucky for me, there was a map in the glove compartment. I forced myself to study it before putting the car in gear. Route 2 then 2A or the 117 all the way? Unfortunately, the Greater Burlington map "featuring complete road network" did not, in fact, indicate all roads. The IBM road wasn't on it, nor was the Rivers Bend Line, as if some private and state property had been rendered invisible. I opted for Route 117, the River Road. I drove cautiously, trying to get the feel of the large car.

Not that I have a problem with driving. I've been driving since the week after I turned sixteen. That's when Lao Wang first took me out in the company car. He would take me out for a lesson whenever neither Mr. nor Mrs. Pirelli needed his services. "Best way to learn to drive," Lao Wang taught me, "you watch Hollywood movies. Hollywood car chases are a crash course in Beijing driving."

The Sunday morning traffic going through Essex Junction was nothing like Beijing's; in fact, here the traffic was non-existent. Once past the IBM plant, I floored the accelerator and raced down Route 117, twisting alongside the Winooski River's many bends. "Never hesitate," Lao had warned. "The bigger vehicle always has priority: pay no attention to bicycles, it is their task to find their way. Do not look left or right, but simply go forward." If you hesitated that instant to glance to either side, the other drivers, cyclists and pedestrians instantly took advantage of your weakness to fill the way ahead. Lao Wang had guided me down the broad avenue of Chang'an, through the heart of the old capital, past Tiananmen and the gates of the Forbidden City, then up for a wild ride on the Second Ring Road.

At last I saw the pale sun caught in the barbed wire atop the cement wall of the Montrose Detention Center for Women. The prison gate was open, so I drove around to the circular lot at the back, and parked next to a rave-green Volkswagen GTI. The only other vehicle in the lot was a Fletcher Allen ambulance backed up against the doors into the facility.

A gum-chewing driver popped her head out of the ambulance and jerked a thumb toward the building. "They're all in there." She stepped down and led the way into the red cement building, and down a small corridor. Before I could get my bearings, we were in a crowd outside a cell door. I remember thinking it was awfully warm.

A uniformed guard in his thirties with a thick shoe brush of a mustache stepped forward to identify himself as Officer Bundell. When he didn't bother to introduce the others, a large, older woman wearing a thick cardigan sweater, in spite of the heat, and carrying a white cloth over her arm, pushed through. "Irene Hill, um... facilitator... staff," she said. She started to offer her hand, but changed her mind. Instead, she introduced Doctor Levy, a young man in a white lab coat over torn jeans. He opened the door of the room and motioned us in. Everyone followed.

I found myself crowded into a stark white windowless cell with a small cot in one corner. It was even warmer than in the hallway. On the floor, in the centre of the cell, lay a woman, naked, on her back, with her right hand covering her pubis. Her hair was black, her eyelids were Asian, and shut. She was dead.

The four of us were jammed together by the cot for some reason, giving her most of the room in the cell.

"Her name's Ho, May Ho. She's Chinese," the staff woman named Hill said.

I looked at the coroner.

Dr. Levy cleared his throat. "There are no signs of violence, no bullet or stab wounds, no bruises or blood." His voice was all wind, the kind of sound one makes the morning after a Saturday night of alcohol and other stimulants.

"Can I take the shot now?" Officer Bundell asked, waving a Polaroid camera in my line of vision.

"Oh, sure," Dr. Levy whispered.

I added, louder, "Go ahead." I think I was conscious that I ought to exercise some authority, not so much because it was my job, but because there seemed to be a lack of it in the room.

The camera flashed in the already blinding white of the cell. Bundell tore off the Polaroid photo, and Irene Hill leaned over for a peek, then quickly stepped away, and drew a white gown up over the body.

"Well? All set? Time to wrap up?" The gum-chewing ambulance driver tipped her cap back over dark beaded hair and scanned the room, finally settling on Officer Bundell. I guessed that the man in the white lab coat and I were probably the youngest professionals she'd seen in her twelve years on the job.

"Wait a minute," I said, digging in the pocket of my new suit for my report form.

"Sorry, you want to go next door," Bundell nodded, and lay a hand on the ambulance driver's arm. "We better go next door, first." He turned to me. "It's this way."

We filed out of the cell and into the hallway. Bundell opened a second door, and waved me into an identical stark white windowless cell. I took one step inside and dropped my report form. On the cot lay a young white female of medium height and weight, with long blond hair. She was lying on her back exactly in the same position as the woman in the first cell, with her right hand over her pubis. Dead.

"No signs of violence, no bullet or stab wounds, no bruises or blood," Dr. Levy repeated hoarsely.

Irene Hill pushed past me to cover the body with a second gown. "This is Liz… um, Elizabeth Rich," Hill said, a note of sadness in her voice.

In her hurry to cover up the second body, Irene Hill had kicked my report form under the bed. Bundell retrieved the paper, while I stood stunned by the doorway. "Didn't they tell you?" he said. "There's two of them."

Dr. Levy fumbled in his pocket for something to wipe his forehead. Bundell muttered, "A tag team."

Not to be undone, the gum-chewing driver added: "Mutt and Jeff."

Irene Hill hugged her sweater, then reached over to touch my uniform's sleeve.

"Let's go," I said, but I really meant let go.

In silence, we proceeded to an adjacent room, slightly larger and with windows. This was clearly a pharmacy, lined with closed cabinets; a window with a slot for dispensing pills faced the hallway. Facilitator Hill sat down at a small desk and began to work on the death certificates. After a few moments, she ceded her place to Dr. Levy. Sweat stained his white coat. He tried to move through the form quickly and nonchalantly under our gaze. Below *Cause of Death* he wrote "Unknown—TBD." Finally his pen hesitated, hovering on the bottom of the page. Irene Hill leaned her large woollen bosom over to point an arthritic index finger at the blank line over the title Medical Examiner.

He signed and stood up. I sat down in his place, more to recover my composure than to check the form. Still I couldn't help noting that he'd scribbled nothing more than a poor facsimile of his initials on the edge of the line. He stepped quickly back from the desk and went to the window looking out into the parking lot, speaking with his back to the room: "I'll have Dr. King sign this as soon as he gets back."

"What do you mean?"

"I'm not authorized to sign death certificates. My boss, Dr. King, has taken a holiday weekend." He turned wearily to face me. "They woke me up this morning."

"Tell me about it," I said, looking down at the form. I noticed several blank spaces. The whole thing seemed so unreal, so uncoordinated, nothing like the simulations at the academy. I fought to recover something of the investigating sequence I'd been taught. "Who discovered the body?"

"She did." Bundell said, nodding at Hill. "Irene Hill." He checked his watch. "I've got 0740. Is that right?"

Dr. Levy moved back to the desk, checked his Wenger Chrono Commander divers' watch and, as calmly as he could, corrected Bundell: "0722, April 23, 2000."

They both seemed to be waiting for me to write all this down. Unfortunately, there was no place for notes on the death certificates and I had forgotten to bring a notepad. I turned to Hill. "You discovered both bodies?"

"Yes, that's right," Hill said stubbornly, as though I had doubted it.

"The cells were locked?"

"Yes, locked. Those are dissociation cells. They're supposed to be in complete isolation."

"And both were exactly as I saw them? Naked, on their backs like that?"

"Yes."

"Where's your superior?" I asked, looking from Hill to Bundell and back.

"Oh, Warden Segal is away on holidays," Irene Hill fiddled with a pendant inside her sweater neck. "Easter, you know."

"I've contacted the warden and she's on her way back as we speak," Bundell added.

I had a ton of questions to ask him, her and the doctor's assistant, but suddenly I remembered Captain Carter's firm order: "Fill out a FOOS and get your ass out of there." Which is what I did.

◘

Monday morning, May 1st, bright and early, I began my life as a Greater Burlington Police Detective. When the police departments of Burlington, South Burlington, Colchester, Winooski, Essex, Williston and Shelburne were consolidated, there was talk about housing the force in a brand new highrise. Instead, in accordance with city planning, the officers had been crammed into 1 North Avenue, a five-storey building that looked like an isosceles triangle fitting snugly between Battery Park and North Avenue and extending to the edge of the city bluff. There were windows on all three sides, with the unit chiefs and sergeants occupying the back offices, those facing Lake Champlain. At first, the fifth floor had been relegated to archiving and storage. The ceilings were lower, the windows narrow and the views made even smaller by the overhanging roof. But, inevitably, by the time I joined the force, overcrowding had forced a reorganization and the fifth floor had become the detectives' floor.

My first week went pretty much as I'd expected. Captain Peter Carter gave me the briefest of welcomes on the threshold of his office as he hurried off to a meeting at City Hall. He had the height and silvery crewcut of a police captain. He was wearing a dark gray suit, and a blue and orange striped tie, which could only be a Father's Day gift.

The Captain handed me off to Detective Louise Moore, who was supposed to show me the ropes. She began by leading the way to a quick coffee break. Louise Moore was only an inch and a bit shorter than Carter, her hair was black and curly, she wore a black pantsuit, high heels, gold earrings, latch and watch, and pearl-pink nail polish. No question, Lou Moore was a real head-turner and she knew it.

In the din of people and machines, it seemed an army rather than a mere fifteen detectives were working on the fifth floor. On the North Avenue side, next to the washrooms, four vending machines and a table with a few chairs had been crammed into a windowless space. It was the kind of spot no one actually sits in, but people are constantly squeezing past each other to get a coffee, chewing gum, aspirins, and a quick word of gossip.

Moore pushed past a thick mustache in a large crumpled suit and punched a handful of coins into the vending machine. She tore the cellophane wrap off a couple of aspirins, while the mustache gave me the obligatory once over.

"What's this, Lou?" he said, "Don't tell me they just doubled the quota."

Lou said, "Rey Pirelli, this is my partner Bill Vance."

Bill Vance slurped his coffee and grinned. "Well. Looks like you've got some competition, Lou. Fresh out of the academy, too, and nary a wrinkle in her blues."

"Bill's married," Louise shot back. "And, as you can see, his wife's a very good cook."

"Rough weekend, Lou?" Vance wasn't really fat; he looked like a retired football player who had slid down the sports slope to golf. As his body sagged, he'd increasingly come to invest his pride of manhood in his mustache. Unfortunately for him, he was shorter than Louise and a step slower.

"Word is you speak Chinese," Vance said to me. "That must've stretched the brain pan."

"Come on," Moore told me, "I'll set you up behind a desk and you can start gnawing at my paperwork."

And that's pretty much what I did for a week: type up reports and file paperwork for Lou, and occasionally the other detectives. It wasn't glorious —

and I had no doubt Detective Moore was taking advantage of the rookie, sister or no sister — but it gave me an idea of the variety of cases the squad was handling: everything from B & E, fraud, wife battering, to the odd murder. By the weekend, I was starting to think Captain Carter had forgotten me. I spent two days emailing back and forth with Huiru in Beijing, walking Otis all over Burlington, and trying to figure how I was going to slip free from my servitude to Lou Moore and get into the Captain's office for a one-on-one. The least he could do was put me on a regular beat. I showed up early Monday morning, determined to cross the floor and rap my knuckles on Carter's office. I marched into the squad room and right into Bill Vance.

"Morning, Madame Butterfly. You sure work fast," he said, and cocked his head toward the rear. "Boss wants to see you."

As I crossed the length of the fifth floor, through the maze of work stations bunched in twos and fours, separated by movable partitions, and the rising clatter of voices, computer fans, mouse clicks, keyboards, printers and fax machines, I started revising my speech, unsure whether to adjust my demands upward or practice simple gratitude.

Carter's door was open. "Come in. And close the door."

Before I'd had time to take off my cap, he was slamming a folder on his very neat desk. His family, a wife and two kids framed in gold, jumped. "What's this?"

I recognized the paper. The Captain was pointing at Dr. Levy's unreadable initials. "A.L., Sir. For Aaron Levy."

"Who is Aaron Levy? I know Dr. King. Dr. King is Burlington's ME. So, who the fuck is Aaron Levy?"

"He's the coroner's assistant, Sir. Dr. King was on holiday."

Carter nodded. "And this assistant Levy fellow, what's his problem, he can't sign his name?"

"Well, he was going to get Dr. King to sign later, sir. He…"

Captain Carter slammed a finger into the paper. "This is a death certificate. It's not a car-rental contract. As a matter of fact, Officer Pirelli, without a signature, this is not a death certificate. This is a piece of shit."

"Yes, Sir."

The Captain took a deep breath. "Okay. Now. Where's Lucille Segal's signature?"

"Lucille Segal, Sir?"

"The warden. Where's Warden Segal's signature?"

"The warden was away on holiday, too," I muttered. I felt like a small child who'd left a trail of cookie crumbs across the kitchen floor.

Now Captain Carter pulled another sheet from a file and waved it in my direction. I could smell the Irish Spring on him. "What's this?"

"It's my FOOS report, Sir."

"At what time did this..." Carter checked the report, "this Irene Hill find the bodies?"

"I... didn't get the exact time, Sir. It's a preliminary report."

Carter snorted. "Pre–lim–in–ary. You do know what facts are, don't you Officer Pirelli? Or did you skip that class at the academy? The class on facts?" He flipped a page. "What's the age of the victim?" He paused, flipped another page... "Victims."

The captain froze for a moment, took a deep breath, then gently closed the file and fixed me with a long, deep stare. "Officer Pirelli, where were the victims' clothes?"

"There were no clothes in the cells, sir."

"Did you think they throw their inmates into solitary in the nude at Montrose?"

I suddenly saw myself standing at a filing cabinet practising the alphabet.

Carter shook his head. "What the fuck happened down there, Officer Pirelli?"

I was looking out past his ear, through a small window, into the sky and lake's deep blue. Captain Carter pushed away from the desk, stood and turned to the window. Silently we both took in the view.

When he spoke, his voice was calm, almost fatherly. "Okay, Rey. You've had a bit of a rough start. Use that, learn from it. Remember the routine. This is not such a tricky case. Start by going back down there. Talk to Warden Segal, first. Interview a few inmates. Take another look around. Get a copy of the ME's report. Write it up. Just go by the book, Rey."

It took me a few of his short sentences to realize he was actually handing me the case. The first question I wanted to ask was: Why me? A rookie, who'd messed up a simple FOOS report. But I knew better. Or thought I did. In retrospect, that's exactly the question I should have asked. Instead, I gathered up my case file and prepared to get my ass out of there before the Captain changed his mind. I'd turned and stepped toward the door when it swung open, and Detective Louise Moore exploded into the room.

She ignored me and went straight for Carter. "Okay, Peter, what the fuck?"

"Come in, Lou," Carter said. "Sit down. I was just finishing with Detective Pirelli."

Lou glared at him. "Why her? Just tell me why."

"She's got to start somewhere. We're paying her a detective's salary."

"Put her on a drunk and disorderly, for chrissake. Somebody sold my uncle a fake Rolex. Put her on that. This is a murder, Peter."

"Not yet, it isn't," Carter said. "So far it's just two bodies."

"I'm the lead detective and that case is mine."

"Sit down, Lou," Carter said.

Detective Moore dropped into the chair opposite her boss and crossed her legs hard and fast, like a nutcracker.

I waved a hand at the door. "I'll just…"

Carter shook his head. "No, shut the door, Detective. We might as well clear the air. I don't want any bad blood in this unit."

I shut the door and stood awkwardly, just out of range of Lou Moore's legs.

Carter nodded and drew a breath. "Rey Pirelli's absolutely the best candidate for the job. First, she's virgin territory. She's outside the politics, and I mean here…"

"So I'm not a virgin," Lou said.

Captain Carter gazed down into his coffee for a moment before replying: "All right, Lou, here it is." He started counting off fingers. "First off, Detective Pirelli's new here, absolutely no connections in City Hall or with the Chamber of Commerce. No friends, no foes. And a clean record. Two, she's humble…" He paused a moment, daring Lou to interrupt. "Three: top of her class in puzzle-solving. And this case is tricky. Two inmates dead, and we've got nothing to go on. In two weeks, a Federal Review Committee is scheduled to start deliberations on Montrose. This case could push them over the edge and shut down the whole experiment. We don't want to stand in front of that fan. I don't intend to get caught in the middle of it. Which makes four: Rey's a fast runner." He turned to me. "You've got 14 days to deliver, Rey. Before the review committee on Montrose opens. Got that?"

I nodded, more to clear my head than anything. I was feeling dizzy.

Lou started to say something, but Carter held up a hand. "Five, the eye-catcher in this investigation has got to be something Chinese. And Rey spent all those years in China. She's practically Chinese." He swept his extended hand back over his brush cut, put the lid back onto his empty cup, and threw it a little too firmly into the wastepaper bin. "Sorry, Lou. I'll make it up to you."

"No, you won't. You'll take the wife and kids out to the sugar shack for a weekend. I've got work to do." Louise Moore spun and stepped swiftly out.

I found myself stranded, floating somewhere between the desk and the door.

"Officer Pirelli," Carter said, turning his attention to a file on his desk. "What are you waiting for? Two weeks."

✤

This time, I parked the unmarked police car in the lot reserved for staff and pre-registered visitors. The car beside mine was marked in pink on brown: "MONTROSE—DETENTION CENTER FOR WOMEN." A black BMW, this year's model, stood out among the sensible Swifts and Tempos. Probably the warden's. I checked my crumbling hairdo in the rearview mirror — no need for a second glance to fix that — I pulled out the bobby pins, rewound the chignon and donned my cap. I practised my new title out loud: "Detective Rey Pirelli, Greater Burlington Police," and then whispered my mantra: *Nan-mo-a-mi-tuo-fo.*

I stepped out of the car and stood motionless for a moment. Faint highway sounds. The smell of spring mud. The river. The pavilion by the water? Was this the best seat to view the moon? And why was I getting it? There were African violets and curtains in several windows. But this domestic touch couldn't belie the barbed wire atop the gray wall. A brand new progressive detention centre is still a prison. I took two breaths from the diaphragm and proceeded to the gate. I pressed on the ground bell. There was no visible camera. "Identity, please?" a male voice responded.

Inside the door, a mustachioed officer sitting at the reception desk in front of a series of televisions, told me to wait without pausing his 180 degrees scan across the monitors. The clicking of little heels gradually superseded the officer's clicking computer mouse. A petite woman extended a firm hand from the cuff of her tight burgundy suit: "Welcome to Montrose. I'm Lucille Segal, Warden."

I followed Warden Segal's Vetiver perfume through the arch of metal detectors. The warden explained that security was tight here, even though Montrose was based on a new philosophy of detention. "The gateway through which you have just entered is one of only two entry points for each and every one, staff, inmates and visitors alike. Everyone in and around the premises of this institution is photographed. We have cameras everywhere except inside the girls' rooms and the showers. But the system here is unobtrusive. And of course, there are no guns! And only one man." She stepped in behind the counter and the guard. "Paul, could you please visualize Officer Pirelli's arrival."

Paul, of course. I recognized Officer Bundell. I could have sworn that Warden Segal's tone softened as she spoke to him. Well, he wasn't unhandsome. Paul pressed the REVERSE button on his console and zoomed in on my police vehicle. I felt my cheeks redden as I saw myself rebuilding my hairdo while my lips formed my private incantation, *Nan-mo-a-mi-tuo-fo*. I was lip-syncing with myself.

"What is that you're muttering?" Bundell asked, leaning in close to the screen. I wondered whether he could read lips.

"A Buddhist chant, actually." He glanced up at me, expressionless. I didn't tell him I'd seen it stuck on the fenders of taxis in Asia and had no idea what the words actually meant.

The warden refrained from commenting on my performance; instead she resumed her role as guide. "All entries and exits from the outside are electronically controlled." At a nod from the warden, Paul prompted the other monitors. First he offered a bird's-eye view of Montrose. I saw the square perimeter wall topped with barbed wire. Beyond the wall, empty fields and the river flowing outside the wall, to the northeast.

"Any escapes?" Don't ask me why I played the curious tourist.

Warden Segal shook her head. "Absolutely none in our two years of existence. And no deaths either. Until now."

On the monitor, a cluster of five buildings, each painted a different colour, formed a large semi-circle. A footpath connected them while a vehicle road linked the back of the red building to the gateway. I was getting my bearings; that's where I'd entered a week ago. I stiffened. Paul zoomed in to show me the signs indicating each building's name, while the warden read them out: Acorn in brown, staff residence; blue Begonia, green Cedar and yellow Deer were all "resident" accommodations; Begonia was the residence for the more serious offenders. "That's where the two victims had been housed. And Eagle, the red construction, is our services building; it contains the laundry room, supply and storage space, as well as the clinic. And the silent rooms. That's where they were found."

"What's at the back of the Eagle?" I was already on a first-name basis with the buildings.

"That, by the automatic doors?" Warden Segal barely lifted a painted index at the screen. "Containers. They're for sanitation disposal."

A silly question. I don't know why I'd asked it. Maybe just to show I was listening attentively. Inside the semi-circle, four additional buildings formed a quadrangle: the Food Emporium, the Gymnasium, the Hollyhock, and the Ivy. Paul cast his roving eye inside the cafeteria, empty at this time of day, but then he zoomed to the kitchen where four women with meshed hair and long aprons were chopping onions, opening large cans of — Paul zoomed yet further in — yes, creamed corn. "Shepherd's pie?" Another of my trivial questions. Neither the warden nor the guard bothered to reply.

"And my office, as you will see, is right in the middle of things. In the heart of Hollyhock and with a link to the public space for visits. Those two southward buildings are for residents' guests. Jay is the visitation hall and Koala, for prolonged family visits."

As though she'd read my mind, Warden Segal concluded: "Perhaps you find the nature names a little outlandish? Well, I thought they'd be less cold than the alphabet. Plus I didn't want the girls to concoct their own names for them, so I pastoralized them, if that's a word. I guess that was naïve; they've changed all the names anyway. Begonia is Bygone; the Food Emporium was the Fat Fodder for a while, now it's simply the Chow. Prisoners are rappers; give 'em words, they'll mangle them."

I was tempted to provide some words of my own to replace the zoological names, but wisely shut up and followed Warden Segal instead, down the long graffiti-free hall. The sound of the warden's needle heels on the immaculate tile floor brought back memories of highschool: the empty halls when I stayed late to work on the yearbook, the echo of the janitor's keys as he mopped the terrazzo floors. But there were no lockers here, no sour smell, no metallic gray. The prison's main hallway was decorated on both sides with gigantic laminated scenes of Vermont's seasons: a maple-grove sugar farm, a clover-green pasture dotted with black and white cows, the Green Mountains in their red and orange fall colours, and then two white horses suspended in mid-flight across an expanse of even whiter snow. The warden's Vetiver perfume evoked spring.

At the end of the hall, they came to a fork: "Hollyhock," headquarters, straight ahead; Jay and Koala, the public spaces, to the right. The warden opened a door to give me a glimpse of Jay, where inmates received pre-approved guests. The large space was clearly designed to provide a homey feel, with settees arranged for groups of four or six guests. Shelves of what looked like amateur artwork adorned the windowless walls. In one corner, brightly coloured toys were neatly stacked. I had no time to explore further because Warden Segal had opened yet another door, leading to the Hollyhock administration building, in which her own office occupied central space.

○

There were two settees in Warden Segal's office, similar to those in the visitation parlour, but Segal's were upholstered in soft brocade, and pink, like the walls. It was a little too feminine for my taste, but when the warden offered me a coffee from a shining espresso machine, I was won over. Lucille Segal motioned me to take the sofa facing the courtyard. She sat in the armchair facing me, lifted her right thigh, then her left, to firmly pull her skirt straight under her buttocks.

"Needless to say, this has been a shock. I've been here for two years, since the institution opened. We've never had a death at Montrose. And now two."

I noticed she hadn't used the word murder or suicide.

"These deaths are terrible. What's worse, they could jeopardize the entire experiment, all the good work I've done here. Montrose, as you've seen, is what we call a Pink Pen: no bars, no forced labour. The girls' rooms are their private spaces. Except for the mandatory searches. That's a concession to the Department of Corrections I had to accept. But these are minimal. Dynamic security and positive reinforcement, that's what I do here. Montrose is not just a custodial facility, it's a place where attitudes and behaviour can be improved, where women can become empowered." She paused and leaned closer. "You're young, starting out in law enforcement; you can appreciate the importance of my work here, I can see that."

I wanted to say yes I could, but I had to remind myself I was a detective working a case. Also, I found her use of the first-person singular irritating. Through the window behind the warden, I noticed a large woman in a royal-blue suit, down on all fours transplanting things in the courtyard. "Does the woman in the garden work here or is she an inmate?"

The warden glanced at her Longines watch. She didn't have to look out the window. "That's Gloria Fletchard. She's a resident here. Lives in

Begonia. Any minute now, you'll see May Ho's duty replacement cross the quadrangle, wheeling a gray container. Schedules are meticulously observed here… I don't have many rules, but they must be strictly adhered to: performance of assigned tasks is one, presence at daily counts, submission to random searches are the others. Our detractors think it's a picnic here. Did you see the picture in the *Burlington Free Press* last year?"

I shook my head.

"The residents organized a Christmas party. There were costumes. As a matter of fact, one of the victims, Elizabeth Rich, was in that photo. The Correctional Services and I were flooded with hate mail. Our tax dollars going to lesbian orgies! Club Fed!" The warden's jaw hardened. "I'd rather not make the front page of the newspapers again, I'm sure you can understand. I need the public's support. Montrose is an experiment that costs an average of $120,000 per woman per year; that's $25,000 more than in a traditional women's prison and $40,000 more than a male convict costs anywhere. With the present trend in public funding, our position is not exactly secure."

I nodded and bit my lower lip.

Warden Segal soldiered on. "Peter Carter did explain to you about the review of Montrose beginning May 15th? There's been ongoing discussions in high places about turning Montrose's management over to a private firm. They want to turn this place into some sort of production farm. Now, with this… This police investigation comes at a bad time."

What about the deaths themselves? Weren't they bad timing? "You were away when the deaths occurred," I said a little sternly.

"On sun and sea holiday, planned well in advance and badly needed. And interrupted."

To my eyes, the warden had managed to pick up a tan.

"I'm relieved Peter… Captain Carter sent you. We have to save Montrose. I think that's why he sent you. You're untainted. Fresh, if you know what I mean. You don't mind me calling you fresh, do you?"

I could have told her I'd been called worse, but I just smiled and held my tongue.

"Of course I expect you to conduct a thorough and impartial investigation into those poor girls' deaths. All I'm asking, Rey," Warden Segal concluded, stressing her use of the first name, "is that you keep the stakes for Montrose and the women here in mind."

Warden Segal stood up to retrieve a stack of folders on her desk. Her two-piece suit accentuated her muscular body. She must be on a Pilates program, I thought. "You'll find more info on Montrose's mandate and finances in the pink folder."

Pink file, pink walls, pink signs. I tried to focus on the case. "What's the connection between Elizabeth Rich and May Ho?"

The warden extended two more folders, lilac-coloured this time. "These reports are Rich and Ho's individual files: admission, assessment reports, medical including psychiatric evaluation, everything right up to their deaths."

"Warden Segal," I repeated, "can you tell me what connected Rich and Ho?"

The warden placed the pile of folders in my lap and sat down again, pausing to straighten her skirt before answering. "Elizabeth Rich had been admitted six months before May Ho. I assigned her as Ho's buddy. They became friends. Very close. Aside from that, May Ho was Chinese — I don't know if this is significant — Elizabeth Rich was interested in things Chinese: she was a professional acupuncturist, she was teaching herself the Chinese language, and she was into that slow-motion exercise routine..."

"Qigong," I volunteered. "Were either Rich or Ho sick?" I tried to reformulate less awkwardly my line of questioning: "I mean, did either have an infirmity, a chronic disease? A condition of any sort?"

"Why on earth would you ask that?"

I suppose the question was strange; it had just popped into my head and out of my mouth.

"No," Segal continued, "no conditions. And we don't pill-pop here at Montrose. Sure, there are those rare cases where sedation is necessary. But we never had to do any of that for either of those two girls. I must remind you that, Montrose is not a regular prison for women. We're not like Singer. Or those jails you see in movies. Montrose is virtually drug-free."

I could see she was building steam. "I'd like to visit the victims' cells," I interrupted, 'and interview inmates and staff who dealt with them."

"You'll want to talk to Facilitator Irene Hill then. You've already met her, I'm told. She can take you to see their personal effects. Their rooms, however, have since been cleared of their contents. You'll find a complete inventory of their belongings in their files. In any case, they didn't die in their rooms. Irene discovered their bodies in the silent rooms. She'll show you." The warden stood up and turned to gaze out the bay window.

I could sense her tension.

Without turning around, she said: "You're going to find this whole affair has been conducted shoddily. Even the autopsy was far too summary — the ME's concluded 'cause of death: unknown.' They found something 'unusual' in Ho's blood, whatever that means. My staff may well have contaminated evidence with their speedy clean-up. Unprofessional..."

I tried to stop the flashback of those two bodies in the clinic a week before.

The warden broke off, massaging her temples. "My people have been reprimanded. But surely that's not sufficient reason to condemn an entire program."

No, I thought, but murder might.

The warden moved quickly back to her desk, flipped her agenda, checked her watch. The interview was coming to an end. I managed to get in one more question: "Who among the prisoners or staff, if anyone, was close to Rich and Ho?"

Warden Segal, still standing, lifted her eyes from her papers. "If you're looking for murder suspects, your best bet would be Chris Morrison and Eileen Shaw. They hated Ho. But then they hate pretty much everybody. Gloria Fletchard, on the other hand," she nodded toward the window and the gardener in the courtyard, "likes everyone. There was another woman, Laura Elmsley, who often sat with them in the cafeteria. Sorry, Detective Pirelli, but your guess is as good as mine. If you're looking to make this into a murder investigation, I'm afraid your case rests on nothing."

"Maybe." Maybe the warden was hypoglycemic. She was suddenly in an awful hurry to end the interview. I got up. "Nothing is *not* mere emptiness, Warden Segal," I said. Which would have been a very effective final statement, except that, unfortunately, as I said it, the stack of folders on my lap tipped over and scattered on the floor. I bent quickly to gather up the documents, and found myself at Lucille Segal's feet.

She offered a thin smile. "Here, let me carry some of these files for you."

I followed her perfume and two-piece suit back to the gatepost. We walked without speaking through the empty halls. It was 12:30, and my stomach was gurgling. Click, click; click, click. The warden, I noticed, wore an ankle bracelet.

Somewhere between the gushing fountain and the white horses on white snow, I stopped in my tracks. "Why were they in what you call 'silent' rooms? Those are segregation cells, right? What had they done?"

The warden paused. "Nothing. They asked to be put in there. First Rich, then Ho. The rooms were empty, so I agreed. Those rooms serve various purposes: sick-bay watch, for example; but also when we, or inmates themselves feel they need some quiet time alone."

"You mean when they feel they need protection? When they fear for their lives?"

"Detective Pirelli, this isn't Singer…" The warden turned and walked on to the prison exit. As we came up to the gate, I saw Paul Bundell quickly gather up the scraps from his lunch and toss them in the waste bin.

◘

Time for a bit of junk food. Around the Champlain Valley Exposition Fairgrounds, fast-food joints had sprouted like mushrooms. The smell of grease struck me full in the face when I opened the swinging red door of Vezina's Kountry Kitchen. Along with the Pogo and chips, I ordered a tomato juice, for my conscience.

Actually, tomato juice has felt like a luxury, since China. I still remember the first tomato juice changing planes at Narita airport on my way back! Seven years without a tomato juice. Not that I missed it while I was in China. There were plenty of good things to eat there. And variety: more dishes than you could try no matter how long you stayed. My foster mother Joy was a great cook. I long for her *gongbao jiding*, a kind of chicken stir-fry with peanuts, her *zhajiang* noodles, and steamed ginger fish. Most foreigners in Beijing stay close to the diplomatic compounds and import their food. But not my family.

My uncle Thomas had gone native long before he married a woman from Shanghai. After my mother's death, Thomas and Joy had adopted me, and taken me back to China with them. I had quickly absorbed his love of the Middle Kingdom and its peoples. And Joy had treated me like the child she had been unable to have. They called me a Beijing brat. Even now, with all the creature-comforts of the West, I guess I'd trade it all to be back on my Flying Pigeon bicycle, wending my way through the crowded *hutongs*, those gray-walled mazes of compounds, or circling the tree-lined artificial lakes north of the Forbidden City, in the exquisite peace at the centre of the city. Later, I'd come to know the narrow paths within Beijing University, the lotus ponds and peach trees. If I were in Beijing right now, I'd be chewing on a roasted meat stick or a pancake purchased for pennies from a street vendor.

But Beijing was a long way away. My life there had come crashing down with Thomas and Joy and Hainan Airlines Flight 29.

I drenched my deep-fried Pogo in sweet honey mustard. What's a Pogo without sweet mustard? I was determined not to backslide into nostalgia. I was going to make myself a place here, in my new-old country. The *National Enquirer* was lying on the counter. "Murdered by Jealous Ex-: 'He Was Stalking Her' Declares Janitor"; "Baby Was Stepfather's Punching Bag." Ugh. I flipped to the sports section. They were still playing hockey in May. I checked the Personals. "WSF seeks WSM, non-smoker, nature lover." That wasn't me. I had Huiru, at least virtual Huiru. And I had a case to solve.

Before getting back into the police car, I smoked a cigarette and watched a bunch of kids in bright tops, jeans and fake Nikes, dragging their feet across the street and back to school. I flicked the long butt, hit the open road, and was back in downtown Burlington in less than a half hour.

As soon as I opened the door at 14A Cliff Street, Otis sprang at me, all tail and tongue. Gently, I pushed him away. First, the police clothes had to come off. No dog hairs, please. I dropped an armful of folders on the makeshift desk and moved to the bedroom with Otis in tow. I changed to my beloved striped cut-offs and navy-blue hooded sweatshirt. Now, at last, Otis got some attention, before I released him into the little garden. He stampeded towards the left corner of the fence. That shrub — was it dogwood? — would grow shit-smelling flowers, for sure.

I sat at Max's small desk. It wasn't much, but a hell of a lot better than the minuscule work station in the midst of traffic Captain Carter had assigned me at the station. I stacked the folders, arranged by colour, into two piles. Rich's stack was thicker than Ho's; she'd done more time. I selected a red felt pen and circled May 15 on the wall calendar. Two rows, 14 days to solve the case. *Nan-mo-a-mi-tuo-fo.* The review of the new reform prisons would start on that date. No wonder Warden Segal was worried. Not just her job was on the line. I guessed a great many people, especially the boys at the top, would like to see the Montrose experiment fail.

In two facing columns, I listed Rich and Ho's profiles. Elizabeth Rich: 33 years old, single, acupuncturist, convicted of murder in the 2nd degree in the death of her 7-year-old son Bing Whitehead; life sentence, admitted to Montrose on November 15, 1999, eligible for parole in 15 years.

May Ho: 43 years old, divorced, university professor, convicted of manslaughter in the death of her lover, Lee Pike; 12-year sentence, admitted to Montrose on February 14, 2000, parole eligibility in 4 years.

Both had pled guilty; neither seemed to have gotten much of a plea bargain.

I spread the photos over the surface of my desk, hoping maybe this would help bring something of the two women's lives back. I was wrong. At the academy, I'd seen a few dozen of that standard shot from the toes along the length of the body up to the throat. The dead look unreal in photographs, perfectly still, without a trace of the tics and twitches of the living, their faces like masks. Ho and Rich's identical positions, right hand on the pubis, were puzzling. Mirror images. A fearful symmetry. Had they made a pact before going individually into their solitary cells?

I foraged through Max's desk drawer until I found a roll of Scotch tape. I began pasting the various photographs of May and Liz onto the exposed brick wall of the living room. Close-ups of their body parts revealed each singular body's particular volume, specks, uneven textures and shades of colour.

Elizabeth Rich was approximately my height, but plumper. Long blond hair, longish nails, pudgy hands. Soft belly, round thighs, very pale skin, a shadow of pubic hair. May Ho, much taller and thinner than Rich. Cool hairdo, probably cut her hair herself? Funny layers. Angular body, almost no hips, small breasts, flat belly, short nails, surprisingly thick dark pubic hair. Certainly didn't look like a 43-year-old. I picked up another photograph, Rich's back: through the long, blond hair, I could make out a tattoo. Possibly picked up in prison. On closer examination, I decided it must have been done before Rich had gone in. This was no prison tat, not something etched by a broken shard tied to a toothbrush. It was too well-done. An eyeless lizard. The Chinese say that if you add the eyes to the representation of a dragon, it will fly away. Ho and Rich's mug shots revealed further differences: Rich was staring downward and her face seemed to disappear into the white background; Ho wore heavy-framed glasses and her sharp eyes looked straight ahead. What was so troubling about May Ho's gaze? The word inscrutable automatically came to mind. A stereotype. Did I think that? Oh, Rey-hee, did you think you were above all that?

In a sense, the pair complemented each other perfectly. One tall, one short; one black-haired, one blond; one angular, the other round. One Chinese, the other studying Chinese. Both had committed crimes of passion, one killing her lover, the other her child.

They were yin and yang, like the two blind musicians in a short story by Shi Tiesheng that I'd plodded through in the original Chinese. The two musicians wander together from village to village, playing their music, the elder teaching the younger the secrets of the *qin* lute. Who was the teacher here? Rich or Ho? The elder musician explained that, once a *qin* player had broken his thousandth string, he could break open his lute and find within the prescription to cure his blindness. After some time, the young player, unwilling to wait so many years of playing and wandering, decided to cheat: he broke his lute open, only to find a blank prescription and death. The secret the blind teacher had tried to impart to his protégé was nothing more than the satisfaction in a lifetime of dedication to the instrument the musician would feel at the moment of death. Had Rich and Ho also tried to cheat some esoteric Chinese riddle and found death within their silent chambers? Or, like the old teacher, had they found redemption and a peaceful end?

Suicide? Expediency? Certainly both women had motives for suicide. Especially Rich. Killing her own child. Sitting in a cell, playing it over and over again in her head. Assuming she'd really done it. Either way, her child was dead.

But Rich had been learning Mandarin. That didn't seem like a project someone suicidal would undertake. Unless it was an escape from thinking. An escape that failed? I had been obsessed when I started to learn Chinese. I'd thrown myself into the task, practising for hours on end, until my hand would automatically and independently of my brain perform the correct order of strokes. Even forgot about boys, for a while. Joy had started teaching me before we all left Vermont for Beijing. She had even sent me for lessons with Lok Cheung, a calligrapher living in the Old North End. I loved my daily morning discipline, copying Joy's and then Lok's characters over and over again, until I'd lost all sense of myself. Maybe that was why the first character one learned was always "you," rather than "me." Joy was a good teacher, even though the Beijingers mocked the slight southern accent I'd picked up from my new mom.

I sat back down at the desk and began flipping through the files. Otis immediately settled under the desk on my feet. I opened the post-mortem report. "Slight anomaly in May Ho's blood." Okay, Rey. What was in May Ho's blood? Poison? Very romantic, but nothing was found in either of the victims' intestinal tracts. If you could trust the ME.

I picked up the phone and dialled Dr. King at the Fletcher Allen. He answered the phone in the rusty voice of someone working alone deep into the night. I identified myself and my case, then remembered to apologize for calling him so late.

"No problem, I'll be here a while. I've got work to catch up. That's the trouble with vacations; you have to come back. What can I do for you, Detective Firelli?"

"It's the autopsy report on May Ho," I told him. "There's something about anomalies in the blood..."

"Hang on, let me see if I can find that paperwork." Dr. King was gone from the phone for a long time. When he returned, the news was not good. "I'm sorry I can't seem to find that file. The place is a bit of mess. I've just come back..."

"Well, maybe you can remember the autopsy. You wrote that nothing was found in the intestinal tract. Can you confirm or be more specific about this?"

"Correct, nothing in the intestinal tract. Actually, I didn't..." Dr. King cleared his throat. "Truth is, Detective Pirelli, I didn't perform that autopsy, an intern did."

I didn't need to know his name. It had to be the young driver of that rave-green GTI, my fellow rookie at the crime scene. "Aaron Levy performed the autopsy and you signed it?"

"A formality, really. Aaron Levy doesn't yet have the authority to sign."

I was stunned. "Maybe you could just give me your trainee's phone number, and I'll call him myself."

"Sure... we can do that for you. But hang on a second, before you get all worked up about a signature. You have the report. I don't see what good talking to Levy will do."

"I'd still like to talk to him."

"We do good work here, Pirelli."

"Your report is incomplete, Dr. King, and now you tell me the autopsy was done by an intern."

Dr. King paused for a moment before replying. "You're new at this game, aren't you, Detective? I think you'll find I have plenty of friends in the department."

I hung up too angry to try talking to the intern right now. I wouldn't get anything out of him, anyway. He'd probably be high on amphetamines, preparing for his finals.

I phoned the lab analyst. Dr. Witz, Witz? was out of the office and his voice mail was full. What a joke.

I got up to stretch my legs and calm down. So did Otis, but he settled back down under the desk when he saw me pacing in the living room instead of gathering his leash and treats. I came up face to face with the brick wall of crime-scene photographs. I began peeling the pictures off. The answer simply wasn't there. I knew I ought to sit down and go through the files again. Apply the lessons I'd learned in police procedure. But I needed something else to trigger my brain. I went to my unpacked box of books and retrieved a scroll. I hung it on a nail already imbedded in the wall. It was a single huge character, in wild broad strokes: *XI*, meaning a kind of free-wheeling happiness. Huiru had made the calligraphy for me on my twentieth birthday. Whenever I retraced the execution of the work, I felt happy and energized. But now Huiru was back in Beijing, and I was here alone with this morbid mystery.

Had Rich and Ho fallen in love? If so, why would they commit suicide? Was the way their hands laid on their pubises a kind of signal they had left me?

The mystery novel by Japanese author Inoue Yasushi came to mind. A man and a woman found dead on a deserted beach are presumed murdered, until the investigation reveals them to be suicides. The reverse could be the case here: Rich and Ho could, in fact, have been murdered, though all the signs pointed to suicide. Had someone else positioned their hands after killing them? How could they have communicated from separate locked segregation cells? Yet they died at the same time on Easter morning. Suicide or homicide?

Either way, the key question was how?

My desk was one messy jigsaw puzzle, my mind was spinning with scenarios. I felt a headache coming on. Otis followed me into the kitchen as I poured another shot of espresso. It would wreck my night, but I'd worry about that later. I didn't need to feel my forehead to know that the old familiar "trying to figure out the impossible" furrow had appeared. I pulled out my barrette, and re-swirled my chignon; then slowly but firmly massaged my forehead in small circular motions. Otis pawed my leg. I glanced at my Swatch. The hands were two blades slicing through Edgar Allan Poe's right eye. The hell with supper, the Pogo was keeping my stomach occupied anyway. I turned to the dog. "All right pal, let's…" Otis, leash in mouth, was already at the door waiting for me to grab a couple of plastic bags and lead the way. Otis bounced out. I hesitated, glanced at the panel of buttons on the incomprehensible security system, shrugged and followed the dog.

I opened one eye to glance at Max's flip-card alarm clock. 05:02, plop, 05:03. I felt the great weight of a nightmare on my lower body. But then relief, as Otis lifted his 80 pounds off my legs and jumped out of bed. I waited for 05:04 before getting up too, took off my sweaty red PJs, put on my forest-green bathrobe and followed the dog to the kitchen, detouring briefly through the living room to fetch my mini-recorder and cigarettes. I settled on a chair while Otis snooped around the kitchen for a little treat. I found myself facing another clock, this one on the microwave. The lime-green light indicated 05:10. I turned on the recorder and dictated:

"The sky is sunset red. I find the lighting soothing, except that there are intermittent flashes of blood on the pavement, which is not! Soothing, I mean. People start popping up. My mother, now old and very fat, stands in her cherry polka-dot shift, her hair in a bob, and wearing starlet sunglasses. Then it's not Mom any longer, but a woman in a business suit, wearing an ankle bracelet. There's also a blond woman smiling at someone she loves behind the camera. They're all standing, as if waiting for a cue. Then my mom is Petula Clark and/or Diana Rigg, covered in sequins, and parading in a beauty pageant for mature women. She moves down the catwalk no, it's an escalator. I notice she has huge breasts and her dress is too tight. She smiles sweetly and begins to sing 'My love is stronger than...' Then she trips on her cheap red sequined dress, falls many stories down. She starts in on some other Pet tune, but I can't see her any more. The singing is coming from somewhere below the pavement. Then it stops and the camera shifts to the basement. Mom, now nude, is sprawled on the floor of a windowless white room under a fiercely bright fluorescent light. She's alone. Unloved. She has a tattoo on her left shoulder blade. I don't know why I still think this is my mom: she would never, NEVER, have a tattoo! I turn her on her back and do a body search, opening up her flabby legs, checking her orifices. Gelatinous goo comes out of her vagina in a mass, it's white then turns bloody red, and prickly with needles. I hear a sped-up Muzak version of 'My love is warmer than the warmest sun.' It's coming from above, but I can't locate any speakers People, officials I think, rush into the cell, carrying files I'm supposed to read; I can't hold on to my mother's legs and take all those files at the same time. Two of the men are Chinese; the other is Caucasian and looks drugged. The Chinese look like old-style cadres in their navy-blue Mao suits. The white guy has a Chinese character pinned to his breast: I can't read it because he keeps on shoving his files at me. I never get a good look. I want to get closer to see the character, but I'm still holding on to my mother's heavy legs."

I pressed the STOP button. "Okay, Otis, you deserve a biscuit for hearing me out." I smiled at the big creature whose weight had most likely triggered the dream. I massaged my legs, still numb, then filled his food bowl, lit another cigarette and turned on my computer. Over there, it was six in the afternoon; he might be at his terminal?

I briefly debated whether to describe my case or my dream to Huiru. Finally I typed out a brief version of the dream. As I waited to see if I'd get back an email, I tried to recall the few childhood memories of my mother. God knows where I'd stored the even fewer Polaroids. There was one of my mom dressed in a polka-dot shift, her hair in a bob, and wearing swirling sunglasses. I couldn't remember the last time I'd dreamt of my biological mother. Why had I mixed her up with this case?

I made myself a cup of jasmine tea and picked up my proverb book. My finger struck page 203, line 3: "The frog inside the well knows nothing about the wide seas." As always, the proverb was to the point. I was a frog deep inside the well of this case; I should not make any assumptions at this point, based on a narrow point of view. I played back my dream, noting the presence of Warden Segal with her ankle bracelet, and blond tattooed Elizabeth Rich. But what about those sequined has-beens singing inanely sunny songs?

Of course, I really didn't believe dreams could magically solve murders, any more than I would let bibliomancy or the *Yijing* determine my life. But ideas, clues, desires that are already there below the surface, can emerge if you know how to read the signs. Nor did I have the slightest intention of informing the captain and Lou Moore about my personal police methods, none of which were featured on the final detective's exam at the academy. I'd wait until I'd solved my first hundred crimes and become a legend in the department before divulging my techniques.

Why would my mother appear as old and flabby? She was 30 when she died, which meant she'd be 46 today. At 43, even in death, May Ho didn't look old at all. Neither did the warden, for that matter; she seemed less a figure of authority than a sexual agent. And tattooed Elizabeth was even younger. My mom had become all of these women. And something else. But what?

Clearly, in the dream, I had given myself the role of the fumbling detective with too much to handle, and probing deeper and deeper into the dark recesses... What was an inverted vagina? No, Rey-hee, forget the penis. From that hole, needles had emerged — Rich was an acupuncturist — but also gelatin and blood: births, therefore deaths? A death linked to a woman's orifice? An infant death? Bing, Elizabeth's boy she'd murdered? But Bing was not an infant. And May was childless. So why an infant? Otis was snoring. The frog inside the well, Rey-hee: don't presume too much. But keep every detail in mind, no matter how arcane or silly.

I replayed the tape of the last segment of the dream: the Chinese men helping me in the investigation by giving me files, written documents; the white guy didn't help, he was drugged — not himself — but the Chinese word pinned to him may have been the answer to this as yet unrecognizable tangram. I realized that, in this investigation, my knowledge of Chinese could become essential. The "pavilion by the water" had to be my linguistic advantage.

So much for dream interpretation and bibliomancy. I figured I'd better do a bit of old-fashioned detective work. After all, I had to have some activity to report to Captain Carter. I started to draw up a list of the people I'd need to interview, friends and family of the two dead women.

On May Ho's side, there was Joe Tuzzo, her ex-husband, and Sam Ho, her only sibling. The ex lived somewhere in the country upstate, and the brother in New York City. That would take another full day. In Elizabeth Rich's column: a friend named Karl Krauss; her parents, Gerry and Gina Rich, and her elder brother Daniel, who still lived at home. And it might be worth looking up some people linked to their work: May's university colleagues, and Rich's colleagues at the clinic where she'd practised acupuncture.

But first and most importantly, I needed to go back to Montrose. The warden had been quite thorough; inside the pink folder was a complete list of the inmates of the Begonia residence, where both Rich and Ho had been housed. I'd have to talk to them, and especially to those she'd mentioned: Gloria Fletchard, Laura Elmsley, Eileen Morrison and Chris Shaw. The computer tinkled a familiar tune. Huiru's love note had arrived.

◊

By the time I slowed the old Ford down to turn on to the muddy Rivers Bend Line, I had put aside my mother, my dream and my proverb readings, and reinstated Detective Pirelli. I was focused and ready for a day's interviews at the penitentiary. I had talked to Chief Carter and my ears were still pinkly ringing with his fatherly advice: "Keep it simple. And don't let the inmates impress you: be tough, Officer Pirelli."

I had done Route 117 at twice the speed limit. Cop's privilege. At the prison gate, I didn't even look in the rearview mirror before stepping out of the car. I wasn't going to give Paul Bundell the pleasure of replaying my unprofessional antics. *Nan-mo-a-mi-tuo-fo;* I closed my eyes and kept my lips tightly shut. That, he couldn't see.

Irene Hill was at the gate waiting for me. "Warden Segal has asked me to be your guide today." I smiled politely and followed her plaid skirt through the four seasons of the pink hall and into the visitation room.

"The warden thought you could conduct the interviews here, in Jay, where the girls receive their guests. For convenience's sake, they've been arranged in alphabetical order: Laura Elmsley, Gloria Fletchard, Eileen Morrison and Chris Shaw. The warden… we hope that's fine with you."

The alphabetical arrangement was as good as any. Mentally I reviewed my notes: Laura Elmsley, convicted of credit-card forgery, and diagnosed with hyperlexia, was the least dangerous of the women. Gloria Fletchard, on the other hand, had poisoned her entire family. Convicted of first-degree murder. Eileen Morrison and Chris Shaw were a team. Both had been convicted of drug-related crimes ranging from burglary to armed hold-up and Chris had recently done some time in the dissociation cell.

Jay, the visitation hall, was painted a sunny yellow — which was a good thing, since there were no windows, except for the panes on the two doors, one for the visitors' entrance, one for the inmates'. The African violets on the coffee tables were presumably meant to create a lived-in décor. I've always felt African violets are the rodents of the plant world.

"I'd like to see Rich and Ho's personal effects first. Where are they?" I asked.

Irene Hill bent and snapped a leaf off a plant. "Of course. We've put them in the Eagle, our services building. You really want to go there first?" She appeared slightly irritated by the change in program.

I followed her through the empty quadrangle. No large gardener in sight on this sunny day, only an invisible woodpecker relentlessly sharpening its beak on what sounded like metal. I wasted no time. "What exactly is your job at Montrose?" I couldn't help adding, "What do you 'facilitate'?"

Irene Hill shook her head before she answered: "Odd jobs, really. I take care of the mail, I chair Sunday get-togethers…"

"And you're responsible for hobbies, right?" By now, we'd reached the front door of the red building. Hill held the door open for her guest, but I waited for her to answer before stepping through.

"Yes, hobbies. And such. I'm a little bit the jane-of-all-trades in this place. You see, I live here, at Acorn. That's the brown residence over there." Her hand fluttered vaguely in the opposite direction. "Others have kept their apartments in town. So I'm the only one who's potentially always on duty."

"You've been here a long time?"

"Since the beginning. Two years already. I took a cut in my salary coming here, but I've never regretted it. The girls need care, but above all, they need to feel they're in a family. We have to give them hope."

It was easy to guess that Irene Hill belonged to a religious order; she had that mix of pastoral goodwill and maternal discourse. As if on cue, a cross popped out of her beige polyester cardigan. She tucked it back in and buttoned her sweater to the collar. I stepped into Eagle. "I suppose," I suggested, "you see it as an opportunity to do a bit of God's work?" In Beijing, I recalled, many Christian Americans taught God, along with ESL.

"Montrose rules forbid staff from proselytizing. You know, some of our girls are First Nations… and then we have many unwed mothers. Most girls here aren't ready for Jesus. Especially our sisters living in Begonia. That's for serious offenders. Our chapel isn't quite overflowing, but I'm hopeful. And careful. Baby steps…"

"So you use hobbies to orient them?"

Hill's smile returned. She listed a predictable inventory based on racial stereotypes. "I try to get Natives and Hispanics working with leather; Blacks, too, though, one or two have learned to make quilts. White women prefer macramé, or knits; those with arthritis go for…" I interrupted her: "Actually, I'd first like to revisit the isolation cells, please. Aren't they right by the clinic?"

For the second time, I stepped into May Ho's segregation cell. I've never been to a convent but these tiny rooms with monk beds reminded me of cloisters. This time the cell was bare.

I decided on a more direct approach. "Sister Hill, tell me, what were you doing in here at 0600 the morning Rich and Ho died?"

Irene was momentarily taken aback. "I didn't come in here… I went to Liz' room. You know, it was Easter morning. I brought her — all right, I suppose it was out of order, but Liz was a good girl, regardless — I brought her, you know, well, holy water."

My principal memory of Easter was of tall cardboard boxes with yellow paper straw smelling deliciously of chocolate.

Liz' cell was totally stripped of any of her belongings.

In silence, Facilitator Hill led me to the storage space and to two superimposed green Rubbermaid boxes, the bottom one identified as Mtrose-178 and the top as Mtrose-203. "Let's see. Yes, Mtrose-178 is Elizabeth's belongings; Mtrose-203, Ho's."

I noted that Irene Hill referred to May Ho by her last name, whereas Elizabeth Rich was granted first name status. I opened May's box first. It contained several books dealing with animals: *Animal Estate*, *Readings in Animal Cognition*, *The Platypus and the Mermaid*; and at the very bottom, the familiar yellow *Book of Changes*, the *Yijing*. What prompted May's interest in animal behaviour, something completely out of her area of study? Was it a reaction against her fellow humans, or was she looking for lessons in survival applicable to her prison environment? A bookmark in the *Yijing* was inserted at Hexagram 18, and Hexagram 36 was earmarked. I jotted down the numbers for further reference. While I dug through May Ho's box, I continued my informal interrogation.

"So, no holy water for May Ho? I guess she wasn't such a good girl." I waited a moment, but Irene chose not to respond. I picked up a box of tea from May's effects. It was high-quality *longjing* tea. I sniffed it a little longer than necessary before replacing it. "We know that Elizabeth Rich was learning Chinese writing. What did May Ho do to pass the time?"

Facilitator Hill sighed. "She never came to me. I never got her involved in any hobbies. She wasn't pro-active or receptive to our programs at all. She did mention something once but I thought it was a joke. 'Pooch therapy,' or something like that. Perhaps it was a joke. Ho could be sarcastic."

"Some detention centres let inmates train dogs for the blind; other centres, just like hospitals, bring dogs in to boost morale. Perhaps that's what May Ho was thinking." Or sniffer dogs. I picked up a tiny Yixing earthen teapot. I didn't have to get too close to detect a powerfully pungent herbal fragrance. Not any tea I had ever tasted. Something medicinal.

Irene shrugged. "Dogs would have been out of my jurisdiction. In any case, it was hard to figure what Ho was thinking." Sister Irene absentmindedly played with the white hairs on her chin. I tried to keep from staring, concentrating instead at the bulging cross under the beige sweater. Hill added: "But then she was Chinese. Did you know the Chinese actually eat dogs?"

"I gather May was the only person of Chinese descent here."

"Oh," Hill became serious. "I'm not ignorant of their ways, if that's what you're thinking..."

"How's that, Sister Hill?" I was more bored than annoyed with the familiar clichés. "Have you worked with the Chinese community?"

That seemed to touch a nerve. "No, I've not worked with the Chinese community. God help me, I hope I never have to. I lived in China."

"Oh? And when were you in China, Sister Hill?"

"I was born there."

"Let me guess: your parents were missionaries."

"And their parents."

"Where?"

"Oh, in the provinces. You wouldn't know it."

"Try me."

Irene cocked her head and looked at me with new eyes. "In Zhengzhou, Henan province. My parents were killed when I was eight. By the Red Guards or the PLA, that's the..."

"People's Liberation Army."

Either she was not impressed or Hill was too absorbed in her own recollections to register surprise at my knowledge. "It was very early in the Cultural Revolution, Mao declared war on Christians. They began to kick out all the missionaries. My father wouldn't go. In the end, I was put on a boat by local parishioners and sent back to America, alone, an orphan. The Chinese..."

"That must have been terrible," I interrupted before Irene could begin heaping recriminations. "Sister Hill, you were the one who discovered the two bodies on Easter morning. Is it possible that you or someone removed anything from the scene or did anything to the bodies before calling the police?"

Irene straightened and pressed her hands against her hips. "Neither I nor anyone else tampered with the evidence, if that's what you mean."

"I had to ask."

Irene exhaled a long breath, visibly relieved. "I'll let you look through the boxes and come back for you in a little while?"

◘

Upon first inspection, the boxes of the deceased were a great deal less revealing than Irene Hill's China connection. I was still mulling over the nun's revelation as I pulled out May's stylish clothes. I would have gladly worn them: the checkered Diesel shirt, especially. I was looking at the size when I noticed it was stained and smelled of the same stuff that had been in the teapot. Whatever that medicine was, she had spilled it all over herself. The accessories were expensive: her ashtray, a silver pumpkin with a cover in the shape of a stem, was certainly one of a kind; her broken eyeglasses were Parisian Miklis. The prescription was obviously severe. Why hadn't she replaced them?

On top of Rich's box was a book entitled *On the Art of Controlling Qi: Qigong for Life*. The inside cover page was autographed: "To Liz — for life," signed, but not dated, *Jane Spitzer*. The book had been much used and annotated in large round letters. Between that book and the others, which were Chinese writing manuals, I fished one of those dime-store rubber lizards that boys all over the world use to scare girls. Must have been her kid's toy. As I looked at Rich's writing exercises, I squeezed the reptile and it unexpectedly popped open at the neck. I smiled at Liz' grade-three level calligraphy, remembering when my writing had looked like that. At first I too had struggled to give strength to each structure, struggled to break the habit of the alphabet's slanted loops, to convert to freer yet more powerful lines and hooks. Under Elizabeth's numerous Chinese dictionaries — many of whom were all-too-familiar — I uncovered a photo album with a goofy golden retriever on the cover. The album contained family photos. There was a little boy in a Spiderman outfit — surely her son Bing. He was very different from her: a dark mane of hair almost reaching down to a set of heavy eyebrows. Unsmiling, he glared at the camera. A bully. I took the photo out of its slip-in pocket. It was dated Hallowe'en 1998, over a year before her incarceration. In Elizabeth's confession, she'd mentioned a Batman outfit she'd made for the boy's last Hallowe'en in 1999. I perused the earlier photographs, all neatly dated. Suddenly, I gasped. In an early picture, a happier Rich beamed at the camera. She was wearing a print shift, blue mascara, pale lipstick, little high heels: the pose and the look were strikingly reminiscent of my mother's. I still had that Polaroid somewhere. I thought back to my dream. Unfulfilled lives of mothers?

"Detective Pirelli? Are you ready to head back to Jay?"

I replaced the photos and closed Elizabeth's box. From May's belongings, I picked up the pungent teapot, and turned to Hill waiting in the doorway. "Irene," I said, locking onto the nun's eyes, "I need to know. Did you tidy up the cells in any small way before calling for help?"

She picked an imaginary crumb or two off her speckless beige sweater, turned her tongue seven times in her mouth, but didn't answer.

Still holding the teapot, I crossed my arms and waited a moment. "Is that what you did, Sister Hill? Tidied up?"

Finally, Irene Hill answered: "I didn't do much. I did pick up the nightclothes that were on the floor. To cover them."

"What else, Sister?"

Sister Hill's voice was very low and her eyes flitted around the room. "Well, I closed Ho's eyes. Her eyes were so wide open. So black. I know I shouldn't have, but they really scared me. There was something… something empty staring. For a moment, I thought they were…"

I closed my own eyes, exercising patience. "What else? What else did you do, Irene?"

"After closing her eyes, I cleaned May Ho up a little."

"Cleaned up? What? Vomit? Urine, feces? What?" It took all of my willpower to keep my voice relatively flat.

"No, of course, not! One doesn't interfere like that with a dead person… Just her eyes, because they were open and so frightening. And… her private parts. I thought, the policeman and the male doctor shouldn't have to…"

"Tell me about the menstruation. Was it heavy, normal?"

Hill reached for the cross under her cardigan, for support. "Must we talk about this?"

I let my steady gaze answer in the affirmative.

"There wasn't much. It was… gooey. And clotty."

"And you didn't report it to the doctor?"

"That young doctor, Levy, he looked so upset. I thought it didn't matter… In any case, she was Chinese. I assumed she might be different that way."

"Different?"

"From other girls." Irene took a small step toward me and extended an imploring hand. "Officer Pirelli, Montrose is my home, we're one big family here. I simply felt it was my duty to… to clean up a little. I certainly had no intention of tampering…"

I nodded. "That's all right, Sister. I just needed to know."

Accepting my nod as absolution, Sister Hill, her head high and a her heart a trifle lighter, led the way out of Eagle's storage area and back to Jay.

✡

Waiting for the first inmate, I examined the crafts on sale: leather bookmarks with kooky gospel sayings: "God moves in mysterious ways," "I really want to READ you LORD, but it takes so LONG." Was this ironic, I wondered? There were also various shapes of multicoloured quilt bits I guessed were potholders, covers for Kleenex boxes and toilet seats — what else could that round furry stuff be?

I was tangled up in a feather-and-pearl mobile when Irene ushered in a wiry 20-some-year-old woman with gray streaked blond hair and a mousy look. Laura Elmsley. Tufts of hair hung limply to either side of her face and her khakis seemed to fall off her hipless body. I motioned her to sit in the armchair in front of me, but she moved instead to sit at another module. So, not such a wimp after all.

Still, I couldn't let her take the lead. "Ms. Elmsley, could you please sit down here, in front of me." Laura Elmsley followed the direction of my finger then moved over to the flowery sofa. She cupped her hands together on her lap. With her fully buttoned-up white blouse, she looked like a convent girl, the kind who did her homework on Saturday night.

"I'm Detective Pirelli, investigating officer in the deaths of Elizabeth Rich and May Ho. You knew these two women?"

"Two? Well, I knew one, Zil; and then I knew another two, I mean one, May. Those two were one, you know."

"What do you mean?"

"Everyone knows they were like this." Laura crossed her middle and index fingers; then, giggling, formed a circle with her left thumb and index into which she slid her right index finger. Finally her fingers became scissors cutting shapes in space.

Before I could entirely decipher the complex of obscene gestures, Laura Elmsley's fingers were back into their initial good-girl position.

"You mean they were lovers?"

Laura raised her hands as though to clap them together, but instead, her right middle finger tickled the inside of her left palm; then she squeezed her two palms together. For a hyperlexic, Laura wasn't much of a talker. Or else sex was a taboo topic.

"All right. I'll take that as a yes. Did you have any contact with them?"

"On a tectonic level, yes."

"Tectonic or platonic?"

"Tecto, Plato. Me, I don't do... no panky-hanky."

I smiled to hear Plato turned into a geophysicist.

"At the Food Poporium, to my left. I sat to my right. I mean they sat to my left."

"So what would they talk about?"

"Zil and May? They sat facing each other, sometimes Liz was to my left, sometimes it was May to my right, no I mean sometimes Zil was to my left, sometimes she was to my right. I get it mixed up, upper left, side left or right left, I mean upper right, side left, uh upper right, side right." Laura struggled with these positions in space, by twisting her slight body this way and that.

"Zil was my friend. Then May after Liz. One letter after the other, or before the latter. You play Scrabble? Inmate? Intimate! Mascara-Baccarat; workmen-..."

"OK, Laura. What did you all talk about?"

"Food, mainly. Kitchen quixotic things like yakiteri, yakisuki, wabisa. Also about writing, that's my field of expertise. One of them — the one sitting to my right — was talking about left-handed writing. The one sitting in front of me, she was talking about left and right strokes and she was drawing in the air. Like this. To tell you the truth, I couldn't tell them apart. After a while. Though I do know one of them was left-handed. When she sat next to me, I mean, sat to my... right, I'd get her elbow in my plate." Laura started drawing in space what was supposed to look like letters or characters. It was difficult to tell whether Laura was making fun of me or not. Unable to tell a short blond white woman from a tall Chinese woman?

I stole a look at my Swatch. Laura checked her pocket watch. She looked at it right-side-up, then upside down and got up. "Officer-Sir, it's time. I'll retire now to my right-wing chamber. A pleasure to meet me, to me you."

I let Laura Elmsley go, thinking Begonia is left, Laura. There were no ashtrays in the lounge. With a sudden urge to fill the few waiting minutes with a cigarette, I eyed an African-violet pot, lifted it. But someone had preempted me. Under the pot, a sticker warned NO SMOKING!

As I replaced the pot, an impressively large woman dressed in royal-blue athletic gear entered the room. "Do you like my African violets? A nice touch, no?" the prisoner asked in a rich full-throated voice. She lowered her generous posterior into the chair, crossed her feet, leaving her heavy thighs open, and proceeded to introduce herself: "I'm Gloria Fletchard. I'm in charge of the garden here. I wanted to work in the kitchen. But they wouldn't let me. So I said to myself, plants are the next best thing."

I smiled. Gloria may have studied at the New England Culinary Institute and graduated as their top Iron Chef, but she would have to be exceedingly optimistic to think the authorities would let her anywhere near the kitchen after she'd poisoned her entire family.

"Have you noticed the herbs growing around the little cedars? There's sage and sweetgrass — that's for the aboriginal inmates, although they don't use it as much as I expected. It smells pretty good when you burn it: ever tried it?"

I shook my head.

"Some people think of sage as only good for vulgar stews. That's not the case. When you burn sage like sweetgrass, it gives off a scent like incense. Pick a little bit up before you leave."

Gloria Fletchard was a smooth talker; she lectured me on her herbal experiments. I let her talk; herbs and poisons were close cousins, and this case tasted of poison.

"Were May Ho and Elizabeth Rich taking drugs?"

"Oh hell, we're all taking something or other in here. Not that I have to. I'm a virtual gourmet. I get fat just reading recipes!"

"What about Ho and Rich?" I insisted.

"Ms. Ho didn't mind a bit of a chat about food. Most people here, they're like dogs, they'll eat anything... I asked her a couple of times about Chinese recipes. She was a great help. Got those mushroom names finally figured out. You know, like everybody talks about shiitake, but who exactly knows what they are?... It's too bad, really too bad. Can't think why she'd want to do herself in like that. If you ask me, she couldn't get used to the food in here."

"What can you tell me about Elizabeth Rich?"

"Esso-teric."

"How's that?" I couldn't decide if this was Gloria's way of deriding Rich, or simply an admission of her ignorance in all things not culinary.

"Well, I saw her a bunch of times standing in front of the maple tree in the yard. I swear, for the longest time, I mean a whole lot of minutes, she wasn't breathing. As though she were in some sort of trance."

"Go on."

"So, one day I finally ask her about it, and she tells me she's getting energy from the tree. Well, at least it's not fattening, I guess. I could use some of that magic myself." Gloria patted herself lightly on the thighs, and the royal-blue mass rolled and wobbled. Her laugh was whole-hearted and contagious.

When we were through chuckling, I asked, "Could they have been murdered?"

"Murdered?! In here?! Nah, impossible. They were kind of cute, actually."

"Come on, Gloria. You can do better than that." I did my best to inject the full measure of the authority of my uniform into my tone. "You're not going to tell me this place is a little paradise. Everyone getting along, everyone chipping in, no grudges, no violence?"

"Okay, so let's say some people here didn't like them. Especially Ms. Ho: the race thing, I guess."

"Who?"

"Hey, Detective Pirelli, Gloria Fletchard ain't no snitch. She's survived Singer and she's planning to see her plants through a whole bunch of four seasons. If it's all right with you, I'll get back to my transplanting."

It seemed they all knew they had the option to end the interview whenever it got nasty, or uncomfortable or just boring. As Gloria manoeuvred her royal-blue-suited mass around the settees toward the door, I tossed her one final question: "You grow seasoning herbs. Do they use your herbs in the kitchen?"

Gloria stopped and put her hands on her large hips: "You're thinking poison, right? Something like white laurel. Why not curare, while you're at it? You've got to be joking. This ain't no five-star restaurant here. Cooks like Chris and Eileen are good for grating carrots; they throw away the broccoli flowers, for heaven's sake. You think they'd know what to do with fennel, tarragon and sorrel?" The arsenic lady departed with a roar of laughter.

✿

It was five to one on my Swatch, which made Poe look like he'd sprouted rabbit antennae. I decided to go out for a quick cigarette and see Gloria's garden up close. The "energy tree," a young maple, stood in the centre of the courtyard where the inmates took their walks. A promise of shade in a couple of years. Both Ho and Rich would have seen it to maturity had they done their time here. The bark was soft. I put my nose to it and then my ear. A long time ago, as a child driving along the highway with my mother, I'd seen a lone horse in conversation with a lone tree in a large empty field. For an instant now, I became that horse. I'd lost my beautiful polka-dot scarf on that ride; it flew right out the window. There was, as promised, sage and sweetgrass under the cedars. Closer to the cafeteria, rosemary, savory, thyme and what appeared to be other seasoning herbs that I couldn't identify. Did Gloria plant them for the sheer pleasure of watching them grow? I sat on a bench with my back to the administration building to finish my cigarette. I stamped it out and added the remains to a little pile of hand-rolled butts half-buried next to the bench.

¤

I knew I would have to "be tough, too" in interviewing Eileen Morrison and Chris Shaw. I wasn't looking forward to the experience. I started with Morrison, but I could just as easily have gone with Chris Shaw first, because she repeated Morrison's statement word for word, if not syllable for syllable. Obviously they'd rehearsed their story. They never talked to or interacted with the dyke and her Chink toy-girl, except when they got in the way, and they knew nothing about their deaths. There were a lot of "nope"s and "yup"s and "dunno"s, not to mention the occasional "Hey?", all punctuated by the harsh "Ma'am."

Shaw, for her part, sat through it all with legs apart, tattooed arms firmly crossed over her tight tank top.

Hoping to open her up a bit, I finally opted for more personal questions. "Your tattoos, they were all made inside?"

"Yup."

"Here at Montrose?"

"Nope."

"But some were made at Montrose."

"Yup."

I tried to show some artistic interest. "Not bad. You did them yourself?"

Which seemed to work. Chris pulled her tank top up her belly to expose a skull head. "That's from Singer."

At the pubic line, I made out what looked like the top of three letters which could have been L-I-Z. "What's that one, below?"

"Mm, fucked that one up. Didn't turn out right." Chris pulled her top back down and crossed her arms on her midriff.

Morrison and Shaw flaunted their relationship: they dressed alike, they had the same bleached hair and, when they did make complete sentences, both used the first-person plural. "Wasn't Eileen jealous when she saw Liz' name tattooed on your groin?" I asked Chris.

"Hey? Fuck that. That's no Liz tattoo. What the fuck would I want to tattoo that Chink-lover bitch's name over my cunt?" Chris Shaw stared down at her sandaled feet. Her black-Cutex-coated toenails were fidgeting wildly.

"Maybe you're the jealous kind, Chris. Hey, I can understand. Liz rejected you. So you went back to your Singer pal. Have I got it right?"

"Nope. You got it all wrong. Never cared for the bitch." Chris scratched her left hand ferociously. Rey noticed a thick welt.

"What happened to your hand, Chris?"

"Kitchen burn. We got kitchen duty. Didn't they tell you?"

"Take your jacket off, please." I expected to find dull red patches of scraped skin and all manner of scars.

"Fuck for? I got rights. You wanna fistfuck me, you bring the papers, Ma'am." Chris zipped her black bomber jacket right up and shoved her hands into her front jean pockets.

"Why were you put in the dissociation cell?"

Chris shrugged.

"You had a fit. Mutilated yourself. Burned your arms. Attacked the other women. That's when they put you in the dissociation cell."

Chris shrugged again. "Diss cell's a piece o' cake. Fuckin' Sheraton. Service is okay, and no cooking." Chris' hands emerged from her tight pockets and she resumed her scratching.

"Why were Rich and Ho in diss cells when they died? Can you tell me that?"

"They were scared shitless is why, Ma'am."

"Scared of who?"

"Of us." Chris made an odd hiccupping sound, a sort of grotesque imitation of laughing.

"Why?"

Chris stood. "Wanna find out, bitch... Ma'am?"

I stood quickly. "Sit down, Chris Shaw."

Chris turned her back to me and leaned over, with her hands extended behind her. "Go ahead, bite me or cuff me, Ma'am."

I dismissed her.

◘

Facilitator Irene Hill arrived carrying two coffees and a yellowed Tupperware containing four muffins resting on a paper towel. She put her peace offering next to Gloria's African violets.

"I wanted to bake you the girls' all-time favourite, my carrot cake, but I was on duty yesterday. These are my low-fat yogurt muffins. I figured a young woman like you would go for non-fattening sweets, right? You must be tired, do have one."

I decided not to please the China-hater. Anyway, I've never liked desserts. The coffee was tepid and lite, unfortunately not the warden's espresso. "I'd like to see Warden Segal, now."

Irene was visibly disappointed, and worried. She left in silence.

The warden arrived in a tailored pantsuit that echoed the sunny walls and the sunny day. Her hair, though short, looked as though it was piled up into a chignon. Her very sober make-up highlighting her green eyes was picture-perfect. She had certainly not done all this for me; there had to be an important meeting later today. In fact, it turned out Warden Segal had no time for me, but offered to walk me back to the gatepost.

Still in interview mode, I managed to get in a couple of questions along the way about working conditions at Montrose. By the time we got to the gatepost and the ever-watchful Paul Bundell, the warden was summing up: "Let's say we're all a little overworked. Everyone has to do more than one job. But it's so worth it." As she said this, I caught Paul turning his eyes up and sighing under his breath.

"I gather, Paul, you don't think so?" I asked lightly. Immediately I regretted the use of his first name. Rey-hee, why this familiarity? It was not my way to call strangers by their first names.

Paul glanced at his boss, "Let's say, it's not exactly a private-sector paycheque." He went back to zooming indifferently into the foyers of the Cedar, then the Deer residences.

"Paul, oh Paul's never satisfied," Lucille Segal broke in harshly. Somehow, her comment, or the tone in which she delivered it, seemed out of line, not what you'd expect from a superior. But then bosses could be unpredictable. Take mine.

◻

I stopped by the river to light up a cigarette and listen to the rush of the Winooski. But I couldn't shake the vision of the tat twins, with their bleached hair, tight jeans and butch look. Admit it, Rey, that's exactly how you imagined inmates would look. Not like wishy-washy Laura, or expansive Gloria. And where had all the tough jail matrons gone? Warden Segal with her Vetiver perfume and ankle chain; Irene Hill with her muffins and wooden cross.

I chose the long way back to town, up North Williston Road and then the I-89. I needed time to sort things out. I drove at 20 miles per hour, smoking with the windows down. Everyone had, in some form or other, acknowledged the fact that Liz and May were lovers, but no one could offer a reason for their committing suicide. Except Gloria, but that was sarcasm. "May had enough of the food…" A prison, even one with curtains, pink halls and African violets, was still a place of detention. Death could be an inmate's only means of self-deliverance. But nothing, no one, all day had given me any evidence that either of the two women had had enough. According to Chris, the two victims had gone into the diss cells to avoid her and Eileen. That was certainly not suicidal. Could Chris and Eileen have found a way into the cells?

I swung onto the I-89 and picked up speed. I wasn't getting anywhere. Somewhere between exits 12 and 13, I passed the sculpture of two giant whale tails sticking out of the ground. As though the pair of whales had just jumped and dived back down into the earth. The frog in the well image, again. No one seemed to know who had dropped them there by the highway. Or why I switched on the cruise control at 50 miles per hour and tried to reorient my train of thought. The idea of a double suicide pact must be, if not discarded, put aside. No motive, no note left behind. Unless Irene Hill had thrown the suicide note away.

Still, I didn't really believe Hill would conceal such material evidence. Suicide, acknowledged in writing by the perpetrator, elevated death into a defiant act of will. To conceal such an act would surely be an unacceptable sin to Sister Hill. The double-suicide hypothesis was out. For now.

Hill had motive to kill May Ho. Revenge, decades later, for the bereaved daughter whose parents were mercilessly slaughtered by the Red Guards. And Hill not only had access to the segregation rooms, she had been first at the scene of the crime. She even confessed to having "cleaned up" Ho and covered the bodies. But she seemed to have no motive to murder Elizabeth Rich. Bringing her holy water? What if Irene were a spurned lover rejected by Liz, who then slept with the enemy? Liz hadn't participated in Irene Hill's hobbies program any more than May had. Perhaps Sister Hill couldn't bear to see a white soul in the grips of the yellow peril.

As my mind sped up, so did the car. I set it back on cruise control. Warden Segal's selection of inmates to interview had been spot on: they were all potential suspects. With the probable exception of Laura. Mousy Laura lived in a world of words and gestures; she wouldn't flirt a lie, I mean hurt a fly. Educated May might even have appreciated her; played word games with her. And Liz, before May arrived, had already been sitting at the same table with her at meals. Laura had lost her only friends at Montrose.

The bleached twins, Eileen and Chris, had clear motives to eliminate both Rich and Ho. They'd worked as a team out of prison; they could still be operating in prison. Jealousy at seeing Liz coupling with May? Rejection by Liz? Race hatred aimed at May? And they also had indirect access to the victims: they both worked in the cafeteria. They could have slipped something in the trays going to the seg cells. No, their stomachs were empty. Moreover, Chris had, shortly before Liz and May went in there, been interned in the segregated area: she could have left something there. What if Gloria was her accomplice, providing a home-grown secret potion? But what would be Gloria's incentive to kill Rich and Ho? Merely to test out the potency of some plant?

By the time I took the Main Street exit, I had narrowed down my most likely suspects to prison staff Irene Hill and inmate Chris Shaw. Murder then, and an inside job, at that? Something told me that I had better have solid proof before I bore such news to my superiors.

◘

I was turning unto Cliff Avenue when all hell broke loose. The car radio crackled to life, a police car passed me at full speed, and I almost hit, of all creatures, Otis darting across the street. I slammed on the brakes, parked the car half up on the sidewalk and got out, only to be momentarily knocked back by Otis. I could see the police parked outside Max's condo. I started running. Then I spotted Detective Louise Moore, arms and legs akimbo, standing by the door and watching me hobble toward her, with Otis leaping and pawing alongside.

"Please unarm it NOW, Officer Pirelli," Officer Moore said gruffly, pointing at the townhouse, before returning to a conversation on her walkie-talkie. Only then did I realize the house alarm was screaming. I rushed inside, with Otis still on my heels, and punched in the code to unarm the system. Officer Moore, gun drawn, moved past me to inspect each room. Nothing in the living room, nor in the kitchen, nor in the bathroom. In the bedroom, the sliding-window door was ajar.

Moore stepped into the bedroom, but before she had time to say anything, I confessed: "I think I forgot to lock the door... I armed the system this morning, but I forgot to lock the door. Otis must have pushed it to go out."

"You realize you alerted the whole station?" Louise Moore said, as she relaxed and shifted from official inspection to snooping around. "Nice place, eh? Big king bed, too big for one, no?"

"It's not mine. Practically nothing here is mine."

"Not even this sexy piece of lingerie?" Moore bent down to pick up and display my red-flannel pyjama bottom on the floor. "So, anything missing, at a glance?"

"Umm, I don't think so." I picked up my PJs and made a promise to myself to never leave the house without tidying up first.

"Well, make sure. And make it snappy, will ya. This is my break." She brushed off Otis's rugged paw swipe across the calves, the dog's futile attempt to befriend her, and left the room.

"Everything's fine. I am so sorry. It won't happen again. I guess I'm not used to this damned alarm system. I left in a rush this morning."

"Grow up. That's no excuse. You should be grateful it was me and not Vance or Cassidy who took the call."

"How can I make it up to you? Can I offer you a bite to eat? I was going to make myself some fried noodles. How about it, Louise?"

"Chinese noodles?" She pushed Otis off with her leg. "This big guy sure looks appetizing."

I struggled to overcome irritation. After all, this was a colleague, a fellow officer. Determined to make friends, I managed a brief chuckle. "No dog, I promise. Come on, join me for an early-bird dinner."

"Thanks, but no thanks. I'm meeting someone." At the door Louise softened slightly. "What are you wearing to the ball?"

"The ball?!" I vaguely remembered someone mentioning a ball.

"The annual Police Charity Ball. Don't tell me you haven't been briefed on the Ball."

"I guess not. I couldn't make it, anyway. I wouldn't know what to wear."

"Detective Pirelli, everyone goes to the Ball. Even us few unaccompanied gals. You've gotta come! If you're one of us, you'll be there. Got that?" Detective Moore pushed past the big hound. She got back into her car, started the engine, checking her lipstick and mascara before zooming off. I immediately went back to the bedroom, red PJs still over my arm. It wasn't an illusion: nothing was missing in the room but, on the unmade bed, lay a document I had never seen before.

✡

I considered not opening the package. Correct procedure dictated I leave it on the bed where it lay, and call police security or the bomb squad. But if I did that, how long would it be before I could get my hands on the contents? I wanted to know right then and there what was inside. There were none of the tell-tale signs of a letter-bomb, no writing at all on the exterior, and why would someone deliver a letter-bomb in this way? Come on, Rey, you're a cop on a case: just open it! I put Otis outside in the garden first. Then I came back into the bedroom. For a moment I considered how I'd want to be found if the package blew me up. Should I take it into the bathroom and save Max the cleanup? In the end, to hell with it, I tore open the envelope. No bomb. Only a copy of the drugs section of the criminal code: Schedule IV to the Food and Drugs Act of the Criminal Code, to be precise. No accompanying note, no explanations, just the criminal code on drugs. I took a deep breath. A quick leaf through revealed no underlining or inscribed comments anywhere in the document. Who could have put it there? And why? My first guess had to be Detective Louise Moore, who'd been waiting for me at the door. Trying to be helpful? Or confuse me?

I was suddenly very tired. I lay down for a moment on the bed without taking off my uniform. Sometime during the night, Otis' barking woke me. I got into my PJs and lay down with the Food and Drugs Act and a pencil.

✡

It was past 0800 when I woke up in the morning, still tired. And troubled. Schedule IV of the Food and Drugs Act was lying on the floor by the bed. I brought it into the kitchen with me and went through it again looking for annotations while the coffee was brewing. When the espresso was ready, I put aside the document. I wouldn't let myself get sidetracked. It was Irene Hill's meddling with May Ho's body that troubled me.

I regretted not having taken the time to visit the Montrose residences, including Sister Hill's apartment in Acorn. I brought my coffee to my desk and picked up Warden Segal's pink folder containing the blueprint of each building's layout. All the inmates' residences had identical divisions: four blocks of 12 rooms each, six on each floor. On the ground floor of the building, a mini-kitchen, a games and telephone area, a television den and, to the right, showers. I checked the location of the victims' and suspects' rooms in Begonia. Liz and May had been in the same block, May in the room right above Liz'. Eileen and Chris shared the same facilities with the victims, but their cells were next to each other in another block. One could easily slip into the other's, even though it was strictly forbidden. Gloria was right next door, which meant she could hear their griping and groping through the walls. Laura lived in Block 1, ground floor. Irene Hill's place was in Acorn, a separate building; not easy to justify a search or even visit her quarters without more evidence.

The phone rang. It was the chief lab analyst at Fletcher Allen. Dr. Witz excused himself profusely for the delay in getting back to me; he had been on his annual leave. He was also sorry he had contracted a bad cold and would be sneezing throughout our telephone conversation.

I went straight to the point. "Can you tell me now what your report meant by 'unknown substance in May Ho's blood'?"

"'Unknown' refers to something not on our list of drugs, therapeutic or mind-altering, i e. illegal substances. It is most unfortunate that a report should contain such a vague term. I'm also sorry about that. I simply cannot further expound."

"Are you sure that the unknown substance you found in May Ho's blood wasn't also present in the body of the other deceased, Elizabeth Rich?"

Dr. Witz paused before answering: "Very sorry, I thought I was about to sneeze. Yes, coming back to your second question: absolutely positive, no such substance in Mtrose-178, Elizabeth Rich. Only in Mtrose-203." There followed a quick series of explosive sneezes.

I waited.

"Please excuse me, Detective. Can I be of any further service to you today?"

"Actually, I have two more medical questions concerning Ho that you might be able to answer. I have a witness says she died with her eyes wide open. And that she was menstruating."

"Yes?" Dr. Witz, perfectly polite, refrained from interrupting me, but I could hear him thinking in that "yes."

"The witness reported that her menstrual blood was goopy and clotty. I was wondering if you might have any insights. You see, we're not sure this is suicide. Are eyes wide open and/or such type of menses symptomatic of anything?"

Dr. Witz was silent. I pulled the receiver slightly away from my ear in anticipation of another sneeze. But none came and, when he finally replied, he spoke so quickly and quietly, I had to ask him to repeat. "First: the eyes could indicate a seizure, such as grand-mal for example, or a respiratory collapse. Second: I was not requested by the ME to take a vaginal biopsy, so I cannot speculate on that issue. But, in the course of my career, I have performed thousands of tests on vaginal fluids, and the goopy and clotty nature you mention is a frequent occurrence that signifies little, if anything, when not accompanied by a putrescine, cadaverine odour, which would indicate a high level of alkaline. A healthy vagina is acidic, you see."

"Could such a vaginal condition be the result of an infection?"

"Correct. It can also be a sign of acute toxicity causing violent death." This last sentence was punctuated with three short sneezes and an excuse-me. "For example," Dr. Witz concluded, "addicts or women transporting drugs sometimes conceal the drugs in their vaginas. I believe they're known as 'body packers,' or 'hoopers.'"

I thanked the doctor and wished him a speedy recovery.

I couldn't help feeling my investigation had taken a leap forward. Well, maybe not forward, but a leap. Thanks to Dr. Witz, I now knew the cause of death was possibly different in the two cases. And that the condition of May Ho's corpse pointed to murder. The identical positioning of the bodies could have been a perverse funereal arrangement by a twisted mind. Sister Hill? But would she have paired Rich and Ho, a Christian and a heathen? It seemed to me that Irene's particular form of perversity precluded that. Sure, Hill had admitted covering her up. But drugs and vaginal insertions were certainly not her MO.

I went back to the kitchen for my legal drugs: cigarettes and another espresso, and returned to my desk. Otis was dozing on the bed, on his baby blanket, on the spot where the Schedule IV to The Food and Drugs Act had been left anonymously.

Until now I had been wondering who had left the document, rather than why. Even though Dr. Witz had confirmed that there was no known drug in May's blood, I was convinced that there had to be a link between her death and drugs. Could the anonymous document have been intended to tell me something about May's case? I began to read again. I knew that Schedule IV, unlike the other schedules, contained drugs which, while dangerous, had therapeutic uses. Simple possession of Schedule IV drugs was not an offence. I glanced at the names of certain drugs, the length of which was impressive: dimethylbenzeneethanamine, methylenedioxyamphetamine, phosphoryloxyindole, trimethoxybenzeneethanamine. Next to them, other drugs sounded deceptively familiar: opium poppy (Papaver somniferum), opium, narcotine, papaverine, poppy seed, also sweetgrass. The entry for sweetgrass read: "used by aboriginals in ceremonies, and for healing. In the past considered but no longer considered a contraband substance." What if May had somehow gotten hold of some other substance, as yet unknown to the authorities, medical or judiciary? So many drugs in their natural form were still unlisted in the West. Eileen and Chris had Native blood, but Gloria knew more about the life of plants.

I crossed Irene Hill off my list of probable suspects, and moved Gloria up. Whoever had delivered the drug schedule wanted me to link the case with drugs, poisons. If it was an inside job, it had to be with Gloria's help. Or she could have acted alone. To kill May Ho. The problem was the mirror image of Elizabeth Rich's dead body in the next cell.

Though I'd put Gloria at the top of the list, there were plenty of other suspects, if I followed the drug-poison lead outside the prison walls. May's brother, Sam, was a pharmacologist. Liz' friend Karl Krauss was a doctor, with access to and knowledge of drugs. Liz, as an acupuncturist, could also have studied alternative medicine. Could Liz have murdered May?

Backtrack. The Schedule, which was part of the Criminal Code, would be known to peace officers, perhaps lawyers and other professionals involved in law enforcement, such as forensics doctors. Not to mention academics. Like May, like those around her. I had been foolish to suspect Louise Moore of leaving the envelope. She wouldn't have hung around and staged an alarm incident if she'd wanted to drop off a document anonymously. There were a hundred simpler ways to do it. Someone from the staff at

Montrose, on the other hand, might have done it this way. They could be trying to tell me that the case was linked to drugs, legal or otherwise. Who? Who would want to discredit the prison? The warden had categorically claimed that Montrose was "virtually drug-free." If it were leaked that the pink pen had a drug problem… well, experiment over.

I reviewed the staff: not Irene Hill; Montrose was her only home. And the other facilitators, Walker and Haynes, played by the book. What could they gain from the shutdown of Montrose? Paul the guard? Hadn't he demonstrated some bitterness, that shrug of dissatisfaction with the work conditions in the state institution? Was he sleuthing with me?

I checked my Swatch: 0900. Straight through Edgar Allen's right eye and the long hand up through the top of his head. Time to get dressed. And feed Otis. My uniform had that slept-in look. We headed back to the kitchen. While Otis crunched lamb-and-rice kibble, I fetched my own police edition of *Martin's Criminal Code*. At a loss where to start, I opened the book at random. Bibliomancy never fails to produce a sign.

My eye fell on the entry "Oysters." I chuckled: the only foodstuff mentioned in the whole book and I had to land on it. How I would have loved to share a couple of dozen raw oysters right now. A wave of loneliness washed over me. My only friend, beautiful Huiru, was so far away. If I asked him, would he come over to join me? Would he be able to adapt to this world, as I had to his? Could his brushes sustain him, or would he slowly wither like so many exiles before him? Even my decision to enter the police force had been incomprehensible to him. And who could blame him? The police he knew in China represented everything he despised and feared. And what about me? Could I give up this strange new career I was just starting and return to China? What, in the end, did we have in common? Our relationship was a hothouse orchid. Some things were too delicate to last. Stop this maudlin self-pity, Rey-hee. Concentrate on the work at hand. Twelve days to solve this case. Or fail. I lit a cigarette. Otis sniffed once and moved away.

I looked up the entry for "Food" in the Criminal Code. The definition included "*any article manufactured, sold or represented for use as food or drink for human beings, chewing gum, and any ingredient that may be mixed with food for any purpose whatever.*" There followed a series of states and degrees of lethality: "*poisonous or harmful, unfit for human consumption; in whole or in part, filthy, putrid, disgusting, rotten, decomposed or diseased animal or vegetable substance; adul-

terated; manufactured, prepared, preserved, packaged or stored under unsanitary conditions."

Well, obviously, some foods, combined with others, were unhealthy at best, and occasionally deadly. Ask the orthodox Jews, or the Chinese. On my first night with Hairu, when we were both students in Beijing University, we'd climbed the university wall and sneaked up to a friend's apartment where I was staying. We'd decided to eat before going to bed. The boy must have been starving. Students the world over are poor, but in China, in those days, so much more so. It seemed odd to me now, that we would have preferred eating to sex. In the fridge, there were two leftovers, crabs and sweet potatoes. To me, the combo seemed a heavenly match, the same beautiful coral colour. But he'd refused to eat both, claiming that if eaten together, the combination would kill you. I'd laughed at him, but in the end, he ate the potatoes, I the crab. In bed, I'd found his skin delightfully coarse. "University students don't get to bathe that often," he told me. "That's why my skin's so rough." A lesson for a First-World student. Since that night, I had never mixed crab and sweet potato. Just in case.

PART III
BLUER THAN THE INDIGO PLANT

May's ex lived in cow country, in Enosburg Falls, some 45 miles north of Burlington. Once I left the I-89 for Route 104 and 105, the green hills became dotted with Guernseys and Holsteins, and the odd postcard red barn. Road signs announced cow crossings and sports-vehicle trails. Finally, a sign declared Enosburg Falls to be Vermont's Dairy Festival Town. I was going in the right direction. My map, however, didn't include the smaller roads called "lines" and Joe Tuzzo had no phone.

Another sign announced the highschool. The institution itself was a gray box behind a chain-link fence way out in a field. I stopped at Leon's diner in the centre of town. There were eight Dodge and Ford pick-ups parked out front. Inside, Leon had painted his walls swimming-pool blue. On top of the women's washroom hung a pair of antlers and a colour drawing of deer grazing. I asked the huge waitress in a voice loud enough to include the six male and two female customers where Weeds Line was. No one knew. But if it was the beekeeper I was looking for, he lived in the old blue house that belonged to the Aubuchons. Past the falls, follow a dirt road for a couple of miles, the house should be to the left, right after the steep hill.

At the foot of the hill, before the little blue house came into view, I spotted eight blue boxes standing some three feet high in a circle. When I turned off the engine, spectacular silence greeted me. No highway sounds, no neighbours. "Nothing is not mere emptiness," my pompous reply to Warden Segal came back to mind. A black dog leaped towards me. Smaller than Otis, but no fiercer. Mr. Tuzzo lived in full retreat. *Nan-mo-a-mi-tuo-fo.*

A man looking older than his 45 years, with very tanned skin, jeans and a sad smile came out of the wood cabin, although the dog had not barked. Both man and dog stood at a polite distance from the police car, giving me time to extricate myself.

"Mr. Tuzzo? I'm Rey Pirelli, investigating officer in the death of May Ho."

"Yes," he nodded. "I suppose I've been expecting you."

We walked up to the house where Joe held the rickety screen door for me. The black dog seemed to lose interest, and disappeared into the woods. The rustic house smelled deliciously of wood. And there was plenty of it: wood beams along the ceiling, log walls, pine floors and logs piled by the stove. The cherrywood table was bare, except for a pack of cigarettes, a box of wooden matches, a half-full cup of coffee and the French newspaper *Libération*. Very tidy. By the stove were stacked a full year's newspapers and some four dozen empty wine bottles, obviously rinsed and neatly arranged upside down. I sat at the table.

"Would you care for a cup of good strong coffee?" Joe smiled and rubbed his hands in a friendly manner.

I acquiesced with a smile. Joe's joviality was forced; the corners of his mouth easily drooped. His mouth was framed in deep grooves. Maybe, I thought, grieving May's recent death. Discreetly I looked around the room; in a corner, a monk's single cot with an Indian bedcover, and many, many books lining the walls.

"Mr. Tuzzo…"

"Joe, please."

"Are you also interested in things Chinese?"

"What? What do you mean?" The question seemed to upset him.

I trod lightly. "Among May's books we found a copy of the *Yijing*. We know that you offered it to her when you visited on March 9."

"And?" Joe's curt reply was reflected in the glare of his blue eyes. "Are you also going to ask me about those yarrow stalks?"

"What do you mean?" I knew that the Chinese book of divination could be consulted using either pennies or yarrow stalks. But I couldn't see his point.

"They were confiscated is what. Prison guards enjoy the momentary power they exercise over each visitor. What else could that mustache take from me?" Joe Tuzzo turned his palms upward, as though I could read in their broken lines his innocence and his poverty.

"Perhaps you can help me understand a little about that book of divination," I said in an attempt to win him back.

"Have you got a couple of months?"

I smiled. "Then you're a student of the *Yijing*."

"I just like to play with numbers. Kabbalah, Tarot, plain poker cards, the *Yijing*, they all interest me." Joe's mood softened. "What's your date of birth?" He asked me.

I took a sip of coffee and ignored the question.

"Just joking." Joe cracked a smile and I resumed my questioning.

"It's just that the *Yijing* doesn't quite fit with her other books, her interests. Nothing else on China. Nothing on film either. Wasn't that her area?"

" May was allergic to what she referred to as 'Oriental Wisdom.'"

"Why do you think? Did she have a problem with her origins?"

"Maybe. Maybe she just figured other people had a problem with it. I remember when she started teaching. After she read her first students' term papers on Chinese cinema, she decided she would never again teach another Chinese film, or Asian film for that matter."

"Why?" I took another sip of Joe's coffee, which was good and strong.

"She was shocked by the racism of these college kids. And her colleagues. After a full term of her lectures on contemporary China, they were still talking about Oriental inscrutability, the gap between the West and the East, the cultural backwardness of China, and so on. She would come home fuming. Anyway, she soon realized she was teaching *petits bourgeois* kids who were eventually going to use the knowledge she was imparting to sell their expertise to big business, and make millions off the 'mysterious Orientals.'"

"I see you were often witness to her outrage…"

"She could get violent."

"Physically?"

Joe shrugged. "Even physically." He lit another cigarette and gulped down his coffee. He turned the cup around slowly, using two fingers. It was one of those cups they sell in Chinatowns, with the character for longevity, *shou*, repeated in a continuous pattern.

I could see I was on difficult terrain. But I overcame my reluctance to follow up. "Are you saying that she abused you?"

Joe, still turning his cup, looked up at me and smiled his sad smile: "It happens."

"How so?" I felt uncomfortable, but I knew if I didn't get all the information I could now, I wouldn't get a second chance.

"She punched me in the back, in the stomach many times. She pinched hard, too. Once she tried to strangle me." Joe was staring straight into my eyes.

I bravely held his stare. "Why did you stay with her?"

"Now we are entering into talk about the *Yijing*. We humans go through life, moving through various situations, or scenarios, if you prefer. The Chinese, despite a common misconception in the West, do not believe in unalterable fate. In any case, it's not in the *Yijing*. If a person studies the rut he or she is in, all the circumstances and the ways out, as well as what came before, what choices he or she made or didn't make, he or she can make way for what comes next, create his or her future. I know it sounds esoteric, but really it's not." Joe's tone had become more enthusiastic and he was speaking with his hands. "I used to give talks on the *Yijing*. May attended one."

"May's copy had a bookmark in at one particular hexagram: 18."

Joe smiled a little mischievously.

"And another hexagram was highlighted, hexagram 36."

Joe's smile disappeared.

"Can you help me out, here?"

"I stuck that bookmark in at 18, 'Work on what has been spoiled.' The hexagram describes a family situation. The offspring have to resolve problems created by the generations that preceded them. What was handed down by the father must be continued, by solving whatever problem it poses. What was handed down by the mother must be dealt away with briskly in order to move on with one's life. I suppose the idea of continuing the father's legacy while discharging the mother is sexist. But the gist of it is that May's situation, in my opinion, was created by her family. Not in the classical Western oedipal way. I thought she might do a little family archaeology, pick up the *Yijing*, eventually figure it out and move on."

"Forgive me, but I thought May's 'situation' was the result of her conviction for the murder of Lee Pike."

Joe poured himself yet another cup of coffee and did not reply. I was afraid he would retreat from the conversation again. I tried another angle.

"Do you think she committed suicide?"

Joe's response was immediate. "It's been on my mind. Hard to tell." He paused again, then shrugged as if to say it didn't matter what he said. "I don't believe she killed Lee Pike."

"You think she was innocent?"

"No, not innocent. But innocent of murdering that writer, yes. Her mother on the other hand. Well, that's another story."

"You think she killed her mother?"

"Let's just say, I'm not so sure her mother died of natural causes." I was about to pursue this line of questioning, but Joe raised a hand and shook his head. "It's all speculation. I haven't got a shred of evidence."

"But you don't believe she killed herself."

"I suppose she could have. A heroic kind of suicide, telling the world to fuck off. That sort of thing. At the same time, there's a lot of racial tension in jails. She could have been a target."

"Did she mention anything like that when you visited her?"

"No, she didn't." He rolled a cigarette. "But her eyeglasses had been broken. She told me she'd decided to see the world in a blur." He started to drum the cigarette against the table. "That day, I was sitting with May in the visiting lounge, a drooling toddler crawled up to her. She moved her leg away. That's all.

"Suddenly some woman yells, 'Hey you, what you doin' to my kid?' something like that. May ignored her. The woman gets up and comes over, still shouting, calling May 'Yellow Slit,' and accusing her of kicking her child. Lots of swearing: 'motherfucker,' stuff like that. The woman's hair was punk, bleached. Anyway, she grabs her kid, and takes a rabbit punch at May. One of the women guards steps in, tells the woman to get back to her table. Eileen Morrison, I remember the guard called her by name. Of course, May never touched the child. But it didn't end there. Some other woman starts talking very loud, about how it smells funny. 'I smell a dead cat, yellow pussy,' stuff like that."

Brusquely, Joe got up: "Listen, let's go outside, okay? I'll show you my bees." He exchanged his well-worn Birkenstocks for rubber boots and pulled a pair out of the closet for me, along with a bee veil which I donned.

"You don't wear a net?"

Joe smiled his sad smile. "They don't sting me much. Plus it's good medicine for arthritis. They probably won't sting you either. Unless you get excited and disturb them. But better not take chances."

We stepped outside, the black dog joining us, leading the way. As a trio, we made our way down the hill, through high grass and thick bushes. Joe picked several mushrooms along the way. "Supper," he told me. "The best time to pick them is right after it rains, like today. This is royal agaric. Very tasty. Of course you need a practised eye." He picked up another specimen several yards further along. "This, on the other hand, is fly agaric. Very similar, isn't it? Also very deadly. Same orange cap. But the stem is longer. And see the white flecks on the cap, which is slightly less rounded?"

The dog backtracked, weaving and bumping impatiently against our boots until we moved on. But not before Joe slipped the poisonous mushroom into his pocket.

"I find a lot of plants to eat, growing wild, right here, on my land." He pointed to thick evergreen shrubs growing a certain distance away. "Not those, though. Also poisonous." Joe smiled a bit condescendingly and added: "It's mountain laurel. The Indians traditionally used the leaves to commit suicide. The flowers also yield honey but it's inedible. Unlike mine." We had reached the blue hive boxes where the dog was waiting.

"My bees are requeening."

"Requeening?"

"Changing queens. It's spring, the old queen, the mother to the hive is killed off. As simple as that. It's a natural process. No sentiment, and no crime involved, Detective."

We circled the boxes in silence, Joe bending down in front of each hive to count the dry bee bodies.

"Look at this one: it's got a new queen!" Joe picked up the old queen's body and held it for me to see. The body was in shreds. "The new queen has to win her place. They fight to the death."

As we walked back up to the little blue house, Joe concluded his zoomorphic presentation: "The Indians called bees the 'White Man's Fly.' That's because the Europeans brought bees to this continent, some time in the 1800s. Hey, let's have a drink. Come try my melliflo. It's only about 15% alcohol."

I turned down the honey alcohol, on the grounds that I was on duty. The truth was I felt nervous about ingesting anything after Joe's tour. Before going, I did however accept a bottle of his brew, which Joe claimed was "good for the spirit." As I backed the car out, I caught a glimpse of the black dog, standing guard among the hive boxes.

✡

Once I was back at home and alone with Otis, my initial queasiness about Joe's melliflo was supplanted by curiosity. The wine went down easily, like cider. Soon I was feeling pretty light. I sat down with Otis to watch a little TV: *Jeopardy*. It occurred to me that Joe's mead was somewhat stronger than he'd claimed, closer to 30%. The effect was similar to Beijing's local brew, Erguotou, a 35-degree-proof sorghum alcohol. Nothing warmed the heart, not to mention the rest of the body, in the dead of a Beijing winter like a meal of Mongolian hotpot and Erguotou outdoors in the *hutongs*. But Joe's honey brew was definitely lifting my spirits. I giggled as I tried to guess the answers, I mean questions, before the contestants. Impossible, they were too quick. I decided to drink a sip every time I got a question right. That slowed my drinking considerably. The remains of tonight's Orchid Restaurant take-out were strewn across the coffee table: limp veggie, *mapo doufu*, lychee with shrimp — actually, no more shrimp; Otis had taken care of those.

"What is White Man's Fly!" I shouted at the same time as one of the TV contestants.

"Correct!" bellowed the quiz master. I turned off the TV, thanking Joe for that bit of info, good for $250 and a sip of melliflo.

Alcohol seemed the perfect mate for divining. It was as though Joe had struck a chord in me. I fetched my own copy of the yellow book, the *Yijing*, or *Book of Changes*. This volume was less worn than my proverb book, used more sparingly. It was a gift from Thomas, my uncle and foster father who had inscribed it with a rather enigmatic note: *The little fox has nearly completed the crossing: Happy 18th birthday!* I decided to ask the book of divination for help on the Rich-Ho relationship. Feeling silly, I fetched three pennies to do an express reading. I was a long way from the police academy. Not that the *Yijing* was common practice in China either. People in Beijing didn't go around talking *yin* and *yang*. Well, maybe when it came to food, you might hear the phrase *you yingyang*, meaning something was good for you. But *Yijing*? Huiru would laugh.

I concentrated on the pennies, shaking them in my fist and conjuring up images of May and Liz, their naked bodies in identical position, while considering the next step. You rolled the three coins six times to obtain a hexagram. Heads was yin and drawn as a broken line; tails was yang and drawn as a full line. Contrary to Western common sense, the minority won: two heads and one tail was therefore a yang.

I tossed the pennies down on a corner of the cluttered coffee table. Two heads and a tail. Tails it was then. I drew an unbroken yang line as the base of the hexagram. My next throw was a yin. I drew the broken line above the first line. Now I threw three heads, all yin. Three of a kind meant a "changing" line. I drew the broken yin line above the other two lines, adding a star next to it to mark it as changing. I threw two more yin and drew the broken lines. My final throw yielded three tails: a yang, but changing. I marked the full line with a double star. The hexagram was complete:

```
**      ─────────
        ───  ───
        ───  ───
 *      ───  ───
        ───  ───
        ─────────
```

I checked the chart at the back of the book: the configuration corresponded to number 27 of the 64 possibilities: "*Yi,* the corners of the mouth. Nourishing the body and soul." Rich and Ho's deaths were linked. Some form of ingestion. I took another sip of melliflo. Something had penetrated them. They'd consumed something. Ingestion could be either physical or spiritual. Like imbibing alcohol, Rey-hee.

I consulted the additional remarks in the book for the changing lines. The commentary on the third line read: "Turning away from nourishment. Perseverance brings misfortune. Do not act thus for ten years. Nothing serves to further." Did Rich and Ho enter into some form of hunger strike? That would fit the forensic report: nothing in their stomachs. Or... had they refused psychotherapy? Although I was swimming deep in ethylic vapours, I took a mental note to interview the prison psychotherapist ASAP.

The other changing line was in the final or sixth position: "The source of nourishment. Awareness of danger brings good fortune." This was more difficult to interpret. Nourishment. Danger. Fortune. Had someone poisoned the two women?

I gathered up the loose strands of hair in my face and reclamped my HB-pencil barrette. My brain was befuddled. Could Joe have masterminded May's death, somehow? But what about Liz'?

I wanted to go to bed, but I couldn't end the *Yijing* consultation before completion. By turning the two changing lines into their opposites, I produced another hexagram. I checked the chart at the back of the yellow book, and rechecked. The new hexagram was number 36, the hexagram that had caused Joe's smile to vanish. "*Ming yi*, 36: Darkening of the Light," a splendid oxymoron. The book's interpretation was political. In times of tyranny, of bad government, you should hide your light. Go into hiding. "Prince Wezi could only save his life by dissembling." I didn't know what "dissembling" meant here, so I read on. The other case cited was familiar: Bo Yi and Shu Qi were brothers in the court of a bad monarch. Both refused to serve the corrupt king. Instead, they took to the hills, hid out in the mountains and resolved to fast as long as evil reigned in the land. In Chinese tradition, these hermit brothers were paragons of integrity; of course, they died of starvation, according to the legend. But some people believed they lived on, because they had discovered the secret of longevity. Maybe they were qigong practitioners. Liz had been into arcane stuff. She and May had been close, maybe close as two brothers...

I closed the book and screwed the cap back on Joe's bottle, abandoning Otis to his shrimp and bone dreams.

○

The next day I was grateful that Elizabeth Rich's family couldn't see me before 5 o'clock. All I wanted to do until then was take a long bath in therapeutic oils. I was nursing a hangover. A half hour of fresh air with Otis in the late morning had not produced the hoped-for miracle. Consequently I was lying in Max's Jacuzzi, controlling the taps with my toes. Controlling in this case meant more hot water. My massage mitt floated on the surface of the water like a penance, but I didn't have the strength to use it. All I could do was lie there, gazing at my feet through the fog. Finally, I rolled over in the bath, letting my breasts and belly soak up some much needed oil. And rolled back again. Outside, the neighbourhood was quiet in the dead of a weekday afternoon. Most people in this gentrified part of town were like Max, out making money by 0700 and back home after my bedtime. Lucky for me, Chief Carter hadn't complained, or noticed, or else he didn't care how rarely I showed up at my desk in the unit. Maybe he felt guilty about the size and location of that desk. I myself felt guilty about wasting the day. I had planned to meet with Karl Krauss, Liz' friend, but the doctor had not yet made himself available for an interview. I would have to start pursuing him more aggressively.

Especially since my supply of days in this case was limited. All right, I told myself, new rule: no more alcohol until the case is closed. My headache was beginning to melt away. I lay in the bath, feeling the pressure dissipate, until the water had drained completely.

As I stepped onto the yellow mat, a thin stream of blood trickled down my leg. Damn it. No wonder Otis had been furiously sniffing me all day. And I thought it was the honey alcohol. I moved over to the pharmacy, grabbed an OB and opened a pink pack of Always. How did they come up with such a depressing name? But was the false optimism of Stayfree any better?

The drive to the Riches led west down a hotel strip. The Sheraton was the only one on the Burlington side of the I-89. The Holiday Inn and the Best Western faced off against the Clarion and the Comfort Inn. Closer to Route 2, the silver Flight Inn and the rustic brown Ho-Hum competed with the Ethan Allen Motel. In between was a string of Vermont souvenir shops. The Riches lived in the airport area of South Burlington, in an older development project built at a time before bungalows were called ranches, and when carports were a fine place to put the two-child, single-income family Pontiac. I was amazed at the variety of categories of motorways for such a small, rather homogenous area: in addition to roads and streets, the map included terraces, avenues, drives, squares, places, crescents and circles. The airport itself was surrounded by a parkway, a drive, a road, and a circle. I drove around in the maze until I found Ledoux Terrace one street behind the airport drive. The Riches' back yard abutted the airport's parking lot. Two cars were parked in the entrance to their garage. I glanced in my rear view mirror to adjust my cap. Too bad for the couple of stubbornly wild strands of hair. I was red-eyed, but safely padded. For the benefit of the Riches, I'd decided to wear my uniform.

Elizabeth's mother must have been waiting by the door, because I'd barely pressed the yellowed plastic doorbell before I was greeted in a cloud of lilac scent. Kate Rich was a dyed ash blonde. She was wearing a black business suit, softened by a fuchsia silk blouse, and black high heels. Her long burgundy nails matched her freshly applied lipstick.

"You must be Miss, oh sorry, Officer, is it? Pirelli. Please come in."

The Riches' living room smelled of tobacco poorly masked by Air Wizard which, like Kate Rich's perfume, was lilac. I was introduced to Liz' father Gerry, and to her grandmother Annie. I nodded politely to the frail old woman rocking by the mock fireplace. Eighty-eighty, I decided: that time of life when one's age and weight are roughly the same. The matriarch did not acknowledge my greeting, continuing instead to rock and finger a rosary with shaky Parkinson hands. Liz' dad Gerry was sitting on the lush green velveteen sofa, wearing a shirt and tie which, from the way he fidgeted, I guessed he hadn't worn in a while. He had a more extreme version of Elizabeth's snub nose, and the reddish hue of a serious drinker. When he spoke, I was taken a little aback by his thick Irish accent.

"'Av' a seat, der you go, m'dear, right 'ere." He patted a place on the couch next to him. But Kate Rich pointed me to a gold armchair, also velveteen, across the room. Mrs. Rich took the seat next to her husband.

"Is Daniel here?" I asked them both.

Kate replied: "Unfortunately, he couldn't be here tonight."

"But he lives here, doesn't he?"

"Yes, he does," Kate said.

"Sure, and we all do, Kate and me, the boy, and me mom as well. But Dan's in and out. In and out. Boys, you know…"

I thought: only parents would consider a 35-year-old man as a boy… "Is he at work?"

"Nope. Me boy's on diss."

Mrs. Rich explained: "He gets disability." Gerry pointed to his head as Kate got up to fetch the tea.

While Kate was out of the room, Gerry became positively loquacious: "Women in the police force, who'd av thunk it. And young as well, real young. Well, well, well. I read about one lass was a bomb specialist. Imagine dat. And do you blow tings up, as well?"

"I'm an investigator."

Kate Rich was taking a while; she must be laying out cakes or sweets. I especially didn't care for sweets today.

"Ah, brain work, is it? I suppose you girls swig a few with the fellas on Friday night, hey? Arm wrestle on the end of the bar with the boys, do ya?" He cut his joking short as Kate Rich returned carrying a tea platter and the dreaded crystal dish containing macaroons, fudge and Rice Krispies squares. She put the tray down on the coffee table and placed a pink plastic covered cup with a protruding straw firmly in Grandma Annie's two hands. No dessert, it seemed, for Granny, who dropped her rosary beads on her lap.

I accepted a cup of black tea, declined Kate's desserts and Gerry's cigarettes, and began the interview: "When did you last see your daughter Elizabeth?"

Kate Rich straightened her skirt, raised her cup of tea and cleared her throat. "First thing you need to know, Elizabeth absolutely did not commit suicide. Elizabeth was a good girl. If she got into trouble, it was at that detention centre."

"Full of bloody Indians in dere," Gerry said. "Dat lot make trouble where ever they goes. And lesbians, 'scuse my French."

Kate coughed politely into her hand. "Elizabeth was definitely not… homosexual. But, sadly, she never met Mr. Right. She was always pleasant to everyone. Maybe she was too nice. I don't know. She was a fool for love."

Neither Gerry, nor Grandma Annie, nor I could think of anything to add. Kate consequently held the floor: "She had a highschool sweetheart, well several actually. And then she met Will, fresh out of school. Too young, I told her so." Kate inspected her long nails. It all sounded to me like a *Reader's Digest* version of a mother's grief. Gerry attempted a poor hen-and-rooster allusion, but he was drowned out by Kate: "Then came Bobby, and Rick." Kate Rich sighed, as though merely the act of enumerating Liz' boyfriends was exhausting.

"Dat would be Slick Rick," Gerry added for my counsel.

"But she got serious and she got into trouble. Kept on getting into trouble. Cons, all of them. She'd give them her paycheques. She was working in a diner then. Imagine that, healthy men feeding off a waitress. I tried to make her see. We sort of lost track of her when she moved in with Don. He had a place up in Essex, by the IBM plant. Worked there a while. Then he was gone half the year. Worked on the oil rigs, up north. I suppose you'd call it co-habitation. Probably had a wife up there, and kids. At least he left her that mobile home."

"And Bing…" I prompted.

"Bing was his. Bing was very much his father's boy: dark and stocky. Not fair-haired like our side of the family." She brushed away an imaginary curl from her forehead.

"Boy looked just like his dad… 'Ere 'ave a look." Gerry waved a hand at the mantel above the fireplace, but stopped short when he realized there was no picture. Two blue ceramic urns separated by a bunch of silk flowers in a cream vase had replaced whatever family photos had once been there.

"Where's Don now?" I asked.

Kate shrugged. "In South Africa."

"Workin' out dere, if you believe 'im." Gerry shook his head. "Not much work up Nort', right, Katie?"

Kate ignored her husband. "We sent him a note, no reply."

I drained my cup of Lipton tea. "Do you know if she had any special relationship at the time of her arrest?"

The Riches looked at each other, unable to answer.

"Does a Dr. Karl Krauss ring a bell?"

More silence.

"Did she have girlfriends?"

"Maybe Dan would know." Kate poured more tea into my cup.

"'E was goin' to Betty's place for dem wacky-pointer treatments," Gerry grimaced. "Can't say dem needles did our boy any good…"

Everyone paused to sip tea in silence. Suddenly a hoarse sound came from Annie's direction. "… spit… spit… ter." Everyone looked at the old grandmother. There were stains on her smock and her mouth needed wiping. Both hands were shaking, sloshing the tea inside her cup.

"No need to say so, Mum, we got eyes to see, ain't we."

Kate Rich went over to wipe her mother-in-law's chin.

"Spit…zer," the old woman repeated.

"She means Jane Spitzer," Kate told them. "Betty brought her over once."

"Well, bugger me, yer right! Dat's me mum, brains fer all of us Riches. Jane Spitzer it was! And a mighty pretty t'ing she was."

"Jane Spitzer and Liz shared a place for a while. She was older than Liz. A teacher of some sort. They came by together to drop Bing off for a couple of days. They were on their way to some sort of retreat."

"What kind of retreat?"

"Some oriental thing. Vermont's full of those, you know. I won't hide from you, we didn't like it when Liz started going oriental… not at all. She was in a rut. I offered to get her into Amway. I suppose she thought she was too good for Amway." Kate lit up a cigarette. It must be cocktail hour and they were just waiting for the police officer to leave before hitting the bottle.

Gerry reached for his third fudge square. Kate eyed her perfect nails, took a long draw on her cigarette. It was my guess that Elizabeth-Liz-Betty had worked hard at keeping away from her family. I got up to leave: "What about your son, Daniel? What does he do?"

Gerry pricked up. "Oh, you should see de basement. 'Recoopuration art' is wot 'e calls it. Makes t'ings outta Popsicle sticks, pop-can tops, an' de like. Basement's crackin' wid it. 'Course 'e won't let us down dere…"

I could picture the Riches' basement designed by an overgrown teenaged boy: a sea of ship and jet models, bits of sticks and metal scrap surrounding an unmade bed buried under dirty underwear, adult comic books; and cigarette butts overflowing from pop cans. Perhaps, next to the washer-dryer, there was still a box containing Liz' cheerleader pompons and high-school reports. But, probably not. Liz had been buried more than once.

✿

A fresh morning and a fresh espresso. The previous night, the blues had come down hard. The menstruation and the after-effects of Joe's honey mead had certainly contributed to my brooding. Liz had been on my mind. She'd tried so hard to make an alternative life for herself, learning acupuncture, qigong and later Chinese. But the family roots were too strong: her rotten boyfriends, probably abusive, a child she had to care for on her own, the trailer life. Boozing, dirty jokes, lottery tickets, the stink of Lysol, spicy after-shave and flowery perfume. Women in skimpy tops and short shorts. The constant cursing and loud laughter, the TV blasting day in, day out. Life, a relentless chain of procreation. Plastic garbage cans stuffed with diapers. A photo album filled with memories nobody wanted.

I had to decide on the order of the day. So many possibilities. So many people yet to interview. On the phone, Captain Carter had said: "Just cover all the bases." I reached for my book of proverbs. My finger fell on the proverb, "The colour indigo is bluer than the indigo plant." A well-known saying in China, it means the pupil surpasses her teacher. For a moment, I thought I might be the pupil in question. Foolish. More likely a frog in a well.

Following the advice of both my boss and the proverb, I headed to the University of Vermont, where May Ho had taught for more than ten years. Williams Hall was a Victorian edifice atop the hill, in the middle of University Row. When I entered the building, I had a *déjà vu*. I was confronted by two eerily familiar staircases, leading east and west. The architecture seemed identical to the Beijing Central Academy of Arts where Huiru had studied. I read the plaque: "Williams Hall is a copy of the Oxford Museum in England, a building designed by John Ruskin." Had Beijing or Burlington first copied Oxford?

I took the eastern staircase up to Room 411. An anorexic secretary typing at a computer paused long enough to tell me Dr. Pescu was on the phone. "She won't be long." There were two seats next to the departmental chair's office, but two students, a serious boy and a nervous girl, both with folders on their laps, were already ensconced. I strolled some more in the deserted hallway. On the Department of Film Studies' bulletin board were pinned the past term's conferences and special film screenings. *Doctor Emilio Lorca, professor at the University of Mexico, will offer a six-week, 3 credit film/theory course entitled, "Deconstructing the West via the Western." January 3- February 13 Deadline for registration: December 10.*

I shook my head. Still, I felt a pang of jealousy as I imagined people my age sitting through such wild lectures. At Beijing University, my 30-year-old professor Zhang's class was always packed with several hundred students, who would listen religiously to his weekly two-hour lectures in cultural studies. In Professor Zhang's class, I had been introduced to the work of Jacques Derrida, and to Mike Tyson, whose Mao Zedong tattoo had made him into a cultural hero in the Third World. I had never endorsed all of Zhang's proposed connections, but I always left the classroom in a happy state of mind. Maybe it was just hard thinking that did it.

The anorexic secretary brought me sharply back to UVM and my own difficult investigation. Doctor Pescu was ready to see me.

"Dr. Ho was, how shall I put it, somewhat subjective. Perhaps unconventional would be a better word. Let's just say her methods were, well, different." Dr. Amaryll Pescu was dressed in a smart fire-red suit and black turtleneck, with a small pearl necklace. Thick dark brown curls framed her rather angular white face. "I suppose I ought to say she was not," the doctor continued, "particularly collegial. She did not, for example, attend departmental meetings. Naturally, we all expected she would teach Chinese film. That, after all, was what we hired her to do. Nor did she deign to participate in the ALANA program. You may not know that ALANA is the acronym for Asian American, Latino, African-American and Native American studies. She never refused, not in, how shall I say, any direct or formal way. But her course outline never quite corresponded to the actual content of her classes."

I listened patiently to the professor's carefully weighed sentences. "How about her students? What were her evaluations like?"

"To say the least, they're intriguing. Perhaps even, dare I say… extreme?" Dr. Pescu opened a gray filing cabinet and plucked a manila file on the tab of which the anorexic secretary had typed: Ho-Student Evaluation-Fall 1999. The doctor scanned through quickly, selecting a few excerpts: 'A pompous cocksure asshole who cares nothing for students: fire her!' Dr Pescu glanced briefly up at me and resumed her reading: 'A superbly gifted prof: best in the department.' 'Can't wait to take another of Prof Ho's courses.' 'Too many digressions, not enough chronology. I was unable to follow: this prof can't teach.' You see my point, Detective?"

I nodded. "I guess they either hated her or they loved her."

"Well, you might say that," the doctor said, putting the accent on "you."

"So, in your opinion, Professor Ho didn't have many friends here, among her colleagues, I mean?"

"Friends?" The professor paused a moment to consider the notion of friendship in the context of the university. "I can't really say. But certainly no enemies, if that's what you're implying. We work in a collegial environment here. UVM is not, how shall I put it, life on the streets!" Dr. Pescu's white face flushed a little, reflecting the red tinge of her suit. "Which reminds me, I must get back to work. I have a thesis defense in fifteen minutes."

I don't think I would have liked Dr. Pescu as a teacher. Or a "colleague," for that matter. I was happy to find a cheerful white and red chip wagon parked in front of the forbidding Williams Hall. It read: *Lucky Chinese Food*.

¤

I walked back home to share a light lunch of scrambled eggs with Otis. I let him out in the yard and checked Elizabeth Rich's file for the address of the Family Health Centre, the last place Liz had worked before her arrest. Although Rich had only worked there for six months, leaving in June of the previous year, I figured it was one of the bases my boss would want me to check. I was also curious to get a closer look at an MHP.

I decided to retrace Liz' likely daily route, from the mobile-home park to her workplace. In Essex Junction, between the Amtrak Station and the IBM plant, Route 117 became Maple Street. On the map, there was also a Maplewood Line and a Maple Street Extension. I deduced that Mapleton Mobile Home Park which, of course, wasn't indicated on the map, had to be in that general area, probably past the railroad tracks. Sure enough, a maple brown sign announced Mapleton MHP at the very end of Maple Street Extension. A huge red Myers dumpster lay tilting behind the rows of mailboxes, next to the entrance. I passed a sign reading *Drive carefully. Our kids at play!* and slowed down to the requested five miles an hour. But on this cloudy day, I saw neither child, nor adult, nor animal along the dirt road which soon forked into three directions. Mapleton was big, way too big to hope I could find Rich's former home without a civic number. The file had just given a postal box. I cruised by miniature lawns and hand-painted signs reading *Home Sweet Home*, or *The Scotts Live Here*. No *Riches' Pair-a-dice*. Of course not; the man's name was Whitehead. So not even a place to call her own.

I ended up in a cul-de-sac, which forced me back on my tracks. I cut the engine and decided to take a walk. A few elderly women in their kitchens peered at me through gingham curtains, a man in his undershirt watched me from behind the curled blinds of his living room. It occurred to me that my police uniform could be keeping these folk inside their homes.

When I turned back toward the car, a young woman in short shorts and a low-cut halter top was walking toward me. The young woman was carrying an infant in one arm, and holding the hand of a toddler, who couldn't be more than two years old. Her name was Sandy, and she'd never heard of Elizabeth Rich. "Everyone pretty much minds their own business here. Anyways, I haven't been living here long. And I sure as hell don't plan on staying in this dump any longer'n I have to!"

I could see the girl's point. I got into my car just as the train chugged by.

¤

The Family Health Centre was a good dozen extra long bus stops from Liz' home. She would have had to take the Essex green line then the blue line almost down to the Winooski River. A good hour's travel-time, I estimated, even with the bus going full tilt.

Thirty-twoC-D Mallets Bay was part of a one-storey rectangle that looked like a storage space or a ramshackle, disused mall. Thirty-twoA housed Roger's Rent & Own (in 12 months) furniture, computer, appliances; Mr. G's Liquidation Centre, a surplus and salvage superstore, was lodged at 32B. There was a handicapped access ramp on the 32D side, which was the entrance to the Family Health Centre. Inside the centre, the walls were painted a serene sky blue, the floor was natural wood and several colourful posters brightened the entrance. I turned to the impressively large directory list. A lot of people seemed to be sharing at most, three or four rooms. Ms. Shu Qi, acupuncture; Dr. E. Gayatri, acupuncture and homeopathy; Dr. F. Salas, holistic medicine; Ms. Anna Lo, herbal medicine; C. White, yoga; P. Kale, tai-chi...

A very old, very dark-skinned woman emerged from one of the rooms and headed purposefully toward the end of the hall which I gathered led to 32C. I decided to stroll a bit. The place smelled nice, a mixture of herbs, moxibustion and Indian incense. The very old woman returned and addressed me: "I have an OB." She chuckled with her hand covering her mouth. "An overactive bladder. I just can't do a full session without going to the double-U-C." She paused to let that sink in, then added. "Have you come to see us? Come on in, come on in. We're all gals in here." I smiled and followed her into the room. I stopped short in the doorway, stunned. Two dozen grannies of various shapes and colours were enthusiastically performing some kind of dance with red pompoms under the guidance of an athletic woman in her early sixties. The leader waved an invitation to join in.

I declined with a nod, stood there for a moment longer, taking in the energy of the room, before backing out into the hall. I headed for the acupuncture and herbal-medicine office and knocked. A gentle voice invited me to please come in and take a seat. I found myself in a small waiting room. On the walls were a series of large outlines of the human form entitled "Wall Map of Standard Meridians and Points of Acupuncture and Tuina." Tuina? It took me a few seconds to realize that this was not a misspelling of the familiar lunch filling, but the Chinese word for massage. *Nan-mo-a-mi-tuo-fo*, let this soft-speaking woman be Rich's friend, I prayed, though I had little hope.

A frail Caucasian woman, with more wrinkles than I would have thought could fit on a single face, came out of the acupuncturist's consulting room pushing a walking aid. A radiant dark-skinned, dark-haired woman in her mid-thirties appeared behind her. She looked kindly at me and beckoned to come in.

"I'm not ill," I said a little too quickly.

The acupuncturist looked at my uniform: "I guessed as much. Mostly we treat senior citizens here. Though we also offer birthing courses for pregnant women. But they're seasonal. Anyway, you don't look like you're pregnant."

I shrugged. "I don't see how I could be these days."

The treatment room contained a very small desk and chair, a second metal folding chair, a counter and a long examination table covered with a paper sheet. I sat on the folding chair.

"We work for free," Eve Gayatri told me. And she'd never met Elizabeth Rich. She'd been working there for only six months. She had heard that there'd been an Elizabeth working in the office the previous year. "I think those slightly grotesque but very useful maps in the entrance, are hers."

I learned that Shu Qi, the other acupuncturist, wasn't in today, nor was the tai-chi woman. In any case, they'd been with the clinic for even less time than Eve. "We all have other jobs, you see. Paying jobs. This is for the cause."

"Has it always been like this?" I couldn't imagine Rich supporting a child alone and working for free.

"No, they were operating more like a co-op before I joined. Everyone chipped in to pay the rent, and charged a minimal amount for services. But then most of them couldn't keep up. They were starving. There's been quite a turnover lately. Now, we're all doctors, well-paid elsewhere, but giving a bit of time here. I'm originally from Winooski. Up on Elm Street. My own mom comes here for bi-weekly tai-chi classes which she wouldn't miss, even in an ice storm!"

I smiled, recalling the women dancing in the other room. I shook my head and the image was replaced by the memory of Liz' dead body. "Dr. Gayatri, I'm wondering if Elizabeth Rich could possibly have come here as a patient herself. Do you think you could check the patient files for me?"

Dr. Gayatri glanced at her delicate Tissot watch, then at her appointment book and said: "No problem. But we only have one year's files."

Dr. Gayatri slipped back into her office with a folder. "An Elizabeth Rich came here Monday, October 18. For an acupuncture treatment. A bad back. Treated by..." Dr. Gayatri paused to decipher the signature: "By Joan Diez." The doctor sat down with the file on the desk in front of her. "Looks like Rich was pregnant; her baby was due end of October."

"Pregnant? This past year? Are you sure?"

"That's what it says here."

There was no record or mention of a second child in any of the Montrose documentation on Liz. I was stunned, so stunned I almost forgot to ask my final question. "Does the name Jane Spitzer mean anything to you?"

Well, I didn't think so.

◘

Saturday morning, I woke up with the early sun in my face and Liz' ghost baby on my mind. I knew I had to talk to someone who knew Liz during the period before her arrest. After my first espresso, I phoned Karl Krauss again. "You have reached eight-sssix-fffour—ffforty-ssseven-eighttteen." A long-winded, convoluted recorded message followed. It was only 0800: the doctor might not be up yet. I applied some Space Odyssey nail polish — tonight was the police ball — and turned on my computer.

I couldn't get access on the web to Births, Deaths and Marriages — also presented chronologically as Births, Marriages, Deaths — to find out whether or not Liz had had a second child. I entered my password in the Police's Persons Data, only to be informed that the bank was temporarily out of service. Big surprise.

Finally I resorted to the telephone. "Welcome to Vital Statistics. Please listen carefully to the 15 options." I waded through the entire recording for option 15: "To speak to an officer, please press 0." Having been, several times, assured that my call was important to them, I was finally requested, by yet another recording, to please try again later, because they were experiencing a temporary communications overload. On a Saturday?

While I waited to call later, I searched for another link to Liz: her qigong teacher, that "mighty pretty t'ing," that had caught Gerry Rich's eye. I tried the virtual white pages. No Jane Spitzer anywhere on the continent. But there were 275 Spitzers with the initial "J" between the coasts. That took an hour. None, however, with an address in Greater Burlington.

It didn't feel like the day was going to be all that productive. I eyed my monthly calendar, a single date circled in red, May 14 — one of the two rows was already past... And I would have to fit a trip in to New York in the next week to talk to Sam Ho. Chasing the Spitzers of the world could take forever. I went back to my computer, googled "Spitzer, Jane." Nothing. I did receive a junk-mail offering an "Online Sleuth" program that promised to find absolutely anyone's personals for a mere $79.99. I decided instead to give old Alexander Graham Bell another try.

Against all hope, my second attempt at accessing a living, speaking person at the BDM Registrar Office was crowned with success: "V'tal St'tistics, Off'cer P'k sp'king." I gave my PIN number. Off'cer P'k checked on the department's birth records. "N', no person born with last name Rich, from a Rich 'L'zbeth in that time p'riod." Since these records were updated every second day and all hospitals, clinics, hotels, hostels, churches, etc., were required, under penalty of law, to provide such information within 48 hours, Off'cer P'k concluded: "'L'z'beth Rich did not have a b'by. O' we'd know 'bout it."

I couldn't help smiling, in spite of my frustration, at the degree of faith bureaucrats put in their systems. Somehow, I was convinced that Elizabeth had given birth to a second child, but I had no physical evidence. I imagined the worst: Elizabeth, all by herself, doing the job. Was the infant stillborn; a girl or a boy; and what did she do with the remains? I tried not to think of the red Myers dumpster at the entrance to the Mapleton Mobile Home Park. Tonight I'd be attending a charity ball with the fanciest frocks in Greater Burlington for the benefit of poor folks like Liz. I shuddered. In Liz' case, suicide was becoming increasingly credible. I decided to seek out the psychotherapist at Montrose, a Dr. Alex Leo, as soon as I got back from New York City.

In the meantime, Spitzer, Jane had to be located! I regressed one further step in communications tech and "let my fingers do the walking" through the *Yellow Pages*. A sort of directed bibliomancy, not quite random. Might Spitzer run a school of qigong? Search under what? Martial arts, aerobics, sports, fitness? Food supplements, weight control, massage therapy? None of these yielded anything remotely close to qigong. I ran down the alphabet in the index. Acupressure, *Fengshui*, Herbology, Magnetic Field Therapy, *Reiki*, Rolfing, and Yoga, were all listed under Holistic Health Services — *fengshui* was also cross-listed under Interior Designers and yoga had a section all its own — but no qigong. Its cousin, tai-chi or, more accurately, *Taijiquan*, had been classified under Health, Fitness and Exercise Services. I checked for *ch'i-kung*, the American romanization of qigong. Still nothing. My fingers skipped from Murder Mystery Dinner Theatres to Pet-sitting services, Pre-arranged funeral planning, Sperm Banks, Square Dancing and War Games. Finally I dropped the phone book, lit a cigarette and gazed at the blue smoke rings. The morning was gone. I had nothing to wear to tonight's ball. Tuxedos and sequins. Silver and silk.

Associations, look under associations! For the next hour-and-a-half, I worked through the list of various associations in the phone book. Finally I hit on three highly promising groups: the Yin-Yang School of Ch'i; the Lotus Breathing Society and the Oriental Vitality Club for Women. This was more like it. I jotted down the phone numbers.

It turned out the Yin-Yang School of Ch'i was not open to women. I tried the Lotus Breathing Society's number and got a recording: "We're sorry, the number you have dialled is no longer in service." The association had expired or transitioned from telecommunications to telepathy.

I took a break, washed my hair, threw together a lettuce-and-tomato salad, and took Otis out for a walk around the neighbourhood. When I got back, Liz' mystery visitor Karl Krauss still hadn't returned my call. I tried his number again. This time I hung up before the long tiresome message was over.

I sighed and went back to the Spitzer mystery. I tried my last option, the Oriental Vitality Club for Women, but with little hope, because what good could come out of an association with such a corny name? A cheerful Cindy MayIhelpyou answered.

"Do you have a teacher or a member named Jane Spitzer?"

Cheerful Cindy replied: "Off the bat, I'd say we don't. Well, she wouldn't be a regular. I know all the regulars. We do have occasional drop-ins in for a session, or a weekend. Those lists, I don't have on hand. You'd have to speak to Mistress Yee."

I identified myself as a detective.

"Detective Pirelli, I'm sorry but you still would have to speak to Mistress Yee. I can't do more than what I've just told you. Why don't you drop by and talk to Mistress Yee? She's here every afternoon, except, I'm sorry to say, today. But that's exceptional."

Before hanging up, on a hunch I asked Cheerful Cindy: "By the way, how old is Mistress Yee?"

"How old? I couldn't tell you, I never thought of it. As old as life itself, I guess."

PART IV
SEVEN ORIFICES BLOCKED

"Ladies and gentlemen, please take your seats." The crowd noise fell momentarily, then immediately rose again as people shuffled around, squinting over the tables at name cards, in search of their assigned places. "Officer Warner and Rita;" "Officer Colrone and Susan." Six couples per table, more than twenty tables. The few unaccompanied police officers, mainly but not exclusively women like Louise Moore and myself, had been distributed two by two, here and there, among the couples. I was sitting across from a young policeman, also single, named Simon Baal. He was medium height, slim, exquisitely dressed, and had a pair of doll-blue eyes. I guessed: gay.

"Before we get to the food... and more drink, let me invite Captain Carter, the head of the Police Association, to say a few words." Captain Carter, who was sitting at the VIP table with the bigwigs, picked up his champagne glass and stepped up to the stage to a round of applause.

"Thank you." Captain Carter set his glass down carefully on the podium, clapped his hands a few times along with the crowd, took out a little piece of paper from his tux pocket and began.

"This year, we've collected a record amount. I would like to give special mention here to the following good patrons who are honouring us tonight by their presence: The honorable Garry Holmes.... Ladies and gentlemen, a special round of applause for our respected senator." The crowd reacted obediently, almost enthusiastically, although it could have been just the champagne working.

Captain Carter moved bravely on: "Burlington's beloved mayor, Rob Trudeau." Again, the audience made noise. "Mr. Coltrane, from the firm Coltrane, Bonno and Sacks." Captain Carter enjoined Mr. Coltrane to get up and salute the audience. He continued: "Mr. Dyke, from …" At this point, Captain Carter needed to check his little piece of paper. "From X-Dress." Immediately, the emcee whispered something in the chief's ear, and Carter corrected himself: "Mr. Guy Dyke, the CEO of Cross-Dress." A few hoots and a whistle greeted Mr. Dyke. Captain Carter soldiered on, glancing again at his piece of paper before coming to the end of his VIP list: "And last, but not least, Ms. Carla Chanadi and Mr. Tim Reiss, from the sky-rocketing dotcom enterprise Nuvo." By now the crowd had gone flat, managing only weak applause for two equally blasé creatures dressed in black. A figure in the distance caught my eye. From afar, the *femme fatale* next to the *noir* couple looked naked in her flesh-coloured satin gown. She wore a Cleopatra bracelet high up her forearm. Why hadn't I expected Warden Segal to be here? After all, Lucille Segal was part of the *crème de la crème* of the community. She, too, seemed to be unaccompanied. Was she wearing a matching ankle bracelet?

"The proceeds of our fundraising and this evening will go to the construction of a gymnasium equipped with the latest high tech facilities in Greater Burlington's most worthy member of our large family, Winooski. And now let's have some fun! A toast to the Queen City!"

The emcee, I noted, was another good-looking guy with blond, spiked hair. He wished everyone a great meal, in a variety of languages: "Bon appétit! Buon gusto! Buen provecho!" until his words were gradually drowned out by Dixieland music.

"Who's the emcee?" a petite, gray-haired woman asked Officer Vance, next to whom I was sitting.

"Oh, that's David Mekham. His expertise is art forgery."

"Heart surgery?" The gray-haired woman leaned closer and screamed above the loud music.

"Sure doesn't look like a cop," remarked Bill Vance's wife. She was in her mid-thirties, and wearing a tight, tight dress and a stiffly spray-netted pompadour. "Looks more like an athlete, or a movie star." Her mouth turned into a sexy pout, as she waited for the other women at the table to confirm her appraisal. I cocked my head, not sure I agreed.

"Oh Diane! In front of Bill?" Officer Ed Twins teased.

"That's okay, she's all talk," Vance said. He nodded in my direction and added: "He's more your type, Rey. Single, too. You are single, aren't you, Rey?"

"Simon's single, too," Vance's wife put in, swivelling her gaze between us.

Simon Baal and I exchanged a look of mutual understanding and retreated to the menu which was rolled up like a crêpe Suzette. Around the time we got to the white chocolate cheesecake with rhubarb mousse, the blond emcee reappeared on stage, parading a turquoise Cinderella gown like a matador's cape.

Simon Baal, who had been rather quiet, suddenly stiffened. "That's a X-Dress gown Wow!"

"We're also giving away: a deluxe set of golf clubs, a romantic weekend in a luxury suite with fireplace, king-size sleigh bed, over-sized whirlpool tub lined with candles at the five-star Inn at Essex, a pair of round-trip tickets to Hawaii. The evening is young, the wine is plentiful, the music is…" Again the emcee was drowned out by music, this time a medley of golden oldies. Several couples began gyrating on the dance floor.

Captain Carter and his wife Anita joined the dancers. His hands resting lightly on her fireman-red moiré sash band, he was earnestly applying himself to the cha-cha. I was the only woman wearing pants. And my top was cut high on the neck, offering only sparkles to any potential oglers. I stood out like a sore thumb among the women in red dresses and powdered bosoms, exposed and slightly flushed. Simon with the doll-blue eyes caught my attention from across the table, waved an index between his heart and me and cocked his head toward the dance floor. We cut across flows of long satin and perfume, side-stepping patent leather shoes and gold high heels. He held my hand and swung me slowly and elegantly to a Louis Armstrong favourite of mine: "And I say to myself, what a wonderful world." I closed my eyes and let the music and Simon Baal transport me. Until I felt a tap on the shoulder. Louise Moore was wearing a Bombay pink low, low-cut sequined dress with a matching bazooka pink boa around her neck. And she was dancing with the blond emcee. Lou winked at me, unashamedly showing off her catch. Then the dance was over, and Lou's big fish was back up on stage awarding prizes. Neither the dress nor the golf clubs held much attraction for me, so I slipped out to smoke a cigarette.

Stepping back into the hall, I felt suddenly lonely. I stood by the door watching the dancers for a moment, and the emcee, until he caught my gaze. Before I could turn away and find my seat he'd jumped off the stage, and was coming towards me.

"Don't tell me you're a wallflower?" he laughed.

"Pirelli, detective, Rey, third-grade," I saluted. I'd got all my words backwards. He was too pretty.

The emcee bowed. "David Mekham. Detective. Art Forgery. I love your wild pyramid of a hairdo. And your silver nail polish and your oh so unsexy-it's-sexy matching top. And those silk pants: Wow."

"I like polka dots," I said, briefly flicking his bow tie.

"Oops," he read the time off my studded Irony Swatch, "Time for the Hawaii trip. Gotta go. Who knows, maybe you'll win. Or I will. Make you a deal: either one wins, we go together." He grinned and raced back toward the stage.

I followed him at a distance, watching as he leaped onto the stage. He was wearing a signet ring, DM in gothic letters, and had a long scar on that left hand. A dog bite, I feared. The emcee yelled out a name: "Simon Baal." The lucky winner of the Hawaii getaway.

¤

"Officer Pirelli, there are a couple of VIPs who'd like to meet you."

"Me?" I was so surprised that I reverted to the Chinese way of designating oneself, pointing my index at my nose.

DM took my silver-lacquered finger and gently led me to the VIP table. He introduced me to the dignitaries of the evening. I was invited to sit at the table beside the boss, Captain Carter.

The chief seemed to have had a few too many. "Detective Pirelli's our China champion," he bragged. "Believe it or not, she speaks fluent Mandarin. Detective, why don't you give us a toast in Chinese?"

Attentive, DM found the China girl a cup of champagne. I made sure to do it properly, right hand on the stem of the glass and the left supporting it from underneath, while presenting it to the guests: "*Gan bei! Dajia ganbei!*" The table applauded my little show.

The lady, seated to my right, tried out her Chinese: "*Ni hao!* Is that right? Isn't that 'hello' in Chinese?"

I smiled and replied: "*Ni hao!*"

"My name's Djuna. Djuna Dyke. Friends call me Dee-Dee. You're very young to be a detective. What are you working on? Can you tell?" Dee-Dee was one of the most beautiful women I'd ever seen. Her black hair cascaded down a red shantung silk *qipao*. From her smooth olive skin and the way she leaned a little on her vowels, I guessed she was Latina, or Mediterranean. Djuna.

"I'm working my very first case. Two deaths at the Montrose Detention Center for Women. You may have heard it about it."

A gray man at least twice her age, wearing an ill-fitting tuxedo whispered something in Dee-Dee's ear. She excused herself and the couple went off to dance to John Lennon's "Imagine." They came back arm in arm.

"Rey, this is my husband, Guy."

"Dee-Dee tells me you've been assigned the Montrose case. How's it going?" Mr. Dyke, barely taller than his wife, with his thinning gray hair and fleshy cheeks, struck me as socially inept, the sort who was all business, business, always business. His wife must be his social-life-support system. "Picked up any serious leads?" Even when he was speaking to me, Mr. Dyke avoided direct eye contact. Perhaps he was cross-eyed.

I gave him a non-committal answer: "Really, it's too early."

Others at the table were listening, maybe because double murders were everyone's favourite dinner conversation, or because when Mr. Dyke spoke others deferred. He shook his head. "Two dead, and no explanations. What kind of prison management is that?"

"State-run," one of the lawyers piped up.

"Places like that are full of drugs," Dee-Dee said. "Isn't that right, Officer Pirelli?"

I shrugged. "According to the warden, Montrose is drug-free."

"Well," Mr. Dyke said, "the warden would say that, wouldn't she."

I noted the use of the feminine. "You're well-informed, Mr. Dyke."

"I read the papers." Guy Dyke leaned closer, his eyes on the room behind my shoulder, and lowered his voice. "I think we ought to have a talk, before you wrap up the case."

"Do you have information pertinent to the case, Mr. Dyke?"

"Information? No, more like concern."

"And what, if I may ask, is the nature of your concern, sir?"

Dyke shrugged. "I'm a concerned citizen. I'm interested in prison reforms, prison-management systems."

"Well, then you know that Montrose is already a highly reformed prison."

"Hmm." Guy Dyke tapped two fingers on the table in a small gesture of impatience. Suddenly the table fell silent. Heads turned to look at me, or no, not at me; behind me. Before I could turn to see who was there, I heard Lucille Segal's voice, full of barely contained rage.

"Well, isn't this cozy."

"Ms. Segal," Guy Dyke said without looking up. "You look stunning, and yet, no lucky escort?"

The warden's laugh sounded more like a brief snort, and I could hear one too many drinks in her voice. "Well, I suppose, if I had your money, I could buy one."

Dee-Dee winced.

"But you don't, do you." Dyke said, his face turned to stone.

I was sitting as perfectly still as I could, not daring to turn around to face her, when I felt Lucille Segal's grip on my shoulder. "Working out the details of your investigation, Officer Pirelli? Congratulations, I underestimated you. Hardly a month, and already cashing in on the job."

I felt my face turn crimson and my body lifting out of the chair, before I'd even thought of getting up.

Then Captain Carter was between us. "Sit down, Rey," he said, his back to me, and facing the warden. "Come on, Lucille," he said softly. "Let's dance."

She glared past him. "You know what he'll do to those women when he gets his hands on Montrose? He'll kick that place back into the 19th century."

I felt DM, standing now, beside me, his hand floating just by my elbow, but not touching. Carter, meanwhile, had turned Segal right around, aiming her away from the table, talking quietly to her.

"Whatever he's offering," Segal shouted hoarsely back over her shoulder, "you hold out for more. There's big money in privatization."

"Listen," DM said to me, but loud enough for everyone at the table to hear, "everyone here knows there's not a shred of truth in what she said. She's had too much to drink."

Finally, I found my voice. "Excuse me," I said to the table, with all the dignity I could muster, "I believe I'm being asked to dance. Enjoy the rest of your evening."

As DM took my arm to sweep me onto the dance floor, Guy Dyke, in a single rapid movement, slipped a business card into my pant pocket. "Come and see me," he said.

David Bowie's "China Girl" was pouring out of the loudspeakers, and the champagne kicked in all at once. I felt as though I'd waded into suddenly deep water.

"I've got to go," I said and tore loose from DM's grip.

✪

As I removed my Space Odyssey nail polish, I reviewed the highlights of the police ball in my mind — red gowns twirling with black coat-tails, Simon Baal's doll-eyes, Dee-Dee's dazzle, Lou's hot pink sex appeal, and DM. The limelight of the VIP table. And then, Lucille Segal. They had warned us at the academy never to let the case take over your life. And here I was doing exactly that on my first assignment. But how could I keep this case from destroying my career, my life? May and Liz had taken over. My two China girls.

Now I was torn between leaving immediately for New York City to interview Sam Ho and staying in town to see DM again tonight. Split loyalties? No, I convinced myself, it was all work. Somehow I sensed that DM could clear up a few things. Anyway, I had promised Captain Carter an interim report. That meant several painful hours of typing.

I found the Bowie CD in Max's extensive collection and put on the cryptic song. A man wants to rule the world. You can see it in the whites of his eyes. He'll ruin "everything she is," give her television, and "eyes of blue." I'd never noticed the critique of imperialism in the song before. What struck me most was the surface of the text, the eyes, the whites of his eyes, the threat of blue eyes for her. Simon Baal certainly was no threat to me, nor to the warden. I shook my head and another figure popped up: Mr. Dyke, who had eyes for no one, but whose every movement was watched by everyone.

The ramifications of the Montrose case were quickly spreading beyond the prison walls. Why did Dyke have such an interest in the prison system? DM, who seemed to know everyone, might know. So, tonight would be a briefing. Not a date. Well, okay, I wasn't totally fooling myself: I wanted to see him again, and tonight was a date of sorts.

Maybe it was because I was leaving town and abandoning Otis so soon, or perhaps I wanted him along as a chaperone, or to put limits on the date part of the meeting with DM, whatever the reason, I decided, as I dressed casual but smart, to take Otis along.

Otis! I picked up the phone and called Lou Moore. Detective Moore answered, but not right away. She was in great spirits and immediately started talking about last night's ball. I could hardly get a word in, and then it was just "No, you looked great, Lou… Yes, he's very nice… No!… and listen, Lou, really…"

Louise Moore's mood was enough to convince me something had happened between last night's bubbly and this morning's java. Well, good for Lou, and so much the better, because I had a favour to ask. "Yes, Lou, I know I already owe you one, not the other way round."

I could hear Lou talking to someone else over the palmed receiver, the discussion taking some time, and there was giggling, followed by what might have been the exchange of a kiss. No matter, Lou suddenly had a heart of gold. She'd come to feed Otis the next day while I was in New York. Who was she discussing it with? Surely not David Mekham. Come on, Rey-hee, Lou wasn't DM's type.

◘

The Common Grounds Café where DM and I had quickly agreed to meet was a mere twenty minutes' walk away. Otis kept the leash taut, I swayed gently behind, taking in the exceptionally clear, warm night. Must be spring fever, I thought. Or the prospect of going to New York the next morning. Adams Street, by Smalley Park, was lined with heavily scented purple lilac. The dizzying perfume made it difficult to walk a straight line. Even Otis seemed affected. He stopped suddenly to point his snout at the moon, stretching his seal neck almost to a 90-degree angle. Swinging my shaggy purse, I kept tripping over him, once, twice, each time excusing myself with a pat on his flank. Otis didn't seem to mind; tonight we were a team and the good mood was contagious. As we approached the café, I spotted DM on the terrace staring straight into the moonlit lake. He was seated in front of a sea of froth which turned out to be a meringue cream pie and a cappuccino. I squeezed in on the other side of the small table, first feeding an "it's-bacon-it's-not-bacon" treat to my pal. I ordered a jasmine tea.

"You walked," DM said and segued into a comment on my sober choice and a compliment about my trim figure.

The word "trim" reminded me I would have to mow Max's little lawn before his return. That's how oddly my mind was working. Clearly the moon and lilacs had made me drunk.

"Won't help me with this pie?" DM pleaded.

"No, I don't think so, but Otis will join you, if you feel like sharing."

DM didn't like dogs. He cast a wary eye at a tongue-lolling Otis.

"That's a dog-bite scar, on your hand?" I ventured.

"Yes, 'fraid so. Four years ago, I was after a con *artiste* living outside Colchester. I was greeted by his dog. Since then, can't help it, I steer away from the canines."

"Did you catch the forger?"

"Oh yeah, but not at his home: right here, and I mean right there." DM pointed at the warehouse by the King Street Dock. "I'd been chasing this guy around for some time, all over the country and, all the while, he was right under my nose… Isn't that the way it often works?"

I lit a cigarette and tried to impress him: "You mean like the letter in the Edgar Allen Poe story?"

DM nodded. "'The Purloined Letter.' Convenient little set-up. His New York customers only had to step off the ferry to get a special deal on a Francis Bacon. Imagine."

I showed a tight smile. Huiru revered that British artist.

"Most people don't like to talk about art and money in the same breath. Truth be told, art is a question of money," DM said. "Always is. Like it or not. Why do you think we've got detectives like me around? For the love of art? It's not Monet, and it's not Manet, it's money. But never mind my exploits.' He played with his signet ring. "I'm sorry about what happened last night. Segal had no right."

I shrugged. "All part of the investigation."

He nodded. "Sure. All right. How is the investigation going? Not that it's any of my business."

"Well, until last night it didn't seem like money was a motive. It's honey, not money," I said borrowing a line from Joe Tuzzo. "I mean, unless it was about a lack of money. Workers at Montrose aren't well-paid. And they're overworked. As for the inmates, they get a nominal salary for participation in programs and for their assigned duties. From one dollar to seven dollars a day. That doesn't cover cigarettes and the occasional dope, assuming they can get hold of any."

"But after last night, you figure there may be bigger stakes. Prison is like art. A business, like anything else." DM pushed aside the creamy yellow pie. "The white chocolate cheesecake at the ball was much nicer than this. I get these yearnings for sweets… Did you at least try the cheesecake?"

I transferred the plate to the ground beside Otis. "I tasted it. It was good, but I'm not big on desserts, or cheese." Otis gulped down the yellow cream.

"Must be your years in China. I'm impressed, you speak Mandarin, so few Caucasians do. You'll go a long way, Officer Pirelli."

DM sounded sincere enough that I decided to trust him. "Tell me what you know about Guy Dyke."

"Not much, except that he's got a ravishing young wife."

"And he doesn't look at you when he's talking," I added. Meanwhile, DM's gaze was steadily fixed on me. I realized I was playing nervously with the handle of Otis's leash.

"Maybe," DM said, "but Dyke has eyes everywhere; he's a man with tentacled enterprises. He may well be Greater Burlington's most powerful businessman. His best known success is X-Dress, because it's out there in all the stores, in more than plain view. But he also has his hand in some less glamourous ventures. DM turned his signet around and around his finger and eyed me slyly.

"Prison management."

DM nodded. "Mr. Dyke's following a national trend. Turning jails into profit-making ventures. He's done it with the men's prison. And now…"

"He's going for the contract to run Montrose."

"I don't know, Rey. Maybe."

"Why didn't anyone tell me about this before last night?"

DM took a careful sip of cappuccino.

Why hadn't Captain Carter mentioned this? Was I the only one who didn't know about Dyke's bid? I realized that I was standing, though I didn't remember deciding to go. I picked up my cigarettes and tossed them in my shaggy handbag.

"Leaving so soon?" DM handed me a rolled-up magazine. "Almost forgot. You like fiction? Check out page 23."

I angled the magazine under the moonlight to get a better look. The journal was named *Queene*. I'd never heard of it. On the cover, a head and torso photo of a man in his late forties wearing horn-rimmed glasses. I had no idea who he was. DM brought the candle closer. I sat down to read: "*Under Influences*: A Posthumous Text by Experimental Novelist Lee Pike."

"How did you know Pike was linked to my investigation?"

"If you read the presentation and the text, it's simple detective work."

I was impressed. And uneasy; how did DM know so much about my case? "Does it mention a Chinese woman, a prof?"

"It mentions a lover, a woman. If you read this text as autobiographical, it may exonerate his mistress of the murder. The protagonist is a drug addict who ends his life with an overdose of methadone."

"So May didn't kill him!" I said under my breath.

"Pike was a serious writer; he wasn't into confessional writing. The female character provides the former heroine addict with the fatal syringe. Technically, then, she could be an accessory to suicide. But the text is a jigsaw which the reader has to assemble. I'm sure you'll be able to get more out of it than me." And he added: "You've got a good nose, Officer Pirelli. And pretty ears, too." DM touched my hand lightly. Even the slight contact felt warm.

"God help those women," I said, "if they privatize Montrose. It's bad enough in there as it is." It occured to me I was repeating Lucille Segal's words at the ball. I stood up again to leave.

DM stood too, glancing down at Otis. "Yeah. A dog-eat-dog world."

I turned to go, but found myself unable to remember which direction I'd come from. I looked to Otis for help, but he just stood there, gazing up at me and panting.

DM touched my elbow and pointed to my right.

"West," I guessed.

"South, actually."

I shook my head, humiliated. "No sense of direction."

DM laughed. "You mean that, without that big coon of a dog to lead you here, I wouldn't have had even the brief pleasure of your company?"

"I guess I'm easily lost."

"I think," DM said, "when it counts, you know exactly where you're going."

Otis had picked up the scent and pulled me away up, toward Cliff Street.

✪

It wasn't a dream; the doorbell was ringing and Otis was barking, all fours against the main door. Oh, of course, it had to be Lou. But it wasn't Lou. By the time I got to the door, there was no one there. Yet, someone definitely had rung the bell, right Otis? On the mat outside, a manila envelope. I opened the door and immediately slammed it shut — I'd forgotten the damn alarm. Must unarm it first. Why the hell did I arm the thing last night? I guess I wanted a good night's sleep before the drive to New York. Frantically, I punched numbers on the panel. Wrong. I tried again. Then, as I heard the first note of the siren, I got it right and silence cut short my panic. I waited perfectly still for a moment, praying I'd made it in time. Should I phone the control centre and cancel the alert? No, I got it in time. Now I opened the door, reached out like any ordinary citizen would for her newspaper, and picked up the large envelope.

The envelope was addressed to *Detective Pirelli*, in very neat handwriting, slanting slightly left. So a left-handed person or someone trying to mask his or her handwriting? Rey-hee, back track. What did you learn at the academy? I recalled the yellow hand-out.

Suspicious mail: anything mailed from a foreign country, fictitious return address, restrictive markings, excessive postage, misspelled words, addressed to title only. Worse: strange odour, no return address, protruding wires, excessive wrapping, tape or string, special endorsements, lopsided or uneven, oily stains, discolouration or crystallization on wrapping. Also: badly typed or handwritten.

The hell with it. I ripped open the envelope. It contained pages of what seemed to be a financial report. I scanned the sheets for a company name, but found only "the Company," with a capital "C." Beneath that, column upon column of numbers. Additions, subtractions, growth charts, net earnings, operating costs, tax rates. Words and numbers, years, percentages and dollar signs. I glanced at my Swatch, as Otis did a tap routine with his front paws on the kitchen counter. I had no time for accounting. Oh-seven-hundred! Lou would be here any minute: breakfast for two, wash, dress... and clean up! I shoved the envelope in the desk drawer.

Later, backing out, I caught a glimpse of Otis and Lou watching me from the living-room window. Would they be okay together? I realized I'd forgotten to brush the pooch, and to tell Lou where I'd put the plastic bags. She'd figure it out. At least she wouldn't leave the place unarmed....

Once I left Route 7 and hit the I-87, my internal jukebox cranked up. "I know a place where the living is fine and the rents are always low, I know a place where weeee can go. Where we can go-o-o-o." Where did these tunes come from? My one great talent, my garbage mind: I'd somehow managed to absorb vast quantities of bubblegum music from four or five decades. In fact, I had absorbed much of it in China, where my friends loved to collect pirated Western tunes. The result was a mix of all-American pop culture that oddly reminded me of China. And of my mother.

The plain, unmarked Ford wasn't too big to handle and it was powerful. I felt the pleasure of speeding on the virtually deserted highway. A day off on the road! I was getting ready to rewind my singing machine when I almost hit two black birds perched smack in the middle of the thruway. That stopped my singing. Once I was past them, I realized one of the birds was dead, the other standing motionless beside it. In the middle of the highway. A glance in my rear view mirror revealed the living mate still hadn't budged, refusing to leave his or her loved one. I felt a sharp ache for the stubborn bereft bird. And then I realized I was crying. Two tears dropped on my navy-blue jumper. Was I the lone bird who'd flown first from my mother's death, then from Joy's and Thomas'? I shook off the idea, thought of Huiru. He was still alive, even though far away. It was noon here, so midnight over there. He was dreaming at this very moment. Perhaps I, cruising down I-87, was merely Huiru's dream. As though we were each other's dreams. Oh, stop it, Rey-hee, you're just being sentimental. Most likely that live black bird was cannibalizing the dead one.

Speaking of morbid, I'd read Lee Pike's posthumous text the night before. In the story, a woman gave the fatal syringe to the protagonist, although she didn't use drugs herself. There was no mention of the woman being of Chinese descent, another clue that would have identified her. Maybe Pike had wanted to protect May, even beyond his death? If so, he'd done a poor job of it. Those who chose death, it seemed to me, had to abandon any hold they might have on the fate of those they left behind.

✿

Sam Ho was already in the Café Ciao! when I arrived at 1400 sharp. People who don't know each other but who are meeting in a public place always seem to pick each other out, whether in Beijing, Buenos Aires or New York. There were other Asian men in the café, but I went straight to Sam Ho's table.

Ho looked up at me and I saw that he was taking in my plain navy-blue jumper and tights. I must have looked like a graduate student to him. He rose to greet me.

"Coffee, Ms. Pirelli?"

"Oh, okay, a large latte, if possible."

"Of course. This is New York. We've got more than Green Mountain Coffee here. We even have something called the Policeman's Grind! Please, sit. I'll get the *grande* for you."

I studied Sam's back as he waited in line for my coffee. His delicate shoulders, stooping a little even though he was short: the look of a kindly person. So unlike his sister. He checked back, smiling and nodding at me, while he waited for my order. His clothes were sporty but sober, expensive. A pale pink linen shirt and designer chinos. Matching argyle socks, Duxbury shoes.

"Dr. Ho, I'm still trying to connect a few missing links."

"Please, call me Sam. Yes. So am I. I'm at a loss. My mother in February, and now May." He shook his head. "I can't believe it."

"Can't believe what, Dr. Ho... Sam?"

"That they're no longer with us, I suppose. But, what's worse, both deaths have yet to be explained. How can that be?"

"The autopsy in your mother's death concluded she died of cardiac arrest."

"Yes. That Mexican autopsy… It was done so quickly. Look, I realize my mother was getting on in age, but she was in excellent health. As for my sister, well, it's simply outrageous: 'undetermined cause of death?' That's all I've been told. And inside the prison. I was hoping you could tell me more, Officer Pirelli."

"I haven't fully discarded the possibility of suicide..."

"Out of the question!" Sam set his latte a little heavily down on the table. "May was full of life. Admittedly wild, but certainly not self-destructive. She was our Zarathustra." Sam paused, slightly embarrassed by his outburst. "Our father used to say, 'May's our little bull in a bear market.'"

"Your father?!!" I realized my voice was pitched way too high. Why hadn't I thought to check on May's father? People had fathers, as well as mothers. I lowered my voice, "Your father passed away?"

"Thirteen years ago. Emphysema, ever since May and I were teenagers. It was a terrible disease, he couldn't finish a sentence without gasping for breath."

"It must have been awful."

"He was a chain smoker."

I detected a cold medical diagnostic rather than filial regret.

"May smoked too, right?" I remembered the lovely silver pumpkin ashtray in May's box of personal effects.

"I'm afraid so. She wanted to take it all in." Sam smiled gently, almost apologetically.

"Drugs, too?"

Sam shrugged, but his smile vanished.

"Perhaps you weren't told; an unknown substance was found in her blood."

Sam's face reverted to a concerned expression and then a mulish look. His voice was strained: "I'm afraid I can't help you there."

I sensed I'd hit on something. Had big brother provided drugs to his little sister? I took a sip of my "grande" and wished I could smoke, but these cafés were all smoke-free and proud of it.

I juggled with another idea: the anonymous document I'd received on therapeutic drugs. That was right up Sam's alley. What if he was involved in some drug ring laundering money through his pharmaceutical business? And the financial document, also dropped anonymously, could be linked to the first. But why kill his sister? Because she knew something, and he was afraid she'd tell to get out of prison? Or more simply: Sam could have killed his sister, because he suspected she'd killed his darling mama?

While my mind was spinning, Sam sipped his coffee and patted his mouth three times with a paper napkin.

I decided to tackle him head on. "Sam, how did you do it?"

Sam froze momentarily, still holding the napkin over his mouth. He cleared his throat, replaced the napkin on the table and smoothed it flat. He looked up at me, a little sheepishly. "I went to see May at the, hum, centre. She asked me to send her some Chinese herbs."

"How? Drugs just don't get in undetected."

"It wasn't an illegal drug! I'm a pharmacologist, not a drug dealer." Sam, although flushed, remained calm.

"Tell me the name."

Sam smiled and lowered his voice to a whisper: "*Barbar.*"

◘

Sam had been waiting at the entrance to the Montrose visitation hall, a wide grin and arms open for his little sister. May wore a superb *Comme un garçon* black outfit. All noir. She kissed him lightly but he took her into his arms and hugged her.

"*Cuir de Russie*? Well over a hundred dollars a bottle, your business must be thriving, bro." She had led him to the quietest corner, by the handicrafts display. Sam produced a handkerchief, wiped the corners of his eyes, and sat down, delicately pinching his light wool pants to prevent the knees creasing.

"Was the trip up here okay?"

"Fine, fine…"

"That's twice in just a few months… Did you come alone?"

"Yes, Henry couldn't take the time off. But with the BMW, it's a breeze."

Neither seemed to know what to say. Inevitably, as might have been predicted, the topic turned to their mother.

"I'm so sorry I didn't see mother before she died," Sam complained. "I still can't figure it out."

May's shoulder muscles contracted.

"I just know she wasn't taking those herbs I sent her."

May waited, silent.

"What happened in Mexico, May?"

May sighed. "She was too old. I shouldn't have taken her."

"Nonsense. It was nice of you. Not your fault at all."

"Come on, Sam, don't you know anything about mothers and daughters? Don't try to turn it into a good deed."

"Oh, May, you always make things sound worse than they are." Sam extended a comforting hand towards her shoulder, but May pulled away.

"You're not going to ask me about life in here?"

"Oh, May, you're so tough. Where does it come from?"

May crossed her legs and started frantically swinging her right leg. "Maybe I got all the bad genes… you're so perfect, Sam."

"Don't tell me your mantra hasn't changed? After all these years?"

"Okay, big brother. Forget it." May shook her head. "Tell me about New York. You look like you're doing well. How's Henry?"

"Fine, he's fine, all's fine. Thank you. We're buying a condo together, if we can finally put together a decent down payment. It's a brownstone on 89th, with a little garden at the back. There's never enough light on ground floors, but Henry can jog in the park and I can sunbathe out there."

"Well, here's a bit of sisterly advice: beware the neighbours!!!"

Sam nodded. "This Lee fellow, he was your neighbour?"

"Correct. There's nothing worse than neighbours. I have a bunch of them here. Hell is the other, right? And if you think same sex is nice, I've got news for you."

The edge was right back into the conversation.

Sam put his left hand delicately in his tweed-jacket pocket: "Oh, I almost forgot, I brought you this." He handed her a box, which was once finely wrapped in delicate rice paper, but had been torn open. "Sorry," Sam said, "the guard wanted a look."

May admired the teapot and breathed in the green tea leaves. "Mm… Listen, speaking of natural ingestibles, think you could do me a favour, Minchih?"

"Minchih? When was the last time you called me Minchih? What is it, Hsio Mei?"

"Don't laugh at me, okay?"

"Promise, on our mother's head."

"All right: I'd like you to find me some…" May leaned close to her brother's ear and whispered, "*Barbar.*"

Sam pulled back. "Are you nuts? What in heaven's name for? Do you know what that is?" Sam had raised his voice. He looked around to see if anyone had noticed. Fortunately not. A kid had just knocked over a potted plant and most eyes were watching the interaction between a stern thin, tall woman, obviously staff, and a young tough-looking inmate with jet-black hair who'd whacked the child.

May seemed oblivious to her surroundings. "It's not really any of your business what I do with it, is it, Sam? Do I poke into your affairs?"

"Calm down." Sam's shock at his sister's request turned first to bemusement, then amusement. He whispered: "Do you think they'll let the stuff through?"

"Is it illegal? No. Far as they're concerned it's tea. So there. What's wrong with a little fun?"

Sam wagged his index finger at his naughty sister and smiled: "Bad girl. okay, Hsio Mei. *Mo mentai*. It's a deal."

✷

"And that was it. A deal's a deal. So, I got her the barbar," Sam told me. He took his signature handkerchief out and patted his forehead. His polished nails looked professionally done.

I could feel my heart racing, but I kept my voice steady. "Is this *barbar* an accepted APA drug?"

"It's a Chinese herbal medicine."

"What is it exactly? What does it do?"

Sam smiled again and shrugged: "*Barbar* is the vulgar name for *suoyang*."

"Can you write that word down for me?"

He laughed lightly. "If I could, would you be able to read it?"

"I might."

"Well! Police training certainly is getting sophisticated." Sam had recovered his bearings. "Unfortunately, unlike May, I can't write Chinese. I'm a banana, as they say: yellow outside, white inside." His hands made a flowery gesture of apology.

"Do you carry *suoyang* in your store?"

"Not as such, no. I sell alternatives to Western medicine: uppers, downers, soothers, I mean, all the ingredients that can be found anywhere in Chinatown. But in my boutique, they are nicely re-packaged with my logo. Here." Sam took out his business card, which read HEXA-BADA and bore his seal in red: the primary hexagram.

"Well, what's this *barbar* for?"

Sam replied a little too quickly. "It's an upper. A feel-good potion. A tonic, if you like." Sam delicately shook his wrist to reveal his Rolex, which showed 1530. "In any case, Detective, it certainly couldn't have killed her."

My heart sank. "Are you so sure?"

"Totally inoffensive."

I let Sam go in exchange for a promise to try and locate some *barbar* for analysis. But I wasn't counting on him to come through. I thought I just might be able to find the magic potion myself.

I headed to Chinatown. You can find pretty much any food and other products from China in New York's Chinatown; everything from any of the many types of leafy veggie, to porcelain tea cups, bamboo matting, cutting knives, woks and tourist trinkets. And yet, I remember thinking it just didn't smell like China. Was it the American air? And where were the beautiful Beijing girls? The short, shabbily dressed women I saw bore no likeness to the *xiaojie,* those tall, pale, shapely and stylishly dressed young ladies of Beijing. A *xiaojie* could bring five red taxis screeching to a halt at her feet with barely a twitch of a finger.

The fragrance of fried and steamed foods rising above the stench of rotting garbage made me hungry. I rejected the chic Sushi & Dumplings, opting instead for *xiaolongbao,* steamed pork shank dumplings, and a Tsingtao beer at the Little Shanghai, in a side alley off Mott Street. The *xiaolongbao* tasted exactly like the ones served in the restaurant of the Peace Hotel in Shanghai. I walked down Canal Street and let my nose guide me through the dried foodstuffs on sale along the sidewalk: lilies, chrysanthemum, white nuts, and longevity mushrooms gradually gave way to mussels, octopus and finally, to deer antlers, scorpions and various black ant-like creatures in huge vats. The majority were potions claiming to enhance virility, occasionally fertility. Here and there, I stopped to ask salespeople if they stocked *barbar* a.k.a. *suoyang*. They all looked at me with incredulous eyes. Those who answered just shook their heads and replied "*Mo*" in Cantonese, "*Mei you*" in Mandarin or "No, not got" in Chinglish. Several giggled, which told me that *barbar* had something to do with sex.

I checked Sam's business card: "HEXA-BADA — fine healing remedies from Asia," 3 Pinter Lane. Which was on the edge of Chinatown, in little Italy. I made my way through the sidewalk stalls of electronic toys and a shopping crowd that was getting larger as rush hour approached. In front of Sam Ho's boutique, an oiled paper lantern read, in black on red: "HEXA-BADA." From outside, I couldn't see the dapper owner. A young man with blue hair and a blue retro suit sat at a computer behind the counter. Two fashionably thin female customers had opened a red box and seemed to be discussing its contents under a Japanese paper lamp. There were no big vats stuffed with dried animal parts in Sam's shop. I probably couldn't have afforded a cup's worth of jasmine tea here, assuming he carried such a basic item. I checked my fake Louis Vuitton wallet and stepped in, greeted by the sound of delicate bronze chimes. In the hushed interior, I strolled between the shelves, on which little red packages were artfully displayed. I overheard bits of the two women's whispered conversation: "a mood changer"… "when the moon waxes"… "female testosterone"… "harder nails."

"Would you have what's called, in Chinese, *barbar*?" I asked the blue young man behind the counter.

"Sorry," the blue boy said. "I don't know Chinese… Perhaps you could describe to me what's in this *barbar*?"

"I wish I could… It's a, a… tonic." I answered sheepishly.

The blue hair was whipped from side to side. "Dr. Ho is away this afternoon, if you could come back tomorrow; or leave your card?"

On my way out, I scanned the names of some of the potions: *qian, zhen, kan, gen, kun, sun, li, dui* — all names of the *Yijing* trigrams. Sam was using the *Book of Changes* as a marketing tool. If he was, as he admitted, a "banana," he was a clever one. I held up a square-shaped box labeled *kun*, which I recognized as the receptive, the earth, and read its prescription: "Heavenly, after a hard day." The ingredients were not listed.

I stared at the calendar and massaged my temples. The trip had been tiring and time was running out. Next Sunday was Mother's Day. I'd be slaving away trying to finish up my report for Captain Carter. Plus Otis and I both badly needed airing.

"Come on, Otis: let's go for..." There was no need to complete the sentence; Otis was already standing by the pile of plastic bags with the leash between his teeth. I took a deep breath, armed the security system and we were off.

We jogged, stopping by a vacant lot to pick lilacs, which I wrapped in an Otis plastic bag. We ran toward the northeast, away from Max' upscale neighbourhood where condo owners even swept the sidewalk, through the pedestrian Church Street, and past the police station, civic number one on North Avenue. We crossed a street corner I usually tried to avoid: North Avenue and North Street. On one side, the Mermaid Building with its beautiful wooden mermaid extending its body toward the other side of the street like a tall ship's figurehead. The building itself was an anonymous gray-beige apartment complex where I had once lived with my mom. We ran faster, still northbound. Posh townhouses, colonial-style mansions on the lakeside; subsidized, run-down housing on the other.

We turned left on Institute Road and slowed our pace. The Burlington High School and the Episcopal Centre on our right; the Providence Orphanage and the Lakeside Cemetery on our left. I glanced quickly at the orphanage, an austere red brick building now empty. The ornate wrought-iron fence of the cemetery was wide open. We went down a side path and stopped in front of a small dark granite tombstone on which was inscribed simply: Iris Pirelli, 1954-1984. Otis, free of his leash, wandered off toward the lake below.

I placed my bouquet atop the stone, and lay down on the soft green surface of the grave, face down, to inhale for a moment the scent of the grass. Then rolling over I stared into blue sky melting into the lake until it enveloped me completely. I became little Rey again, feeling the grip of a lady's white-gloved hand. I looked down at my white tights, and black patent shoes. Then, oh so slowly, raised my head just a little. The earth was wet and very brown. I knew there was a big hole, and if I moved my foot just a little, I'd fall in. The coffin was in there. Someone was throwing earth into the hole, a little girl started to cry in a shrill voice. I closed and re-opened my eyes a few times and looked around my mother's grave.

To my left, a stone at the head of a mound of freshly upturned earth read, "Ross McDonald, beloved son, 1943-2000." Ross had joined several other McDonalds in the family plot: James and Kathleen, beloved grandparents, 1900-1980 (engraved twice) — a double suicide? a car accident?; Sean, beloved father, 1922-1982; Dorothy, beloved mother, followed by an open date: 1925-   . Dorothy, it seemed, was the one burying them all, stubbornly maintaining a more natural chronology in a round of births and deaths gone awry. Aged mothers surviving their adult sons; young mothers leaving younger daughters behind.

At my mother's wake, next to the food-laden table, little Rey had overheard a woman in a pointed velour hat stage-whisper, "The stain is still there," before popping a triangular salmon sandwich into her mouth.

"I know, darling," the gloved lady holding my little hand had agreed. "The janitor tried but he couldn't wipe it away."

A few days later, the gloved lady had taken me back to the apartment. While she went through the drawers and closets, I had stepped over to the window and dared myself to look down. On the asphalt below, I saw the shadow of my mother.

I sat up, facing my mother's inscription. What would my life have been like if Uncle Thomas hadn't taken me under his wing?

I stood up, reached over to touch the wild lilacs, and wished my mother a Happy Mother's Day. Turning to my left, I added: "Same to you, Dorothy." I thought of Joy. And of May and Liz. It occurred to me that the blue of the sky and lake today was the same colour as the two cheap ceramic urns sitting atop the Riches' *faux* fireplace.

○

When I returned with my empty backpack and a contented Otis to 14A Cliff Street, I found another package, this time small, by the door. Like the two previous offerings, it bore no postage marks, and none of the tell-tale signs of dangerous parcels. The handwriting was steady and straight: *Detective R. Pirelli*, and the wrapping was clean and smooth. Not the same handwriting as on the last parcel. Nevertheless, I handled it carefully. Immediately I noticed a distinct smell, close to but not quite mildew, or ink, or geranium leaves. I stumbled into the apartment, my hands full of package, dog leash, dog and backpack, and my head full of the mystery of this third missive. For a moment I stood there, trying to remember something. Then I dropped everything and scrambled to cancel the red signal AWAY just in time.

I returned to the package. Someone out there was trying to tell me something. But what, and who? The inside of this anonymous parcel was wrapped in a Chinese newspaper: *Xin Shijie, The New World*, an overseas Chinese rag. A gift from Sam? Too roughly wrapped to be from Sam. Or anyone Chinese I knew. Wrapping, after all, was a Chinese art. I thought of the women in the tea shop down the road from my apartment in Beijing, with their fairies' fingers, nimbly enveloping tea leaves in pink ricepaper.

Nor did I think that what I found inside this third package was tea: a solid dark mass, slightly oily to the touch. Of course some teas come in a solid dry cake. But this was not tea. Could it be *barbar*? I knew I ought to bring it in for analysis.

While I paced a little, considering this, I noticed there was a message on the answering machine. A muffled, masculine voice spoke very slowly, pronouncing each syllable. "Try it, Detective Pirelli." Impossible to tell the age or whether he had an accent. There was a pause, during which I could make out traffic in the background, and then: "Infuse it. Drink it like tea."

Someone was definitely following my investigation. Or leading it. Stalking me. Yet I felt no fear. It was more like someone wanted to help, but not in the open. Still, just in case, I armed the alarm system to STAY. I brought the package into the kitchen. I broke off a little piece of the black cake, sniffed at it. "Curiosity killed the cat, Rey-hee." Nevertheless, I put the chunk in a brown betty teapot. While it infused, I smoked a cigarette at the kitchen table and described the situation into my mini-recorder. Just in case. Otis, sensing the solemnity of the occasion, lay down a respectful distance from my feet. I went into the other room, turned on my computer, and typed in a note to Huiru.

The black mixture was ready. I brought it over to my work station. I took a first sip. The taste was bitter. Now to wait. In the meantime, I took a clean sheet of paper, drew three circles, like Russian dolls, one inside the other. In the central and smallest circle, I wrote the names of the Montrose suspects: Eileen, Chris, Gloria. In the second, I listed the people who had been in contact with the victims while in detention: Irene Hill, Paul the guard, Joe the beekeeper, Sam the pharmacologist, Krauss. Dr. Krauss! He had never returned my call. I highlighted his name in an urgent yellow hue. In the outer circle, I wrote two names: CEO Guy Dyke and the qigong adept Jane Spitzer. I went back to the first circle to add Irene Hill's name. And in the second circle, Warden Segal and Dr. Leo, the prison psychotherapist. I highlighted that last name. What about DM? He seemed to know more than he was telling about Dyke's operations. And Lou? Even Captain Carter, himself. Were they in on some sort of corporate scheme to discredit Montrose? At least, the investigation was taking shape, however large and ungainly that shape might be.

Murder or suicide. Or murder and suicide. Liz and May could have been either active or passive agents of their own deaths. In both cases, both options were possible. Liz was positive, studying Chinese and qigong; May was anything but, and she was suffering the relentless abuse of her racist inmates. Try switching those two diagnoses around: Liz was depressed, having lost her boy Bing, and if my hunch was right, a newborn, too. She must have been barely hanging on, clutching at her self-improvement projects for meaning they couldn't deliver. May, on the other hand, was willing to risk everything, throwing herself into any available extreme sport. A Dionysian figure, not depressed or suicidal, but hungry for life.

So, who was helping me? I went back to the drawer in which I'd shoved the second surprise package, pulled out the pages of charts and numbers in the anonymous financial report. You didn't need to be a diviner or a financial whiz to see that the "Company" in question was thriving. Its growth potential and revenues were dazzling. More interesting were the operating costs and expenses. There were entries for "government-owned facilities," the mention of "1,000 beds," and a host of what looked like medical equipment. The company could be an amalgamated hospital. Further along, I found reference to projected costs and loans to finance start-up costs relating to new construction and contract commitments. There followed credit agreements, but also a list of subsidiaries: I counted thirty-some names on one page of the earning calendar. The subsidiaries were varied: hardware stores, children's toys, water services, biogenetics. I looked at the quotes for the children's toys company ABC&Me, but couldn't decipher the charts, except that the graph lines all seemed to be going up. It's not Monet and it's not Manet, it's money, Rey. All right, so who would send me the financial report of a conglomerate? If these were the figures for Dyke's little empire, it couldn't very well be him showing off. Conclusion: someone, not necessarily the same person, had sent me a breakdown of Dyke's finances, a copy of the law on drugs, and a chunk of some sort of drug. Warden Segal? But she had no need, not to mention penchant, for anonymity. Suddenly I felt like May, like Liz, might have felt: there was no one I could trust, not even my colleagues. I was all alone with this mystery. For the first time since I'd been assigned the case, I despaired of solving it. I threw myself down on Max's red sofa.

◘

I woke with a start, head clouded and body heavy. Tea! I'd been dreaming, something I couldn't remember, something wild. The condo was very quiet and dark. I called out "Otis!"

He was in the kitchen, splayed across the floor, motionless, but with his eyes open. Beside him, only dust remained of the unknown black substance. He'd eaten it. I felt a surge of panic for my only friend on this side of the planet. I felt his jugular for a pulse — slow but steady — and he was breathing evenly. With difficulty I lifted him, all 80 pounds, and carried him over to the red couch. He didn't seem to be in any pain. I sat with him, stroking his seal neck and head.

After a while, the memory of my dream started coming back. I turned on my mini-recording machine and lit a cigarette: "I'm in a long hall, with a line of doors on either side. Everything is beige, an endlessly long beige corridor with nothing and no one but me in it. Suddenly, all the doors on both sides open simultaneously. People start pouring out, all rushing toward the end of the long hall. I notice that the people are dressed for a costume ball, Mexicans in large sombreros, toreros in tight pants and gold stitched jackets, senoritas with black veils and wide red crinoline skirts, Batman and Robin, Mao Zedong. I don't recognize anyone. At first. Then I notice, at the edge of the stage, Warden Segal in a pink bikini sitting astride Paul Bundell. I can't believe my eyes: she's stretching his penis with one hand and holding a martini with the other. Her breasts have popped out of her bra, she's laughing her head off. I'm the only one who notices. I stand still, watching. Everyone else is purposefully moving towards the exit.

Then the end of the hall opens up, revealing four women facing the crowd and me. I can hardly see them, they're too far, and there are so many people between us, but I make out Elizabeth Rich arm in arm with my mother and, behind them, May Ho with Joy, my foster mother. All four are glowing. They're waving people on, I think they're waving at me too. They're shining, I tell myself, because they're wearing funny hats that have sequins or stones of some sort. I worry about my mother: what is she doing with Rich? Are they buddies and I didn't even know? Then I ask myself, what is Joy doing to May Ho? She's got one hand tightly around May's neck, as though she were trying to strangle her. That's when I wake up."

In my torpor, I vaguely heard a ringing somewhere in the condo. The sound gradually gained strength and clarity. In the bedroom. The phone was ringing in the bedroom. Leave it. No, get up. I staggered off the couch and into the bedroom to pick up. "Max?!! Where are you?" I moved to the wall calendar: Max was calling to say he would be home in exactly a week. And he wanted to know how Otis was doing.

It didn't occur to me to tell him the truth. Where would I begin? It was all I could do to keep up my end of the conversation. "He's fine. No trouble at all." After I'd told Max what he wanted to hear, I made my way back to the living room and Otis. He hadn't moved. He looked okay, though he lay where I'd stretched him out on the couch, dozing. I, on the other hand, was wide awake.

Using my jade chopsticks, I carefully extracted the dregs from the brown betty teapot and transferred them to a Ziploc bag. I'd leave the stuff, along with May's tiny Yixing teapot, with Dr. Witz, before my appointment with Captain Carter. The forensics lab was out of my way, at the hospital on Colchester Avenue, but I preferred to bring it in myself rather than leave it at Headquarters all morning.

✡

I was greeted in the lab by a woman wearing a turquoise uniform that might have been made of paper and what looked like a shower cap on her head. A nose-and-mouth mask dangled from one ear. There was no receptionist. Cutbacks, the tech told me. She also informed me that Dr. Witz would return to work only tomorrow due to complications from a bad cold that had turned into some form of pneumonia. This was the moment when a good detective would collect on a past debt or make a deal to move her mysterious black substance up on the list of priorities. Unfortunately, I had no debts to recover and nothing to deal with.

I hurried back to the station, amending and re-amending the on-the-spot oral summary of my report I expected Carter would demand. Oddly, the fifth floor was empty. I wandered a bit among the unoccupied cubicles, sat at my assigned desk, listening to the unanswered phones ringing, then walked the length of the floor to the closed door of the captain's office, and back to my desk. My Swatch told me fifteen minutes had gone by. Still no sign of the usually punctual Captain Carter. Suddenly the doors leading in from the staircase flew open and in poured the captain, followed by Lou, Bill Vance, Simon Baal, and many more, the whole station in fact, or so it seemed to me. The faces were all grim and no one paused to offer me a word. When Captain Carter moved toward his office, I approached, but he motioned me to stay put and wait. Lou gave me a quick nod in passing, and followed Carter into the office.

Another five minutes passed before Lou emerged and brushed past me. The Captain called out from inside his office. "All right, Pirelli, let's go."

It was the first time Carter had addressed me by my last name only. Nor did I relish his dismissive tone. And why hadn't Lou at least said hi? So much for the support system. Could my fears about Carter's links to the case and Dyke be founded?

I entered the Captain's office slightly demoralized and unsettled. By the time I emerged, and it was very shortly thereafter, I was completely down.

"Too friggin' esoteric," the Captain said, looking me in the eye, and tossing my progress report down on the desk. "Are you planning to write a report built on hunches and astrological charts? Get real, Pirelli!"

I was at a loss. Carter banged his fists down on his desk, stood up, shoving his chair back, and turned to face the window. His gray-flecked crew cut was uncombed, a few bristles had broken free here and there, and when he turned around to face me, I noticed his eyes were blood-shot. "Look, Pirelli, you're on your own. I can't help you out on this one. I need all my men, right now." He attempted a smile. "I mean, all my officers. Just wrap this case up, Pirelli. And keep it simple." Again, the Captain had addressed me without using my title or first name, but at least he sounded less like a bulldog. I picked up my manila file and exited meekly.

I didn't dare ask anyone in the office what was going on, but in the parking lot, a friendly voice called out my name. DM was waving from his open car window. He drove up alongside. "What's wrong, Rey? You don't seem your usual sunny self." DM knew something. But then DM seemed to know everything.

"What's going on in there?" I asked.

"Red ball." DM explained: two children, a boy and a girl, respectively 12 and 11 years old, had been found murdered at the King Street Ferry Dock, one last night, one the night before. Both had been sexually assaulted and brutalized. And the killer was promising more deaths. Notes, printed from a computer, were pinned to both bodies: "I am not the last one."

"The problem is," DM said, lowering his voice, "the notes were signed Captain Carter, Metropolitan Police. You can imagine Carter's not happy. This is a red ball, Rey. You and I are basically the only ones not working on the case. Lou Moore's the primary, but everyone else is chipping in time. Carter's getting phone calls and hate mail from the whole city. Rumour is even his wife's not sleeping in the same bed with him. Not that he's got time to sleep."

I was tempted to ask how DM'd come to know the intimate details of their boss' marriage, but I decided against it; the situation was too horrible.

"On a far more agreeable note," DM said, putting his hand through the open window of his car and laying it on the open door of my car, "I'd like to invite you to dinner at my place, say this Friday?" Before I had time to reply, DM had extracted an embossed lime-coloured card from his fake croco-skin wallet and handed it to me.

"No," I blurted out, as I put the card in the breast pocket of my uniform. "I can't. I've got too much work. My case. I've only got a few days. I'd like to but…" I had turned the key in the ignition, pulled away, and was out of the lot, into the street before DM moved.

✪

"DOWN-TOWN. DOWN-TOWN: When you're alone and life is making you lonely, you can always go…" Images of Petula's brightly lit downtown clashed with scenes of the grizzly children's murders down by the bay. I was thankful I wasn't on the children's murder case, one area I wasn't sure I could handle. Lou seemed to be in full command, though. She looked awfully professional, in her emerald green suit, Bill Vance on her heels, riding in her wake. The lab would be busy with that case, which meant I could forget about a quick analysis of the "tea." They'd be poring over the notes pinned to the dead children's chests.

I thought of Liz' son Bing, his breath crushed. If all life was sacred, and all beings equal, why was a child's murder more horrifying than an adult's? May's death had certainly been horrible; no time to even shut her eyes. "Keep it simple," repeated Carter. But there was nothing simple about this case. It was like the Chinese character on the man's chest in my dream: indecipherable. I forced myself to sing: "Just listen to the music of the gentle Bossa Nova…" but the happy-go-lucky feeling just wasn't there.

The fields off the 117 flashed by, tender green. I pulled DM's lime coloured card out of my breast pocket, and sniffed it. A light, very light lime fragrance. Good thing I was going to see that shrink. Get your act together, Rey. Get REAL!!!

✿

The guard called Dr. Leo down for the detective. I waited in silence, watching Paul apparently rubberstamping what seemed to be correspondence. I tried to forget that part of my dream; I definitely felt no sexual attraction to him and hadn't the slightest desire to find myself in Warden Segal's bikini.

After a few minutes listening to his stamping, I spoke up: "Officer Bundell, may I have a word with you?"

He didn't get up, but stared at me with his very blue eyes.

"There's something I don't understand. Remember Joe Tuzzo's visit to May Ho, March 9, and Sam Ho's visit to same, a few days or so later?"

"Sure." He looked relieved, but quizzical.

"Good. What I don't understand is: why did you confiscate the yarrow stalks Tuzzo brought for Ho?"

"Those home-made Pik-up-stix tied with a red ribbon? She got them back all right, didn't she?"

I pursued my line: "What about the little box that her brother Sam mailed her?"

Paul didn't speak immediately. He replied, "What was that, again?"

I figured he was buying time. "A red box containing a black substance. Why didn't you confiscate that?"

He shook his head. "No, no little box. Don't remember any little box."

"That package is in the log."

Paul stared right at me, though I could see his brain spinning.

"The man brought tea when he came to visit her. This looked like more tea. Well, the sort of tea Orientals drink, anyway. So, I let it pass. What about it?"

"So you did that out of respect for an inmate's ethnic difference? I'm impressed."

While we studied each other, Dr. Leo arrived. Why had I thought Dr. Leo would be a man? Rey-hee, shame on you. Alex was a name for girls as well as for boys. And that a prison for women would hire a woman doctor made sense. The doctor was 40-something, quite trim, and with straight thick brown hair cut at jaw-length. She wore a barely noticeable but expensive French perfume and an impeccable charcoal-grey suit. Together, we walked through the pink halls and across the quadrangle to the Ivy Institute where the doctor received her patients. Neither of us spoke along the way.

"It's odd for me to be discussing patients," Dr. Leo began. "Quite aside from the issue of doctor-patient privilege, there's an irreconcilable discrepancy between what I write on assessment reports and what goes on in here, between the patient and me. The written, on one hand, the spoken on the other, and then the unspoken, beyond that. Three worlds." I figured this was Dr. Leo's compulsory preamble; I let her go on. "A penal institution is a very bureaucratic place, you know. Montrose, with all of its innovations, is still a prison. I have to fill in the blank on a form with a yes or a no, check an impairment, a disability, a handicap, mild or severe. Everyone here has some kind of disorder."

Don't we all, I thought.

"Though I have to say that women, whether inside or out, have always been too easily classified as mentally disordered, as soon as they behave or do something unconventional. A British study on female inmates came to the conclusion that, contrary to general opinion, they are 'depressingly normal.'"

I was a little taken aback by Dr. Leo's progressive discourse.

"To tell you the truth, Montrose's inmates might benefit more from some form of social psychotherapy. Some penal institutions have implemented it successfully for men. Results are faster, in terms of interaction. It's even had some effect on APDs." Dr. Leo immediately apologized for the acronym. "That's Antisocial Personality Disorder. Group therapy is bound to be offered here, more likely sooner than later. Better suited to a work environment. In any case, that's not my field."

I preferred not to imagine Liz, May, Gloria, Laura, Chris and Eileen sitting on folding chairs arranged in a circle, and discussing their problems together. I got back to the object of my visit: "Dr. Leo, I'd be grateful if you would share your insights on Elizabeth Rich and May Ho? Your unwritten professional opinion."

Dr. Leo produced a practised Mona-Lisa smile and proceeded to share. "I followed Elizabeth Rich for almost six months. May Ho, for only two. Time, its passing, is decisive in therapy. Nothing much came out of my meetings with Ho. Nowadays, educated people seldom believe psychoanalysis can remedy situations. They often claim problems are political or social. Which isn't entirely untrue. But May Ho was also a very subjective person. I really can't say anything about May. Except to describe the way our sessions went."

¤

Dr. Leo's expression was impassive. It was 1430, and with 20 minutes left in the session she still hadn't extracted a word out of May, who sat, legs apart, in the stressless chair, directly facing the doctor. The doctor re-crossed her legs, this time from left to right. The woosh of the nylons. There was something sexual in the way May stared at Dr. Leo's knees. The doctor had caught the inmate looking her over when she'd come in for the session.

"Tell me, May, what are you thinking about at this very moment?"

May smiled. "Shall we play you tell me and I'll tell you, or would you prefer show me and I'll show you?"

"May, you agreed to see me. Can't we get some work done?"

"Listen, Dr. Leo, how can I put this to you? I'm not a great believer in psychotherapy. I don't want to discuss my mommy-daddy, peepee, caca."

"Fine, let's talk about you, then." As May said nothing, gazing instead at the poor Miro ersatz on the wall, Dr. Leo added: "Any dreams lately?"

May laughed briefly. "You're joking."

"Humour me."

May shrugged. "Thanks to Ma'am Pill, no dreams, thank you very much. My nights are a dark void, which suits me fine."

"What are you afraid to dream about, May?"

May made a spooky face and fluttered her fingers. "Murder. You've read my file, Doc. Would you sleep well?"

"So what occupies your mind during the day?"

"I try to think as little as possible. I smoke. I savour the institution's fine food."

"Maybe we can offer you something more interesting."

"Actually, there is one thing I wouldn't mind."

The doctor detected a note of sincerity. "I wonder would Montrose consider offering dog training? I'd go for that."

"You like animals?"

"Let's say they're more interesting than we are. And more reliable."

"How so?"

"Ever heard of unconditional love?"

"But why would you want such a love? Do you want a slave? Or to be a slave?"

May shrugged. She eyed the doctor for a moment, seemed to make a decision, and shut down the conversation. The session ended in a game of staring, Dr. Leo Mona-Lisa-smiling at May, and May fixing a spot 25 degrees from the doctor's knee.

◘

I detected a note of regret in the doctor's narrative. After a short pause, she resumed: "Elizabeth Rich, on the other hand, was, I think, on the brink of self-discovery. She'd been in denial about almost everything, including her crimes."

"Crimes. Plural?" I asked.

"I believe that Rich arrived at Montrose with a severe case of post-partum depression."

"You're saying she'd just given birth? Did she tell you that?"

Dr. Leo put her elbows on her desk, joined her hands under her chin and leaned toward me. "Not in so many words, no."

Dr. Leo was slowly turning her wedding ring, on her finger. The big diamond flashed occasionally, distracting me. I shifted in her chair to escape the diamond's rays. "So, how do you know Elizabeth Rich recently had a second baby?"

"It's a guess, I admit, but a professional one. Before taking this contract at Montrose, I was working with new mothers at Fletcher Allen, the campus in Essex. I recognize the symptoms of PPD, sorry, post-partum depression. Rich didn't have to tell me, I could read it, in her speech and in her silences. I considered some sort of medication, if not anti-depressants, at least mood stabilizers. But here at Montrose, we're very anti-drug."

Infanticide! Dr. Leo had confirmed my suspicions. The doctor seemed to read my mind: "Oh, it may not have been infanticide. Rich may not have killed her infant. But something happened to it. A crib death, maybe. Or a stillborn. Whatever the case, she never reported the birth nor its death."

"Which is a crime!" I blurted, repressing that sinister image of a baby in that huge dumpster among the rotting lettuce, bloody tissues and empty cans of pork and beans. More quietly, I added: "Were you aware of the danger, I mean the possibility that Elizabeth was planning to end her life?"

"I detected no suicidal ideation for Rich, and certainly not for Ho. But then, psychotherapy is not an exact science. The difference between a suicide and other deaths is a question of agency: suicides are subjects who perform their deaths for the world. That's why they leave a note, a message of some kind. Elizabeth was just starting to come to grips with issues of agency."

✣

Lying on the red couch, Liz repeated for the umpteenth time over the past forty minutes, just how fine everything was in her family. "I believe in looking good, in dressing well, and in being nice to people. I was raised that way. We were always in a good mood in my family. No sulking no whimpering over spilt milk. I'm rarely in a bad mood. What else can I tell you? People say I have an easy-going personality."

"Perhaps too easy?"

Liz looked up, a little surprised.

"Perhaps you don't make your own decisions, you go along with other people's? Do you let other people decide your life, Elizabeth?"

"I've had a life of my own… hey, what can you expect when you're a mother." Dr. Leo had stepped away from her usual non-committal listening role. Liz seemed to sense that. She asked her a question: "You have children, Dr. Leo? I don't see any family pictures in your office."

"Elizabeth, we don't meet here to talk about me. Let's get back to you as a child. Were things always so rosy in your family?"

Elizabeth sighed like a poor piano student who can't seem to hit the right note. "Swell, really. A normal family. Father, mother, brother, the whole deal."

Dr. Leo insisted: "How about your mother? Did you feel close to her?"

"Sure, like any daughter would. My mom was busy. She was a working mom. I told you, she works for Amway. I guess I was proud of her. Every morning she left the house, all dressed up, lips, eyebrows, nails: everything glossy."

"You didn't feel neglected?"

"She had to work to feed us. Sure, she loved earning her own money. She liked to buy clothes. She'd show them off for us, like a model. 'She called her stuff 'commission.' See this new black and white hat, kids? Well, that's last week's commission.'"

"No fights, no disagreements? Every family has disagreements, Elizabeth."

"Sure, every normal family has fights."

"Describe one. A bad one."

"I must have been nine; she came in just as we were finishing supper. She was wearing a real sharp Irish-green suit. She started, with her usual, 'Look at what I picked up with my commission this week.' Dad grabbed hold of her arm and took her into their bedroom. We couldn't hear, but we knew something nasty was happening in there." Liz' voice shifted slightly, into a little girl's. "Dan... that's my brother... Dan disappeared down to the basement. I guess I was scared. I didn't budge. But then they both came out, Dad first. She'd changed into a pair of black slacks and a white turtleneck. I remember she did the dishes that night. After that, she never showed off her new stuff."

"So, whose side were you on, Elizabeth? Your dad's or your mom's?"

Liz closed her eyes.

What psychotherapists define as a meaningful silence followed. Dr. Leo waited.

At last, Liz piped up again, in that little-girl voice, barely audible. "I was on Dad's side. I guess I was happy she was getting it." She started sobbing.

Dr. Leo waited a moment, until the minute hand ticked up to 10-to. Softly, she said, "I'm afraid we'll have to stop here for today."

○

I listened carefully to Dr. Leo's description of her session with Liz, but something was bugging me. "With all due respect, Doctor," I said when the psychiatrist was through, "do you really think all suicides leave a message?"

"Well, any generalization is dangerous. But for the most part, yes, I think so. Why?"

"My mother committed suicide. Defenestration. All she left behind was a stain in the parking lot."

"How old were you? You must have been quite young. Perhaps you were not told about or shown her note."

A wave of nausea swept over me. I closed my eyes and swallowed. Dr. Leo waited, absolutely motionless, while I exhaled slowly.

"Officer Pirelli, allow me another impertinent remark. Shoemakers wear badly worn-out shoes. Perhaps detectives have difficulty solving their own personal enigmas."

I shuddered. I breathed from the belly until the nausea passed. "Tell me, Doctor, do you do dreams, I mean in your analysis?"

"Tell me your dream, Officer Pirelli, I'll see what I can do."

I told her how my mother had been popping up in my dreams since the beginning of the Montrose case. I recounted my last dream, in which Elizabeth Rich was buddies with my biological mother while May Ho was being strangled by my adoptive mother. "The only connection I can see is that all four women are dead."

Dr. Leo twisted her diamond. Her well-manicured nails were cut short and lacquered with varnish, *au naturel*. "Dreams are not always a mirror or inverted image of reality; sometimes our unconscious has already figured out the solution to a problem, which only rises to the conscious level much later. That's why people take dreams to be premonitory. No such thing. Prescience is only a temporary time lag. Dreams don't tell us anything we don't already know. I can't tell you more: seems like your unconscious has already put the pieces of the puzzle together."

I saw it now, as clear as daylight: I had paired my mother and Liz, because they were both suicides. Liz had killed herself. But Joy had died in a plane crash. An accident. Which meant that Joy and May were paired because they were both accidents. But why, in my dream, was gentle Joy strangling May? Because May was murdered? Death by murder and by accident? How was that possible? Accidental murder. May had been accidentally murdered?

I realized that several long moments had elapsed, and that the doctor had allowed me this time to reflect, treating me like a patient. I stood and said, "I should be paying you for this..."

"I don't think so. Now I can close these two patients' files."

We smiled at each other, and Dr. Leo escorted me back to the gate. As we crossed through the quadrangle, I spotted Laura Elmsley, grayish hair down over her face, entering the gym. But Laura was not dressed for sports. She must be lost again, I thought. Dr. Leo, probably seeing me smile in Laura's direction, once more read my mind: "Laura's not lost, and she's not going to play basketball. She works in the gym, hands out the equipment."

I shook my head. I imagined Laura handing out ping pong rackets, badminton shuttlecocks, a volleyball net, a medicine ball. The doctor chuckled, as though she was sharing the unspoken image.

Warden Segal was waiting for me at the gate. She was dressed in a smart maroon pantsuit and holding a plain white envelope in her hand. Her expression was grim. "Officer Pirelli, I wonder if you could spare me a moment in my office."

"I'm in a bit of a hurry," I said.

She nodded, bit her lip. "Of course. I understand." But she was barring my way. "Officer Pirelli, I owe you an apology." She extended the letter. "That's a copy of a letter I sent to everyone who was sitting at that table at the Policemen's Ball, when I said those awful things. In it I admit to having been under the influence of alcohol, and to having made baseless accusations against you."

I took the letter. "Warden, do you have any information on Guy Dyke's bid to take over Montrose that could help this case?"

"I'm sorry." She shook her head mournfully. "I wish I could help you. Officer Pirelli, I've put my whole life into this place. Not just my career. Montrose is these girls' last chance."

"I know," I said. I tapped the envelope against my forehead and slipped it into my pocket. "Thanks."

She stepped out of my way and the gate swung open. "Rey," she called after me, "just solve the case."

◘

Four days left and still no sign of Liz' friend Karl Krauss. I knelt down beside a stretched-out Otis and massaged his belly. He half-opened an eye and made a low cow-like sound. Okay, I told him, that's it. Today the good doctor would get an unsolicited caller, me. My determination to act now may have been influenced by the fact that, during my morning bibliomancy session, this time using Martin's Criminal Code instead of my usual Chinese proverbs, my finger had fallen on the entry "double-doctoring."

I let Otis out into the back yard. He snooped a bit and produced a desultory spray before flopping in the grass. I gazed up at the blue sky. I decided to start with Krauss' residence, which was walking distance from Cliff Street. "Come on, Otis, let's hit the bricks."

"Miss, no! Sorry, you can't leave your dog here." The uniformed doorman had stepped out from his little desk at the corner of College and Battery and onto the sidewalk, probably motivated more by the deep blue sky than any professional sense of responsibility.

I led Otis to the back of the building and looped his leash around a lamp post in the alley. I guess I should have worn my own uniform.

"Miss, may I ask whom you're calling upon?" The doorman was back behind his little observation post.

"Apartment 6A-2."

"Ah, the doctor, yes. He's just come in. That'll be the penthouse, the farthest elevator on your left. I'll announce you. You are Miss…?"

"Detective Pirelli. I'm expected," I bravely added and walked quickly to the designated elevator.

There were only two doors on the sixth floor of Unit A. Not bad, the doctor had a semi-private elevator.

Karl Krauss opened his door almost immediately. He was tall and startlingly thin, beyond lanky. If the word brown came to mind, it was because he was wearing a brown suit, brown socks and brown shoes, and a buttoned-up beige shirt. His hair was brown, cut short, and his features were sharp, birdlike. His lips were thin, purple. He managed not to show too much of his displeasure at the unexpected visitor, leading the way into an open space, which he had transformed into a hi-tech haven. I noted the 48 inch flat-screen Sony TV, with integrated DVD. On a shelf next to the TV, a Sony digital camera, and neat stacks of DVD-ROMs. There were also row upon row of VHS tapes and CDs. Plus an arsenal of remote controls lined up on a shelf. I sat in a snow-white Scandinavian leather recliner. Doctor Krauss offered me Japanese green tea, which he served in black lacquer bowls. He sat down on a twin recliner at least ten feet away, thus creating a chasmic distance between doctor and detective. The only other furniture in the room was a metallic side table, next to the doctor's chair.

I sat very straight, holding my bowl of green tea, and began: "Dr. Krauss, first I'd like to know why you've been avoiding me." This sounded odd even to my own ears. So I rephrased: "Why haven't you returned my calls?" Now I sounded like a slighted lover. Neither formulation elicited any response from the doctor. I ignored his silence and pressed on: "How long had you known Elizabeth Rich? And what exactly was your relationship?"

Karl Krauss took a long, slow sip of his tea, licked his lips as though he were tasting a rare wine, delicately centred his cup on the little metal table, and crossed one thin long leg over the other. "I can see how you might find it cu-cu-curious. Someone of my st-st-stature associating with someone like M-m-mizz R-r-rich." He glanced around the living room, as though inviting me to recognize his stature.

Or maybe he needed to confirm it for himself. I had to admit the view from the turreted window, unobstructed down to the lake and to the distant Adirondacks was probably the best in town after the Wyndham Hotel. These apartments sold for half a million. Nevertheless, I refrained from commenting.

"M-m-m-mizz Rich and I met at a co-con-conference entitled 'M-m-m-anipulating Consciousness: Acupuncture, Anesthesia and Hy-hy-hypnosis,' a few years ago. We hap-happened to be in the same workshop… I was be-be-besotted."

I had read somewhere that trying to help a stutterer along only makes matters worse. So I waited him out before asking my next question. "When did you become lovers?"

Doctor Krauss raised his nose and sniffed. "I do not take on l-l-love-lovers. Ms. Rich was my b-b-bad object choice." He still hadn't looked me directly in the eye.

I decided to take a chance. "Did you know, Dr. Krauss, that Elizabeth Rich had given birth just prior to her arrest?"

Krauss's nose remained perched, but its wings fluttered a little. He answered without looking at me: "I… I was the genitor." Krauss leaned heavily on the last syllable, giving it an Italian twist.

"A girl or a boy?"

"I'm afraid I can-cannot say. Irrelevant now, wouldn't you s-s-say?"

I did not say.

"Detective, don't be j-j-jud… j-j-j-judge…" Krauss took a deep breath and tried again. "Judgemental." The word exploded from his mouth. "Sh-sh-surely, in your profession, you have had occa-ca-occasion to witness all manner of se-se-sexual arrangements."

"Why did you visit her at Montrose? Isn't that a manifestation of some sort of relationship?"

"I'm not unca-ca-caring." Dr. Krauss licked his lips. "I wanted to give her a special me-me-memento. Perhaps I felt p-p-p…"

"Paternal responsibility?" I butted in, despite my best intentions.

Krauss shook his head violently. "P-pity."

I mentally went through Liz' personal belongings. "What did you give Elizabeth Rich?"

Dr. Krauss smiled and, in two clear distinct syllables, told me: "Diamonds."

"Diamonds? We found no diamonds in her belongings." I was sceptical, though clearly, Dr. Krauss could afford them.

Krauss shrugged. "Yes, tiny di-diamonds. In the belly of a li-li-li-little rub-bub-bub-rubber li-li-lizard. M-m-mixed with ca-ca-candy." Suddenly, he broke off and produced a series of high-pitched staccato sounds vaguely reminiscent of laughter. "I su-su-suppose she ate them."

"Weren't you searched before you went in?"

Krauss smiled.

✡

The guard had picked him out of the line of women and children waiting. "Your suitcase, Mr...?"

"It's an attaché ca-case, and my name is D-d-doctor Krauss."

"All right, Doctor..." the guard smirked, "my name is Officer Bundell. Let's have a look at your visitation form." He read off his own list. "Karl Krauss, to see Elizabeth Rich, relation: friend; profession: medical doctor. Dr. Krauss, your attaché case, right here, please." Bundell tossed the brown leather case roughly under the detector, and reached out for Karl's beige raincoat. The detector alarm rang.

"I'm on ca-call. M-m-my t-t-tools... instruments," Krauss stuttered in answer to Bundell's quizzical look.

"Open the case please, Doctor." It contained the usual medical equipment, stethoscope, orthoscope, otoscope, ophthalmoscope, hypodermic, speculum and splints: all the invasive instruments a professional could wish for. The officer made sure to leave his fingerprints and germs all over everything before waving Krauss through.

Elizabeth Rich was seated in the crafts corner. Dr. Krauss walked slowly toward her, trying not to touch anything. Liz was wearing her usual sporty outfit and a ponytail. And just a touch of baby-blue eye shadow and pink lipstick.

He spoke in a hoarse whisper, because, in a prison, someone might be listening in. "Is this the uniform?" meaning her jeans and sweatshirt. "D-d-dreadful."

Liz re-tied her ponytail, crossed her arms and gazed toward the exit. "Why'd you come?"

Krauss stared at her long nails. His tongue darted out briefly over his lip and disappeared. "I've m-m-m-m." He paused, closed his eyes to concentrate and tried again. "I've m-m-missed you."

Liz twirled her ponytail.

Krauss shook his head, leaned in even closer. "I m-miss my little p-p-p-p... my little p-p-p-pricking lizard. My organs t-t-t-ingle." He sat back, pink with embarrassment, or was it the effort of producing that sentence? "My nip- nip-nipples..." He cast a quick furtive glance at the nearest tables and puffed up his shallow chest. "My whole...."

"For chrissake, shut up. Get another slave."

Krauss opened his attaché case and took out a box marked *Latex Gloves*. "This is for you, Ba–ba–ba-beth… S–s–s-something harrrd, that lasts for ever-rrrrrrr." He extracted a rubber lizard from the box, delicately placed it in the palm of her hand and shook it a little with two long bony fingers.

"Fuckin' sadist." Liz wrenched her hand free, got up to leave. Out of nowhere, a runny-nosed toddler reached up for the lizard. Liz grabbed the toy and stuck it in her pocket.

◘

"You see," Krauss concluded. "P-perhaps she swallowed them. Or they were s-s-stolen."

"Or, considering where they came from," I said, "she may have tossed them in the toilet." The doctor had paid his paternity debt and didn't seem to care what had happened. I tried a medical approach. "Dr. Krauss, we believe Ms. Rich committed suicide. What's your professional opinion?"

Immediately he was more at ease, only stuttering here and there. "Self-deliverance, whether de-de-deliberate or accidental, accounts for more de-de-de-deaths than laymen imagine. In this country alone, officially, there are approximately 31,000 su-su-suicides out of an annual rate of 2,250,000 de-de-deaths. The actual rate is certainly double and perhaps triple. M-m-ms. Rich might very well have been contributing, in her own small way, to increasing those f-fi-figures." Dr. Krauss took a sip of his tea.

Assuming Liz had flushed or swallowed the diamonds, why hadn't she gotten rid of the lizard, too? I asked to use the washroom. Krauss cringed, then sighed and pointed towards the back of the apartment. As I'd expected, the washroom turned out to be clinically clean, with an oversized cabinet, lined with row upon row of vials, too many to inspect. There was also a bidet. On my way back to the living room, I passed a half-open door and peeked in. The room was in stark contrast to the metallic living room. Drawn velour curtains bled into Pompeii-red walls. A huge 18th-century candelabra hung above the centre of the room where, rather than the four-poster bed you might have expected, there was a doctor's examination table. I decided not to go looking for the whips and leather à la Masoch. Instead I walked down the hall, bypassing the living room, and quietly let myself out of the apartment and into the elevator. Only once I was out of there and in the alley with Otis did I breathe a long sigh of relief. Oh, Liz, you sure were one tough girl.

◘

"Enough bad vibes, Otis! Let's go see a friend." I grabbed a stray take-out box Otis had been picking at in the alley. He gazed up at me, his snout covered in brown goo. Such garbage right by a posh building like Dr. Krauss'. Like diamonds mixed in with worthless candy. I resisted the urge to go back in and threaten the concierge with a citation.

Otis and I walked a good forty minutes before we got to what was still called the Old North End, a place often frequented by the police, where the poor locals and the new Chinese, Indians, Pakistanis and Filipinos all tried to live, if not in peace, at least cheaply. North Street was the boundary. Beyond it, Burlington city planning had abandoned its neat grid pattern; narrow winding streets shot off in all directions until they seemed to fall off the edge of the city bluff. All the way, I talked to Otis, more to dispel my sadness than because I thought he could be mollified. "You'll see, where we're going, you'll get some noodles instead of that garbage, how's that? You know those longevity noodles in a clear broth? Or maybe he'll be cooking home-made *jiaozi* dumplings with lots of ginger."

Lok Cheung always had something cooking. Lok Cheung had been Joy's only Chinese friend in Burlington. During the Great Proletarian Cultural Revolution, which Lok Cheung always referred to as the GeePeeCeeR, treating it like a terrible disease, or the acronym for a virus with a scientific name too long to remember, his wife, also an artist, had hanged herself. He'd left his native Chaozhou in the seventies. Since then he'd eked out a meagre existence teaching Chinese ink painting to the occasional student, and to elderly ladies in search of another arts and crafts course to enrich their retirement years. Joy had sent me to Lok Cheung to learn the basics of calligraphy.

At the corner of Hyde and North, we paused in front of the Like Grocery Store, a name folks in Burlington generally greeted with a shrug and a shake of the head, or at most a quick sarcastic jibe. In fact, "Like," pronounced "Lee-ko," was Chinese for immediate, meaning fast service. As we ascended the dirty stairs of 72 Hyde Street, even sleepy Otis perked up at the pungent aroma of ginger, anise, Chinese cabbage and unidentifiable herbs. The television was set to a Cantonese station, and the volume was loud. Or maybe it was just that the door was nothing more than a slice of air between two sheets of pressed wood.

Master Lok was working on a giant calligraphy. He smiled at me, pausing with his brush in mid-air. But he didn't speak. I understood: he must follow the impetus. I stood back respectfully, holding Otis on a very short leash.

Lok Cheung completed the last character, which I recognized as *wan*, meaning "late." He turned his full attention to me. "My friend, my friend, she come back. Aya!"

"What is it? A poem?" I asked. "May I see?"

"Poem, yes. Liu Zongyuan. Tang dynasty. Very sad. About old age. Like me. But very wise. So, not so much like me." He eyed his work critically.

"Very much like you, Lok Cheung." I kissed him and, as always, he backed away a little at the Western familiarity.

He bent to apply his seal to the work and then looked at me: "You eat something?"

"*Hao*! Okay!" We followed him into the kitchen where fresh noodles were waiting to be thrown into a broth. "Add some for the dog, okay?"

"Dog?! Hsio Lei, I eat dog, I don't feed dog." Lok Cheung laughed. "Okay, okay, noodles for dog, too. And shrimp for you, me and he! Okay, Hsio Lei?" Hsio Lei, or Little Rey, was the Cantonese name Lok Cheung had given me years ago. Gently he brushed the coon's back. Otis cocked his head, giving Master Lok his most charming gimme-something-to-munch pose.

"Are you adding salt to the noodles?" I was trying to figure out exactly how he made these delicious noodles.

"Soya sauce, ya. Salt, no. Salt very bad for you."

"But what's that white stuff, then?" I pointed to the pinch of white granules he was getting ready to throw into the soup.

"*Weijing*. magic potion: *Um-us-gee*."

"But, Lok Cheung, MSG is bad for you."

"Ah-yo! We eat *Um-us-gee* already five thousand years."

I made a mental note to try adding monosodium glutamate to my next bowl of noodles. I picked up my courage to ask about yet another potion. "Lok Cheung, have you ever tried *barbar*?"

"*Barbar*?!" Lok Cheung's wooden chopsticks froze in mid-air.

Obviously he knew what it was. I couldn't believe my luck. "Yes, barbar. Do you have any?"

"No, no. Not for you. Not for girls… For men, old, dirty men. Not me. I do not eat this *barbar*." Lok Cheung stared into the soup, but I could see he was blushing.

"What is it?"

"*Chun yao.*" He repressed a smile as he uttered the two syllables in a low voice.

"Spring medicine?" I was pretty sure I knew what that meant, but I wanted to hear it from the master's mouth.

"Sex medicine."

"Aphrodisiac? How do you write *barbar*?"

Lok Cheung sighed. Carefully, he set two bowls down on the makeshift table, and a third on a newspaper on the floor for Otis, and then drew the character in the palm of his hand. "This not in dictionary. A people's word."

"Oh, *benrbenr*... the root of roots, right?" Of course. I'd been stupid. I'd spelled it "barbar," a spelling which didn't exist in the *pinyin* romanization of Chinese.

"Yes, you know, male root. Double root." Lok Cheung motioned for me to eat. The three of us dug in, Otis outslurping both of us.

Finally, I took a break scooping noodles into my mouth. "I was told it's also called *suoyang*. Do you know those two characters?"

Lok Cheung shrugged. "Maybe I can guess, okay? First, *yang*: that is not so difficult. *Yang* is 'male.' *Suo*, maybe..." And he drew a few possible characters in his hand. "Maybe this one?" Lok Cheung made a firm fist of his hand: "Lock. Lock *yang*." He held his hand as though he were gripping an iron penis. We both laughed. "But why you look after these filthy things, Hsio Lei?" he asked.

In Mandarin, I told Lok Cheung about the case. He let me speak without interrupting, though he grimaced and frowned from time to time. When I was finished, he thought a bit, before declaring: "No need to look about outside people. Inside prison is torture. Torture everywhere. Those two women kill their selves." Lok Cheung crossed his arms, in a pose I recognized as an imitation of a steadfast *wuxia* warrior on TV. But then, maybe because he felt he hadn't convinced me, he added: "Look with your eye."

"My eyes?"

"No, no, your eye." He pointed to the space between my two eyebrows. "Not visible is visible."

"I don't understand." I knew my old friend was too down-to-earth to dabble in esoteric ideas like the third eye.

But Lok Cheung insisted. "All things leave trace. But not always visible." He took my arm and led me to the calligraphic work he had been completing when Otis and I came in. "Look," he said, pointing at the empty space between two characters. "Between the *bu* and the *wan*; or here, between the *yi* and the *liu*. No trace the eye can see. But you, Hsio Lei, you can see the trace, *shi bu shi*, yes or no?"

◘

Locked *yang*. My Chinese dictionaries were still in a box. I retrieved my *Cihai* encyclopedia, mini *Xinhua* dictionary and my Chinese-English dictionary. "All right, Otis, you and I are going to figure out what this upper called *barbar*, a.k.a. *suoyang* really is." I put a fresh espresso on the table by my dictionaries, Otis lay down at my feet, and we settled down to work. Although, looking at Otis, you wouldn't have called it that. Since his ingestion of the "tea," Otis had been extraordinarily placid. He'd become a couch potato. On a lined legal paper, I wrote the characters Lok Cheung had drawn in the palm of his hand: *suo* and *yang*. But I couldn't remember the *suo*. I was losing my Chinese, a lock, to lock, how do you write that again? The difficulty using a Chinese dictionary is that there are hundreds of homonyms, so that the sound *suo* could be any number of different words. You have to know which of the many written characters pronounced *suo* you are looking for. And the characters are listed in the Chinese dictionary by order of the number of strokes in the character. I was forced to check the different characters for *suo* in my mini *Xinhua* dictionary and then countercheck them in my Chinese-English dictionary. Finally I found the right one: the character was composed of the radical for "metal" and the phonetic *suo*. Now I counted the number of strokes in the "metal" radical: five. I opened my *Cihai* encyclopedia, turned to the index, and looked in the section of radicals with five strokes and let my finger run down the column to find the "metal" radical. The reference sent me to page 25. Then I counted the number of strokes in the phonetic part of the character: seven strokes. I proceeded to the seventh section, where the radical was combined with phonetics of seven strokes and again let my finger run down the columns until I found the character *suo*: page 1717. At last! And "*suoyang*" was the very first entry. And what was equally marvellous, the Latin name for it was provided in parentheses: *Cynomorium songaricum*.

I sighed with pleasure, the kind of pleasure only true detective work can provide. Now came the hard part. I stood, retied my hair with my HB-pencil barrette and stretched my body before attacking the paragraph explaining *sucyang*, a.k.a. *cynomorium songaricum*. My Chinese reading skills had also deteriorated, and it took me a good half-hour of dictionary work, from Chinese to Chinese, and from Chinese to English and back to Chinese to translate the following: *The plant, shaped like a penis, is comprised of a stem with no leaves and a large oval flower at the top. The plant contains a lot of starch and can be eaten. It can be applied to the affected area. It is used in Chinese pharmacopoeia as a tonic, especially for erectile dysfunction.*

I recognized the Chinese way of treating diseases, which I had experienced firsthand. During my university days in China, I had contracted hepatitis A. The doctors had given me pork liver to eat. Treat an organ with that organ, or something resembling that organ. But what would May have wanted with a treatment for erectile dysfunction? This question prompted more linguistic sleuthing.

Feverishly I dived into my unpacked boxes of China-related books and found Robert Van Gulik's *Sexual Life in Ancient China*. I flipped to the Index. No *suoyang*. "A" for Aphrodisiacs: still no *suoyang*. I went to W for Women and was quickly buried in a maze of sub-entries including pernicious effect of; inferiority of; inferiority of under Confucianism; Taoism and; Buddhism and; satisfaction of. I looked up this last sub-entry and found lovemaking positions and times of the menstrual cycle to avoid sex. Nope. Back to Women, and down the column, until the final entry piqued my curiosity: "compared to a cauldron." One of the references was interesting: a woman's womb was like the vessel of transmutation in alchemy; her vital essence, like mercury. But that was a digression. I moved on. I tried Lesbianism: no such entry. Homosexuality, female: see Sapphism. I flipped to "S" for Sapphism, Sapphist techniques, and there it was, on pages 211-212-213. Women's playthings, dildos, here termed "olisbos," from Latin, perhaps? And it mentioned... *suoyang*! "Resembling *Boschniakia glabra*, it is inserted in the vagina. In contact with the *yin* essence, this plant swells and lengthens. Its potency is 200 times that of the *Boschniakia glabra*." Naughty May! And, in Mr. Van Gulik's usual scholarly way, there followed a list of references to real cases, mainly from the Ming dynasty, but some dating back to 360 CE.

I took a moment to go into the kitchen and take the dozen smelts I'd planned to fry up for our dinner out of the fridge. The odour was not reassuring. I might have waited too long. Had the smelts evolved into the category of Otis food, or even beyond into garbage? The odour of day-old fish. Vaginosis. Bacteria unbalancing the vaginal flora, becoming putrescine, cadaverine. Irene Hill's statement came back to me. "Gooey and clotty." Of course, because May's vagina contained more than menstrual blood. Perhaps no menstrual blood at all. Yes, Sister Hill, May was "different from the other girls," she was packing aphrodisiacs! I decided against phoning the nun again to inquire about the smell of May's vagina. Sister Hill would be only too happy to go on about how May was unclean, how the Chinese not only smelled funny, but certainly had inverted vaginas and orifices entirely different from those of Western women.

May wasn't hooping drugs. Dr. Witz had found no trace of drugs in her blood. Yet May had died a violent death. Could *barbar* a.k.a. *suoyang* be the culprit, despite Sam Ho's claim that it was inoffensive? I picked up the phone and called the police lab. Dr. Witz answered: "Thank you, thank you so much. I've recovered finally, yes. But we are very, very busy. The red ball, you know: my plate is full…"

I commiserated, but wondered if the "tea" substances I had asked to be analyzed had been shelved.

"We have analyzed the substances, as per your request, Officer Pirelli."

I was silent, stunned.

"The tech must have been so busy, she forgot to call you. I guess she figured you'd get back to us."

"I see."

"Welcome to the real world of forensic medicine and law and order, Officer Pirelli."

I was too angry to speak.

Dr. Witz gave me a moment, then asked: "Well, don't you want to know what it was you brought in?"

I waited, but clearly Dr. Witz was relishing the suspense. Finally I said, "I guess I better ask, if I want to know…"

Dr. Witz laughed. "So sorry. It's opium. Pure opium. Rather rare and very expensive."

I took a moment to digest the news. Opium. I recalled the muffled voice on the telephone: "Drink it like tea…" Someone had wanted me drugged. I shivered. Poor Otis. But I quickly got back to May's case.

"Dr. Witz, is it possible that opium could be masked by some other substance so that the lab wouldn't pick it up in an autopsy?"

This time Dr. Witz paused for many seconds, during which I heard him shuffling through pages. A reference book, maybe. "I cannot refute that absolutely. Opiates can be concealed — not annulled — by some plants. I can't find the list of plants as we speak. But then it's not exhaustive. So many plants from other continents are yet to be studied."

"Have you ever heard of *Cynomorium songaricum*, Doctor?" I wasn't going to confuse him with the Chinese nomenclature.

Dr. Witz chuckled. "Detective Pirelli, you surprise me." I could tell he was truly surprised, but it wasn't just surprise at my scientific knowledge. "Are you sure you haven't spoken to my assistant? About the content of your second specimen, I mean: the substance in the tiny teapot?"

"No, why?"

"And you don't have your own little lab stashed away somewhere?"

"What's in the teapot, Dr. Witz?"

"Yes. Well it is, indeed and in fact, *Cynomorium songaricum*. The traces in the teapot are actually of the same family, but much more potent, and I use this word correctly, than something called *boschniakia glabra*." He chuckled again.

Before I had time to ask him what was funny, he continued: "I'm so sorry, Detective Pirelli. I had a flashback to my old country. Where I come from, a small town near Lodz, peasants make a living from *boschniakia glabra*. It's an aphrodisiac that sells well among the émigrés..." He chuckled yet again. "If they only could get their hands on this *Cynomorium songaricum*... sorry."

But I hadn't been listening. My pulse was suddenly beating very fast. *Barbar* and opium: a deadly combo. "Doctor Witz, in your professional opinion, is it possible that this aphrodisiac could mask opium?"

"Hmm, well it's not impossible."

"And what if the mix had been inserted vaginally?"

"Ah." Dr. Witz didn't chuckle nor cough. He paused before responding categorically. "Yes, I see. Definitely, it would most certainly have induced toxic shock."

"Toxic to the point of being fatal?"

"Absolutely."

"Thank you, Dr. Witz!"

"Officer Pirelli, I'm going to refrain from turning this line of inquiry into a poor joke."

"I'm very grateful, Dr. Witz."

I put the receiver down on its cradle and threw the smelts into the garbage.

✡

I hesitated before donning my uniform to visit the Oriental Vitality Club for Women. If it was a sect, a uniform would be off-putting, Spitzer or no Spitzer. If it was an exclusive club, they might respect a fully decked-out policewoman. I opted to wear the blue suit and cap. In any case, the uniform would ensure I would not be taken for one of them. The club was way out in Colchester, in Malletts Bay, past the Champlain Marina. "Turn right at the end of Route 127 on Lakeshore Drive. Turn right again at Shore Acres Drive and go down to the end. That's Whispering Pine Line. There's a sign, our logo, a yin-yang symbol and our acronym, OVCW, in pink underneath." Cheerful Cindy's instructions were not only precise but accurate. And Route 127 was quite scenic, overlooking the Winooski River, then passing through Half Moon Cove. I made a mental note to come back to try out the Sunset Drive-In. What would Huiru think of a drive-in? The truth was, it wasn't Huiru I was imagining in the seat next to me; it was DM. I shook my head to erase the image.

The Whispering Pine Line was a dirt road not unlike the prison's. The afternoon sun glanced off the cars in the parking lot. I parked the patrol car between a Mercedes C-43 and a Saab 9-3. Stepping out to have a cigarette before my meeting with Mistress Yee, I surveyed the lot. The European Community seemed to be assembled here: BMW 318is, Porsche 911, Carrera 4, Volvo S80, VW JT8, even a convertible Jaguar XKR. The colours ranged from midnight blue to persimmon orange. So, not a sect. Rather, the other thing: select. A glance at the license plates of the cabriolets, coupés and sedans told me they were not all local. The twenty-some cars all seemed to have the club's sticker, a mini reproduction of the pink road sign. I searched for an unobtrusive place to put my cigarette out. Finally, I hid it under the Ford, which looked sadly out of place on this lot.

The building, a single-storey structure that seemed to extend back into the woods forever, looked like a chic *après-ski* lodge: plenty of wood and windows. There was no bell on the door. I knocked and waited a good five minutes before a woman, dressed in black with her hair in a tight chignon opened. "Cindy?" I asked, knowing full well this older, Eurasian lady couldn't be Cheerful Cindy.

"Cindy is out. Please take your shoes off, Detective Pirelli. Mistress Yee will be with you shortly."

I bent over to undo my oxfords, and when I straightened up the woman had vanished. I stepped into the enormous entrance hall, a cloak room filled with ladies' street clothes, shoes, sweaters, hats. I looked around in case slippers had been supplied. I found none, and then I remembered the Eurasian woman was barefoot. "Okay," I thought, "maybe a little bit of a sect. *Nan-mo-a-mi-tuo-fo…*" The ceilings, walls and floors were all hardwood. A small box had been installed in the panelling by the door. A flip of the index revealed the dreaded electronic red STAY of a Chubb alarm system. In the absence of chairs, I stood there in my socks, listening. All I could hear was a gentle swooshing sound which seemed to be coming nearer. Two women, one dressed in the same black cloak as the Eurasian woman, the other in white, came in backwards on all fours, swinging the doors open with their bare feet. They were waxing the floor in tandem. When they reached the hall, they shifted into forward and waxed back into the inner rooms. I was left without a word, only the dizzying smell of wax.

Finally, a woman of indeterminate age with a serene expression on a smooth moon face appeared out of nowhere, or so it seemed. In fact, she must have come from the inner rooms, but ever so quietly. This woman was also barefoot and wearing white. Her white hair was in a tight chignon at the very top of her head. She had long well-manicured nails and a pleasant smile. "Welcome to the Oriental Vitality Club, Detective Pirelli. I'm Yee." Mistress Yee who, despite her name, did not appear to be Asian, led me into the inner rooms. They were all empty of furniture, very Zen. Here and there, women were standing facing walls, or sitting on the floor gazing through the windows into the surrounding woods beyond. Mistress Yee proceeded slowly and silently, allowing me to take in the serenity of the light-flooded rooms.

She led me through what looked like a dance studio without the mirrors, then through a sliding door, and invited me to step outside. "We can speak out there without disturbing anyone." Mistress Yee pointed to rope sandals by the door, which we put on. We walked to a wooden bench and sat down next to each other, facing a path that reminded me of those enchanted trails in children's books. Or of a *wuxia* film set. Then I noticed, about fifty yards into the forest, a white-clad silhouette hugging a tree.

"You may wonder what that woman is doing over there, with her body glued to that old pine tree," Mistress Yee said quietly. "She's collecting *qi*. Life-energy. The *qi* of a pine tree is yellow; the *qi* of a poplar tree is white…"

"Are you Jane Spitzer?" I asked, as I watched the woman and the pine tree.

"My name is Yee. 'One,' if you prefer."

"What was your name before it was One?" I insisted.

"Nothing."

I paused, glancing at the white-haired lady's mischievous smile. "Why do some women here wear white, like you, and some black?"

She took my left hand in hers and said, "You would be wearing black today. You're full of the worldly life, out there. That's black. White is life, unhampered."

I drew my hand back. "Do you always wear white?"

Mistress Yee let loose a cascade of laughter: "Yes, now, I do. I wear white, always. You would too, if you practised. I feel you're very, very pure. It's a simple question of breathing, learning how to take it in and take it out. All of life."

I felt uncomfortable all of a sudden; I fidgeted on the bench. My pants were too tight at the waist and I kept on turning the police hat, round and round, in my right hand. "Tell me, Ms. um…Yee, could a person control her body — and mind — to the point of tipping life into death?" Even to my own ears, my question sounded wildly esoteric.

Mistress Yee, however, was unperturbed. "Yes, anyone can control her breath, her life and hence also her death. But people seek life, they want to live, no matter what. Most women who come here have impure hearts. They want to stay young, to eliminate blemishes, wrinkles, crooked postures. We teach all these things here." Mistress Yee put her two hands on her belly.

I fidgeted again, feeling my own belly tighten. "What if a person should want to end her life? Can your training teach that too?"

"We do not teach people how to die. But someone could use our techniques to end life as easily as to prolong it."

"Without leaving a trace?"

Yee stared straight ahead, but she was smiling ever so slightly. Finally she said in a flat tone: "You're referring to the Montrose Penitentiary deaths. Elizabeth Rich and the other woman."

I closed my eyes and felt a rush of happiness. Inside my eyelids, orange tones gave way to little stars, and then to throbbing veins, the force of life. I reopened my eyes and, without looking at Yee, spoke calmly. "Yes, I'm the investigating officer in that case. I know that Elizabeth practised qigong. And acupuncture. Acupuncture without needles, acupressure: isn't that a form of qigong?"

"Yes..." Yee's voice was barely audible.

I closed my eyes again. Somehow I was not surprised when Yee took my hand; I had somehow expected it. Yee placed my hand below my sternum and pressed firmly. "Feel that vacuum there? With one finger, you could stop your life, if you wanted to. Life and death, poison and remedy, it's all a question of dosage."

Yee rose to lead me back inside the club, but as she stepped onto the path, the teacher tripped on a fallen branch. I reached out and grabbed hold of her arms. For a moment, we stood face to face and I found myself staring into lifeless eyes, deep milky pools. We walked back through the lodge in silence, I following her, after she declined my arm. Before I left the lodge, Yee handed me a glossy brochure with the OVCW logo. "Perhaps you'll want to join us some day?"

I smiled, accepting the brochure. "I doubt I'd be able to afford even an afternoon session. It seems to me, Mistress Yee, that your club members are rather well-heeled, not to say well-wheeled. Who are they?"

Mistress Yee produced another mini cascade of laughter. "We have many wives of CEOs here. The big firms, you know, like IBM, Verizon, Rutgers, Adelphia... We offer a haven of peace and natural rejuvenation which is hard to find."

Looking into the parking lot, Yee added, "See that cute red cabriolet next to the purple Audi? That's mine." Her voice had become so light and young that I had to steal another look to make sure it was coming from the same 50, or was it 60-something-year-old woman? As old as life itself, Cindy had said. She was right. What a strange mix of death and life in this creature. Something I had seen in her eyes. In a flash, I realized what it was: Mistress Yee was suffering from some terminal disease. The sudden understanding must have shown in my eyes, because my host smiled and shrugged. "We are all dying. How we live that death is up to us."

As I turned on the motor of the police car, heavy rain began to fall. I turned the windshield wipers up to top speed, but even then I could barely see the traffic lights leading into the inner city. How had the weather changed so fast and unexpectedly? I couldn't have cared less, I was on top of the world. Liz' case was cleared. Thanks to many women, my own mother, Dr. Gayatri, Dr. Leo and now Mistress Yee. I picked up speed, singing at the top of my voice, "Raindrops keep falling on my head," until I remembered the cigarette butt I'd forgotten to pick up, and which was now soiling the Oriental Vitality Club's otherwise pristine parking lot.

❑

"Seeing as this one's on you, I'm going for a high-class beer. A Leffe. Belgian. You have one, too?" Louise Moore was waiting for me at a corner table in La Cucina Italiana, in the Church Street Marketplace. Lou was gorgeous in her fluffy pink mohair twin-set. "Ooh, everything's so tempting here," she told me before I had a chance to return her greeting.

"Been here long?" I guessed Lou was a little inebriated.

"Today's my day off. Plus I'm celebrating." Her black curls bounced as she shook her head and swung her long legs decked out in stretch black jeans.

I sat down. "Tell me: what's the good news?"

"Promotion. I've been promoted. To sex crimes. Senior investigator."

"Congratulations! This does call for a special drink: champagne?"

"Nah, Leffe will be fine. The champagne of beers, you'll see."

Though I wasn't much of a beer drinker, I acquiesced. "So when did this happen?"

Lou lit a cigarette. "The Carter case. I mean the child murders. I cracked it."

"Gee, I am out of it. I haven't been following anything but my own Montrose case. What happened?"

Lou glanced at her freshly painted nails, one shade darker than her sweater and looked up, unable to conceal her pride: "In a nutshell, the perp was some rich kid gone wrong. A real cuckoo."

I nodded. "He'd have to be, to go around killing children."

"Shrink said, problem with authority figures — Daddy, the police, you know, the usual."

"How'd you get him?"

"Traces of his clothes he left on the scene. Matter of fact, when I went to nab him, he was wearing high heels — higher than mine!" Lou showed off the needle-thin heels of her sandals with a jerk of her long leg. "I only grabbed him cause he tripped."

The waiter, a sexy Mediterranean guy, arriving with Rey's Leffe, paused to admire Lou's ankle.

"Well, congratulations, Lou!"

We clinked glasses and Lou's gaze met the waiter's. She eyed his silhouette as he crossed the trattoria and headed back to the bar. "Yeah, turns out the guy was wearing Daddy's clothes…"

"High heels?" It wasn't easy to follow both Lou's conversation and her roving eye.

"Daddy owns a big clothing company. For women." Lou chuckled and took another sip of Leffe. "Also a toy company and a cosmetics chain. And I hear he's also the CEO of some jail management — Rutgers or something. So, Sonny will be right back under Daddy's wing!"

"No way!" I laid my glass down hard. "Dyke? The guy at the ball? I met Daddy Dyke. With his wife Dee-Dee. She's my age, more or less. They don't have a son that age."

"The name's Dyke, all right. Mick Dyke. Check out today's *Free Press*. First page: 'X-Dress Heir Crosses the Line.' Jesus, where the hell have you been hiding, Rey? China? Ever heard of second marriages?"

Feeling stupid, I shook my head. "Dyke. Wouldn't you know."

"Name like that, kid was predestined to cross-dressing." When Lou realized that instead of laughing, I was lost in thought, she changed the subject. "What's up with your case? Deadline coming up pretty soon."

"Matter of hours." I was about to launch into a discussion of the case, but Lou had begun to study the menu. "Matter of fact, I've figured it out."

"Oh? So have I. I'm having the osso bucco, but first snails. You?"

I was about to correct her, but something made me change my mind. I turned my attention to the menu. "Oh, I'll have the special: shrimp with sambucca and the penne arrabiata first."

"Great choice. I'm not crazy for anise-flavoured food. Can't stand liquorice. Poorly educated palate, I guess." Lou, eyeing me, adopted a less-than-convincing air of concern. "All right, Dick Pireli, let's hear it. What's the story?"

"Have you ever had a baby, Lou?" The ephebe chose this moment to reappear. He smiled and pretended he hadn't heard my question: "And what will the lovely ladies have today?"

Both Lou and I giggled, the same thought having crossed our minds.

"So, have you ever had babies?" I repeated, lighting a cigarette, when the waiter had gone.

Lou lit one too and took a long drag. "Nope. But I've had a couple of abortions. Who hasn't?" She looked at me and cocked her head. "Well, maybe not the lady fresh off the boat. You're not a virgin, are you?"

I dismissed the question with a look, and said flatly, "Well, one of my two victims was suffering from post-partum depression. I don't know whether there's a direct link or not, but she killed herself."

"But how?" asked Lou with what seemed real interest.

The waiter returned with our entrées. Silently, we watched him lay down the little fork for the snails, grind parmesan for the noodles, and fresh pepper for both. When he'd finally gone, I answered Lou's question. "She was a qigong practitioner. And an acupuncturist. She stopped her own breathing."

"You mean, she was a member of the Falungong?!" Maybe it was the hot snail in her mouth, but Lou turned the word "Falungong" into something like "far-and-gone." She swallowed the garlic-drenched gastropoda, took a morsel of bread, and added matter-of-factly, "Those weirdos are all over the place, these days."

"Actually, no, I don't think she was into Falungong. But qigong has a fundamental principle which is similar. Controlling your vital energies. Prolonging life, keeping healthy, curing diseases, that sort of thing, halfway between the physical and the spiritual. Thing is, you could use those same techniques to kill."

"I told Captain Carter your head was totally screwed up by those Chinese. Of course the big boss wouldn't listen. Post-partum depression, though, that I get. Makes sense. Not my turf, but I hear a lot of infanticides get off with that defense."

My mouth was a big ball of fire; wow, that arrabiata was potent.

The waiter returned again with fresh pepper and parmesan cheese — why the cheese again? — for our main course. We ordered more Leffe. Lou plunged into her dish and soon her lipstick was ringed and shadowed in orange. Nice touch, I thought, with the pink sweater. I attacked my broiled shrimp.

"Are you starving or something?" Lou asked, staring at my plate, which contained no shells; only the tips of tails.

"I think I like the shell as much as the flesh." I laughed, adding in a low, conspiratorial voice: "Is that too weird for you? 'Cause if it is, you're not ready…"

"Not ready for what?" Lou asked, a fork full of bone marrow suspended in mid-air.

"If so, you're not ready to hear how the other inmate died."

"Try me, lady." Lou waved her almost empty beer glass at the pretty boy waiter.

"She died from an overdose," I said.

"Big fuckin' deal." Lou shrugged and stuffed a huge bite of veal shank into her mouth. "I've done the drug beat, honey." Lou lowered her voice and confided: "On both sides of the street, matter of fact. Once upon a time. I'm surprised I'm still alive. Most of my friends OD-ed." Lou let the confession sink in, took a long gulp of beer. The glass was empty now. "You know what, there's quite a few of us ex-addicts in the corps. Of course, you're the exception, Rey: a virgin who never smoked a joint."

I didn't take the bait. "What about aphrodisiacs?" I asked. "Know anything about them?"

Lou smiled, tilting her head slightly. "Hmm? Well, let me think... You mean like Spanish fly?" Lou was less sure on this terrain, and maybe reconsidering her opinion of me.

"Without boring you with details, the other inmate died of an overdose of an aphrodisiac called Chinese *cynomorium*, that was laced with pure opium..."

Lou had definitely stopped eating. "The Big O? It would have come out in the blood tests. And they had clean intestinal tracts." Lou was all ears.

"You're a woman, Lou. What other orifices come to mind?"

Lou put down her glass and lit a cigarette: "Holy Christ! In the safe?"

"Yup, she stuffed her vagina with aphrodisiacs. Hooped it, if you prefer."

"Well I heard of drug mules putting it in there, but shit... You mean the Chinese girl?" She shook her curly head. "Man, those Chinese..."

"Lou, the Chinese have been doing things unimaginable to Westerners for several millennia. They may be as sexist as we are, but they have aphrodisiacs for women, too. Just imagine: nuns, palace consorts, second and third wives, leftover concubines, even plain unmarried women, giving themselves pleasure." I explained how the *barbar* worked.

"Fuck!" Lou's mouth was now completely devoid of lipstick.

I signalled for the bill. "Thing is the stuff is harmless, really. I mean, it can't kill you. May Ho died because someone mixed opium in it. I don't even think she was meant to die. Anyway, I think I know why, and now, thanks to you, I think I know who."

"DM told me you were smart!"

"Have you and DM been talking about me?" I tried to conceal my displeasure. Lou stopped re-applying her lipstick to glance up from her compact and straight at me: "DM likes you. He said you'd figure it out." She finished applying her lipstick. "He said your China connection would help you crack it." I picked up a trace of resentment in Lou's voice, or was it jealousy.

To maintain my composure, I counted my cash, adding a fifteen-percent tip for the ephebe.

Lou stood and kissed me on both cheeks. "Well, good luck. And thanks for the super meal. Gotta go. Day off. Loads to do." She heaved her large handbag onto her shoulder. "One thing, though, free advice from an old cop: forget the aphrodisiacs and the accidental drug OD: call 'em both suicidal manic-depressives. Easier for everyone to follow. Get my drift?" And Lou hurried off, leaving me to wait for the ephebe to return my change. I could feel the marks of her fresh lipstick on my cheeks. The thought occurred to me that Lou might be on her way over to DM's.

✿

I could still see Lou's pink lips whispering, "There's quite a few of us in the corps..." And her final friendly advice, "Make it two suicides, easier that way," echoing Captain Carter's "Keep it simple, Pirelli." But could it be simple now that I was pretty sure that a powerful man like Dyke with his multiple companies was involved?

Nor was it easy to arrange a meeting with Mr. Dyke. I phoned the Correctional Corporation of Rutgers down in South Burlington and got an elderly female voice, obviously exhausted by the numerous queries following Mick Dyke's arrest. "Mr. Dyke is not available for comment." I identified myself and the tired voice sighed and referred me to X-Dress as a likely place to reach the boss. After crossing the first receptionist hurdle at X-Dress, I got a Mr. Readings, who identified himself as the general manager of X-Dress. "I'd like to speak to Mr. Dyke, no one else. He asked me to contact him." Dyke did not come to the phone, but Readings told me the CEO could spare me 15 minutes at precisely 1630 hours.

X-Dress was located in Winooski's most prized heritage building, the Champlain Mill, right by the Falls. I counted 28 windows per floor on one side. X-Dress, of course, occupied the top floor which was where, in the old days, they spooled the wool. I was glad I'd changed into my police uniform because, once you stepped inside X-Dress, it was difficult not to feel shabby and out-of-style. Certainly, none of my mix-and-mismatch duds would have passed muster in this *haut-cool* office. Even the androgynous receptionist's lipstick fit the *noir sur noir* design.

Mr. Dyke's corner office was all tinted windows, slate tiled floors and sleek black leather upholstery. In the midst of so much chic, the small ordinary man looked shockingly out of place. He glanced at his Rolex, pointed to the armchair across the desk, then fixed his gaze on the paper-free surface, where it would remain for most of my allotted 15 minutes. On the positive side, he wasted no time getting to the point. "I'm afraid when I asked you to come by, Officer Pirelli, it was because I was interested in the eventual outcome of the Montrose case. As you certainly know by now, my company has made a bid to take over the management of Montrose. We think we can run that prison efficiently and productively." Mr. Dyke tapped two fingers on the edge of the desk. Ebony? "Unfortunately, with Mick's arrest, all that will have to be put on hold. As a result, there's not much for us to talk about."

I decided to be equally direct. "Was your son Mick using drugs? Or dealing hard drugs like opium?"

Mr. Dyke stopped his drumming. He appeared momentarily to be considering whether the subject of his son had any place in our discussion. It didn't take him long to decide to accept my line of questioning. "Drugs, girls, boys... My son's got all the bad habits. He lost his mother too early on, and Dee-Dee, well, she's his age. Now he's gotten himself into a situation in which not even I can help him." He paused for a moment. "I'm not sure how my son's situation is related to your particular investigation."

"One of the victims at Montrose died of an opium overdose."

Mr. Dyke shrugged but continued to focus on the clear surface of his desk. "There are unfortunately a great many sources of illegal drugs in prisons. Do you have any evidence my son provided opium to inmates in Montrose?"

"Whoever smuggled this opium in, did it without the knowledge of the inmate, who took it by accident."

Guy Dyke resumed his quasi silent drumming against the ebony desk. "You mean they planted the drug?"

"Is it possible that your son might have wanted to use the opium to frame someone at Montrose, to make the prison administration look bad?"

"You're suggesting Mick would have done all this to help Rutgers win the Montrose bid?"

"Drugs and drug-related deaths certainly don't hurt your bid."

To my surprise, Guy Dyke expressed an emotion: he chuckled. Then he shook his head and spun his chair around to look out the window behind him. He lowered his voice. "My son and I haven't spoken to each other since he turned 18. I doubt very much he would even be aware I own

Rutgers, let alone entertain the idea of assisting me in my endeavours in any way, no matter how perverse and illegal." He turned back to face me, and this time he looked me in the eye. "If my son decided to meddle in my affairs, it would be to ruin me, not to help."

"So, until his arrest in the child killings, you hadn't had any contact with Mick?"

Dyke's gaze returned to the surface of his desk. "Not before and not since his arrest."

"You haven't spoken to your son since his arrest? You are hard-nosed."

"He won't see me," Guy Dyke whispered, suddenly drained, as though I had forced a confession from him.

But I wasn't done yet. "Mr. Dyke, if not your son, do you have any idea who might want to try to help your bid along?"

Dyke brushed off the desk in a gesture of impatience. "Officer Pirelli, no one connected to me or my company did anything like what you're suggesting. Never mind that it's illegal, I would never do anything so stupid. The consequences, if a scheme like that backfired — and chances are damn good it would backfire — would be disastrous. I'm not an idiot. In any case, why would I even consider such an insane tactic? I don't have to. Montrose will be privatized. It's just good business, for everyone. Oh, we'll have to wait until the scandal… until my son's case dies down but, sooner or later, Officer Pirelli, I'll get Montrose." His tone was less triumphant than resigned, as though he were weary of the way things just seemed to work out for him.

I could think of nothing further to ask. Only vague suspicions had brought me here and I had no evidence to lay down on the bare desk between us. Anyway, my time was up. Mr. Dyke glanced at his Rolex; it was precisely 16:45, and the androgynous receptionist was standing at the door, waiting for the uniform to exit. It didn't matter; I had somewhere to go.

✿

I went home first. I began by tidying up my desk, neatly stacking the Montrose folders that I no longer needed. I took off my uniform and put on my cut-offs and navy-blue hoodie. And running shoes. Then I dialled Montrose. A male voice I didn't recognize answered my call. Paul Bundell was out on sick leave.

Paul Bundell lived in the Decker Towers on St. Paul Street. I ran all the way over. I slipped into the seedy subsidized apartment building with the mailwoman, who took me for a tenant. I took the elevator up to the 8th floor and rang the first door to the right. Paul Bundell, in cut-off jeans and a torn T-shirt, with one hand on a vacuum cleaner, opened the door. We were dressed like twins; it took both of us a couple of seconds to recognize each other. "Officer Pirelli!"

"Officer Bundell," I said.

For a moment we sized each other up. I was wearing thick-soled sneakers and he was barefoot.

Finally he stepped back and pointed me toward the plaid upholstered hideaway sofa bed in the living room. I went straight into the kitchen and sat down at the marbled melamine table. I put my mini-recorder next to the Pledge, Pinesol and Ajax cans and pressed RECORD.

"I hear you're on sick leave. Is it the Dyke affair made you sick?" I pointed at the other chair.

Paul sat. His eyes were glued to the slowly spinning recorder.

"May 13, 2000, 1800. Detective Rey Pirelli interviewing Officer Paul Bundell in his residence," I said. "Officer Bundell, was it Mick Dyke who gave you the opium?"

Paul sprang to his feet. "Hold on, Pirelli. What the fuck are you talking about?"

"Paul, sit down. I know you planted that opium in May Ho's cell. How much did Dyke pay you to do it?"

"You're making a mistake here." Paul sat down and pointed to the recorder. "Turn that thing off."

"You made the mistake, Paul. You planted that drug document in my apartment, to put me on to the drug angle, then you delivered the "O" to my door, and then you phoned me. That opium could have killed me. It almost killed my roommate. Why? Did you really think I wouldn't figure it out? And what made you plant it on May Ho? Why not Gloria, or Laura or …" I stopped abruptly. I'd bombarded him with too many questions. I thought I'd better wait to see which one he'd answer.

"I don't know Mick Dyke," Paul said. "Read about him in the newspaper, like everybody else. You got it all wrong."

"All right then. What about Mick's daddy, Guy Dyke?"

"Never met the guy."

"So you acted on your own? You had access to May Ho's cell. You saw the contents of the package her brother sent her. You knew you could easily mix opium in with that black paste of hers and May would never know. All I need from you, Officer Bundell, is motive. Why, Paul? And why her?"

Paul rocked back on his chair and crossed his muscular arms over his T-shirt, across which was inscribed *Bens': If we don't have it, you don't need it.* "That's a load of crap. Any inmate could have gone into her cell. Elizabeth Rich, for example. Anyone could see the two of them had some kind of suicide pact."

"You're behind in the news, Paul. The double suicide scenario's out. I have proof. That's not how it went down. Forget about Rich. May Ho is your problem."

Paul shrugged. "You're nuts."

"You messed up. You let May's brother's package containing a drug in; you also let Elizabeth Rich's lover Karl Krauss smuggle in stuff that put her deeper into her depression. And then you confiscated a handful of twigs! And..." I was out of breath, I'd run all the way here, and now he was pacing between the kitchen table and the door to the living room. It occurred to me that he might bolt.

Finally he returned to the table. "It's all circumstantial. You've got no proof."

"I've got enough to lay a charge."

Bundell shrugged.

"A charge of murder."

Paul leaned suddenly over the table. I almost leaped out of my seat, but before I could move, he pressed the STOP button on my tape recorder and sat down.

"Not murder. Listen, Pirelli, I swear to you, there was no way she was supposed to die."

I could see he wasn't going to spray Pledge in my face. In fact, all the air had come out of him. "All right, what happened?"

Paul eyed the tape recorder, and ran his tongue over his mustached lip. I flipped the EJECT button and tossed the tape to his side of the table.

He let it lie there. "A room search was scheduled for the next day, see. I figured she'd get caught with the shit in her room. That's all. I swear. How was I supposed to know she'd ask to go down into diss?"

"Why?"

"I got the idea from Lou..."

Now it was my turn to pale. "Lou?"

"Lou told me Dyke was applying to get the contract for Montrose. I figured..."

"Wait a second, Bundell. Lou?"

"Yeah, Lucille Segal, the warden."

I felt a sudden rush of relief that left me dizzy. I vowed, in the future, to pay closer attention to people's first names and nicknames. In the same instant, I recalled my dream of a bikini-clad Warden Segal straddling Paul Bundell. I closed my eyes to remember the moment, and moved on: "All right, so you planted the opium in May's cell to make Montrose look bad."

"Yeah, the joint's supposed to be drug-free, and all that bullshit."

"So the contract would go to Dyke…"

"Yeah."

"Then what? Mr. Dyke would reward you with a big private sector salary and a bonus for setting up Montrose?"

"Something like that." Paul suddenly slapped the table. "Hey, listen, Officer Pirelli, do you know what I take home at the end of the month at Montrose? Shit, those goddamn inmates are living better'n I do. So I smuggled in a fist of "O." What about it? Happens every day in every pen in this country."

I shook my head. "You thought up this hare-brained scheme all by yourself, didn't you? You did it on spec."

Paul slumped in his chair glaring defiantly.

"What were you going to do? Go and tell Dyke what you did? Did you really think he'd thank you? Give you a job in his private prison? You do realize salaries in those non-union jobs tend to be lower than in public sector pens? Or did you think he'd make you management? Maybe warden of the new and improved Montrose?"

Paul had absently picked up the Pledge aerosol can and was shaking it vigorously. "Why not?"

I ignored the violence in his gesture. "What about your pal Lou Segal?"

Paul shrugged. "I didn't kill May Ho. That was an accident. I didn't know they'd let her take her dope into diss with her, for shit's sake."

"Hey, you know what? I believe you, Bundell." I got up and collected my tape and recorder. Paul had done it on his own. I had been naïve to think Dyke would orchestrate anything like this. Why take the chance? Certainly not murder. Not even planting the opium. A corporate bigwig like that didn't need to stoop so low. The system would provide others, people like Paul, to do the dirty work, voluntarily and free of charge. While people like May Ho and Liz Rich, like Eileen and Chris rotted and died in his prisons.

At the door, I turned to ask: "Think your Lou'll smuggle goodies to you in jail?"

Max's desk was clear of everything, save my laptop. It was time to write my final report on the Montrose deaths. I would get it in just under the wire. Sunday, Mother's Day. My last day on the case. I'd given myself the ideal circumstances — Otis had been walked, I'd made a pot of jasmine tea. If Captain Carter approved my report, it would certainly be made available to the Review Board looking into the viability of the new reform prisons. I typed in the names of the deceased and stopped. "Keep it simple," Carter had said. SUICIDE.

I stood up again and opened my book of proverbs at random. My gaze settled on a saying I really didn't want: "*Qi qiao bu tong* — the seven orifices are blocked." Not so! The proverb implied that I understood nothing, my ears, nostrils, eyes, and mouth being clogged up. It seemed to me I understood this case all too well. And yet the book of proverbs was never wrong, was it?

Captain Carter had chosen me, rookie Rey Pirelli, rather than Lou Moore or even Simon Baal for the Montrose case. Had he wanted to avoid taking sides, at least until a clear winner emerged? He had calculated I'd never get the politics. Well, he shouldn't have paraded his China girl at the ball. I might never have met Dyke otherwise. Although DM had introduced me to the economical ramifications of the case. And DM, I mused, could be the subject of an investigation all by himself. But that was another sort of investigation: a very personal one. I fetched his lime-coloured name card and sniffed it again. Hermès, *Eau de citron vert*. "You've got a good nose, Officer Pirelli." DM's warm touch on my hand.

I set DM's card aside and sat down again at my neat desk. I thought of all the people I'd interviewed during the course of the investigation: Joe the beekeeper, Sam the herbalist, Mistress Yee, Krauss…: none could be blamed for the deaths of the two women; and yet, not one was blameless. Each one could have, at some point, in some way, done more to stop the downward spirals leading to Liz' and May's incarcerations and deaths. It was as though each of the people in the two women's lives held one piece of the puzzle. If only each person had revealed his or her piece, if only the pieces could have been assembled and read, those two horrible destinies could have been transformed.

I understood it all too well. A penitentiary was an expensive institution. Female convicts cost a tremendous amount. Montrose was understaffed. Its staff was underpaid — when it wasn't composed of volunteers — and overworked.

Unprofessional was a term that kept popping up. Officer Paul Bundell, absolutely, but also Facilitator Irene Hill, Dr. King and his intern Aaron Levy. A little voice in my head added: And what about yourself and your FOOS? I had come a long way. But there was also Warden Segal, as well as Dr. Leo. A botched job all around. All right, it was Easter, but did that mean the system couldn't afford competent personnel during a holiday? Did Dr. Leo think it wasn't worth the cost to provide a convict suffering from depression with medicine? Careless or callous. MURDER.

I knew all about the scepticism with which law enforcement generally regarded psychological factors. PMS was still a joke among my colleagues in the police force, and certainly not a viable defense in the courts. Probably, an accused would have less trouble pleading SAD, Seasonal Affective Disorder, because it affected men. But surely post-partum depression ought to have been taken more seriously. Montrose was criminally negligent in the death of Elizabeth Rich.

Both Liz' and May's lawyers, and the respective courts that had sentenced them had all been negligent in their failure to understand the women's situation. Liz, alone and broke, had just given birth. Despite Off'cer P'k's categorical affirmation that "Rich did not have a b'by." But where was that newborn? Liz Rich's killing of her son Bing had to be linked to that second child's disappearance.

And they had falsely convicted May of killing her lover. Methadone had more likely killed Lee Pike. The writer had been "under influence," like his protagonist. Expediency.

I stopped typing. Great, now I was accusing the entire system. Way to keep it simple, Rey-hee. I took a sip of jasmine tea. The worst part was that discrediting Montrose was likely to lead to, if not a more traditional, at least a harsher prison system. If my findings were made public, Warden Segal's reforms at Montrose would be history.

And what about the Chinese connection? How much good would my report do to further inter-racial understanding? I could imagine the headline in the *USA Today*: "Falungong Ritual Suicide in Pink Pen." May's case would provide an even juicier title: "Dragon Lady Dies: Opium Laced with Oriental Aphrodisiacs."

A wave of anger swept over me. Dyke the elder would never be held accountable for May's death. Bundell would go to jail, sure. But wasn't he also a victim of the penal system and the juggernaut of privatization? Would he have done what he did had he been earning a decent wage?

In the end, ironically, Lou Moore's investigation and capture of his son Mick would probably do more to block Dyke's company's chances of running the women's prison. Montrose might well survive, for a while at least, on subsidies And volunteers.

What was it Irene Hill had said? "Montrose is my home." She'd have had to go if the prison were turned into an efficient, profit-making enterprise. If Paul knew about the Dyke bid, so surely did Hill. She must have feared that possibility and hated it, hated Dyke.

Which explained the one mystery I had not yet resolved. Paul had attempted to fool me with the "tea" and drug-related info, but who had left the financial document on the stoop of Max's condo? I logged on to the internet to check out Dyke's prison-management company, Rutgers. I rummaged through my files for the computer print-out anonymously left for me. I compared it with the financial statement on the Rutgers website. No surprise: they were identical. I smiled at Irene Hill's little ploy. The good sister had delivered the financial statement to me, hoping to put me on to Dyke's trail, and somehow involve him in the murder. Maybe Irene Hill had watched too many episodes of *Murder She Wrote*.

I stood up, paced the living room, noticed in the mirror that my furrow, trying-to-understand-the-impossible, was more prominent than ever. Junior officers never get a clean case. That my report could change anything was an illusion.

Otis woke up and stretched. I opened the terrace's sliding door wide. Dog and detective stepped out. While Otis was spraying the little bush, I stopped in front of the dogwood and admired the budding leaves. Spring. I rolled a tender green bud between thumb and index finger, breathed in the fresh tangy scent. Then I got down on all fours beside Otis, to bury my nose in among the bushes.

Could prisons change people? Please check only one box: yes/yes. Should Montrose be saved? No. Yes.

I went back inside to type my report. I told the facts, omitting none. Let the chips fall where they may. I punched SAVE, and PRINT. The pages drifted out of the printer onto the floor. At the bottom of the final page, I signed: *Rey Ir's Pirell*. Then I changed my mind, reprinted the last page and signed: *Rey I. Pirelli*.

I logged on again and bid for a one-way ticket to Beijing. I emailed Huiru: *My beautiful Huiru, I'm coming home: May 16. See you soon, your Rey.* And then Max Foe: *Hi Max: I'll be gone before you get back. Thanks for everything. And for Otis. Be aware that there's now an alarm system in your house.* **CODE: 6423. BEWARE!!!**

I turned off my computer, brought down Huiru's *XI* calligraphy. I rolled it and stored it back in my China box. From that box, I retrieved my CD of Chara and the Yentown Band. How many people outside Asia had ever heard Chara sing Sinatra's "My way?" Maybe Petunia and the Metallica girls from the girl's bar in the pavilion by the water? I could imagine Petunia singing "She don't care" along with the inconsolable Chara. For the girls, inside and out.

I went into the kitchen, opened two cans of smoked oysters and laid them out on two separate plates. I put lime on one and took out my jade chopsticks. Then I poured myself a tall glass of Joe's melliflo and put everything on a serving tray.

I returned to the back yard, set the tray on the grass and sat down next to Otis by the dogwood. I toasted to my bittersweet victory. "To the little fox who completed the crossing: *Ganbei!*" The two of us settled down to wait for the moon to clear the hedge and begin its night journey.

- 30 -

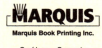

Québec, Canada
2007